Pay Back Is A Bitch

Debbie Ross

DEDICATION

I would like to dedicate this book to
Stuart Ross

Thank you for giving me the inspiration
to write this

You are a worthless piece of shit!!!

DO NOT LET YOUR PAST DICTATE YOUR
FUTURE

ACKNOWLEDGMENTS

In loving memory of Reesa Brady

CHAPTER 1

Oh, Jesus Christ Matty will you just shut the fuck up and order the pizza. It is a Tuesday and every Tuesday Dominos do a two for Tuesday. Two pizzas for the price of one. The two weirdest pizzas ever. Matty is gluten free and I do not eat cheese. I always take pelters for that. Oh, Murrin how can you eat a pizza without cheese? easy, its rank! It is always an argument on a Tuesday who is going to phone the pizza, then we argue who is going to serve customers when our pizza comes. I always win because it is my shop, so I get to eat my pizza in peace. I always pull rank when it comes to food. It is during the week, well obviously if it is a Tuesday. The shop is always quiet during the week you get the odd stragglers for bugs and rats. It is an exotic pet shop. What can I say, I love animals? We have the best exotics around, and we have a blue Nosey Faley. People come for miles to see him. I called him Blue. He has the most electric blue colour, with a white stripe down the middle and he has bright red and yellow too. He is the shops mascot. Everyone wants to buy Blue, but he is not for sale. In fact, most of the reptiles and exotics in the shop are not for sale. I tend to get attached to some of them and then I end up keeping them. So, if anyone comes in to buy something Matty will always say Ill double check with Murrin. We are total opposites, Matty is tall, over 6 feet, slim build, with green eyes and blonde hair. Thinks he knows everything about everything.

I am a small 5-foot 1 red head with a fiery temper, brown eyes and I wing it. I may not know everything about everything, but I will wing it. That was why I hired Matty. He had a fountain of knowledge about all reptiles. Me? I did was I always do. Bought a shop knew absolutely nothing at first and started getting all these weird and wonderful exotic animals. The story of my life, I flip from one thing to another. I always do it. I do not know why.

The pizza comes, and yet again it is another argument, because the shop is so quiet during the week, I got a tv and DVD fitted into the shop which was only to be used after all the work was finished. We were watching Sons of anarchy, so it is another argument who is going to get the money to pay the pizza guy. So, we are sitting watching sons and the door goes, Matty automatically got up because I pull rank over food, I looked over and there was this guy who just walked into the shop. I quickly grabbed Matty and said, oh its ok Matty it's my turn he was about 5 foot 6 ish he had obviously just finished work, he had his working gear on, but even though he had his working gear on I was instantly attracted to him and his smile. He has dark coloured hair, he has a skip hat on, but you can still see his dark hair underneath. He has olive coloured skin. The minute he smiled at me I knew; I just knew he was going to be trouble. He is younger than me, much younger than me. I am 43 I tend to go for younger guys, but he looks a lot younger maybe mid 20's. It is the way he is looking at me, it is making me go all squishy. He is not my usual type. I like tall buys, I like bald guys, I love tattoos. I like a man's man. He is far from a man's man. His eyebrows have been plucked or waxed. Jesus fuck he is more feminine than me. I am not into hair and makeup, it has never been anything I tend to do. What you see is what you get. This guy has neither and yet I have just given up my pizza to talk to him. I do not share food with anyone, I love food. I'd let Stephen take a £1000 sale rather than give up my food, yet I have literally just given up my pizza for a guy I don't know, he isn't my type but oh my god he had me at hello.

4

Now I cannot hear the words. He is saying something, but I am not even listening, I am just looking at him, staring even. I am staring at him and I do not have a clue what he is saying because I am just staring right at him, staring into his eyes, his eyes, oh my god the way he is looking at me. I am gone, my legs are like jelly he is still asking me something and I must look like a right idiot because all I can do is stare. Matty starts shouting at me, and then I come to. Murrin I've told him he's not for sale. Eh? What are you talking about, the guy has just asked about Blue, I said he's not for sale. I quickly get myself together, so I do not look like a total plank, but he is looking at me again with that look, it is like he can see right through me. Shit Murrin think, think. Oh, Blue isn't for sale, but I can get you one maybe. Matty is bumping my arm because he knows we cannot get anymore, I've hit him back as if to say shut the fuck up. Oh, if you leave me your details I can see if I can get you one. You would need to know how to look after him first before getting one. We do this with everyone getting new reptiles. If you cannot tell me how to look after them properly, I do not sell them. I had a total cheek, because before getting the shop I knew sod all about most of them. I learned myself and went to college to study. If you want to come back to the shop and I can go over the set up etc. that you will need. This is all total bull shit. I cannot get another one. I have absolutely no idea why I have just lied to this guy, but I know I need to see him again. He says he will go away and look up what he needs and about the species and come back. Thank fuck, I did it, hopefully he comes back. He walks out the door and Matty says what the hell was all that about? You know you cannot get another Blue, I said I know I just liked him. Matty says are you joking? He is about half your age. I said I know I do not care. It was eye candy, when do we ever get eye candy in the shop.

The following day I am in class, I am doing an animal care class in college, maybe I should have done this before I bought the shop, but oh no, not me, I do everything arse from elbow. I do not even remember what class I was in, but my mind is not on whatever I am being taught, my mind is in one place and one place only. Thinking about the guy from the shop, his face, his smile, how it turned me to jelly. This is not me. I am like the ice queen. I have been through so much stuff in my past to say I have a great wall around me would be an understatement. I have the great wall of China, then metal shutters, behind that is a brick wall. No one is getting through that, yet I am still thinking about that guy. God, I do not even know his name. Why didn't I ask his name? The guy with the smile, the smile that could light up a room and the way he looks at me with those eyes. Why can't I stop thinking about him? Maybe he will come back into the shop to see about the set up. I hope he does. All day this is what I have thought of. Every bloody class today, I may as well not have bothered coming today as I have learned nothing except this man with the eyes and the smile has made me go all wobbly.

I get back to the shop to let Matty go. I go to class a Monday, Wednesday and Friday. So Matty runs the shop while I am in class and then I take over. We all work at the weekend because that is when the shop is busiest. So, I am pottering away in the shop, and the wee chime goes. When the door opens a wee chime goes so if we are in the back, we can hear someone come in. I walk out to the front and there he is standing there looking at me and then he smiles. Oh fuck, I am standing, please do not let him see my legs go wobbly, oh please do not then he will know. It is probably written all over my face anyway.

Oh hello, wait to I part my legs and you can spread me like margarine. He knows, he must know, he is doing that smile thing again. Oh fuck. He is opening his mouth and saying something but all I can hear is I want you, I need you, I am going to have you. I am thinking great let us go. Then I come back to earth, why does this guy have such an effect on me. I just do not get it. He has come back into the shop with stuff he has printed off about Nosey Faleys. Oh, that's great I said, it means your seriously thinking about getting one. However, inside I am thinking I do not give a fuck about that, it is you. I am only interested in you. He starts rhyming off what he has learned about the set up and there I go again, I'm off in the world of, I want you, I need you, lie down, kiss me, have your wicked way with me, do what you want to me. I can see his mouth moving but I cannot hear what he is saying. Only what I am thinking. Right now, I am thinking will you shut the fuck up and kiss me.

Then the chime goes, someone else has walked in and to say I am raging is an understatement. It is the guy across the road. Oh, fuck and he will go on and on and on. He lives alone, I swear to god he saves all his talking for the day and then comes into the shop and unloads. His name is Frank, he is in his early sixty's, about 6-foot-tall, he is old school, dressy trousers, shirt and jacket type guy, but he can talk. Oh my god he can talk, and then you can never get rid of him. He talks seven shades of shite. Absolute shite, another thing we always argue about in the shop. Who is serving Frank? He comes in for one thing and leaves like an hour later, and it is just my luck, I've got the guy that makes my legs wobble and the vagina go all warm, and now this fucker has decided of all the times he could come into the shop, he comes in now. What a bastard, I hate him, I bloody hate him. I am thinking will you just go get whatever the hell it is you want and get to fuck so I can stare at the guy, with the nice eyes and the smile.

He sees Frank, and he says, Oh I'll let you get on with your work. Now I am fizzing, I want to take the brush in my hand and shove it right up Franks arse for what he has done. The guy with the nice eyes and smile is going to leave and I am going to be left with Frank, Frank the arsehole, Frank who talks so much shite. Frank who has literally just ruined my life. He goes to walk out the door and before he left, I asked him his name. It is Dexter he says.

As sure as I know my own name Frank stayed for over an hour. One hour of listening to absolute shite. I could not even tell you one thing he said because all I was thinking about was Dexter. Dexter with the nice smile, nice eyes, and makes me all warm and fuzzy inside. Not Frank, Frank the bastard, Frank who has just ruined my life, Frank who made Dexter leave. I would have happily spent an hour talking or staring at Dexter, but no. I got Frank, Frank the fucker. I ended up shutting the shop early to get rid of him. I had enough, I was still fizzing with him for ruining my time with Dexter. I went across the road to the off license to get myself a bottle of wine and drown my sorrows. If only I could have drowned Frank.

All I could think about when I got home was Dexter, I wonder what would have happened if Frank did not come into the shop. Would he have stayed longer? Is it just me? You know when someone looks at you in a certain way. It is the I want you look, I fancy you look, I want to rip your clothes off look. The look that sees right through into your soul. It is all I can think about, I cannot stop thinking about it. I cannot stop thinking about him. He is all I think about until I eventually fall asleep

Chapter 2

A few days have gone by and every time the chime goes on the door, I turn around hoping itis going to be Dexter, I have only just seen this guy twice for two short amounts of time and I cannot stop thinking about him. What is wrong with me? I am never like this. Since my divorce If I need a good seeing to, I have what you call friends with benefits. No need to hump them and dump them. Just get what you need then get them to fuck. It works both ways. I love being by myself, I can do what I want, eat when I want, get drunk when I want. I do not want tied down to one person ever again. I wasted too much of my life already with an arsehole. I will never trust another man in my life, after what I have been through, so why can I not get this guy out of my head. I think about him in class, in the shop at home. I basically think about him all the time. It is like being a teenager again, see when you fancy someone in class or just someone you know, and you cannot stop looking at them and thinking about them. Thinking I wonder what they are doing now. Will they notice me if I do my hair like this or if I wear that. This is what it is like. It is like being a teenager again.

I am always late for everything. Jesus I will be late for my own funeral. My friends have got wise to it. If you want me there for 2pm then say 1pm and just maybe I will get there for 2pm. I am a nightmare, I have always been the same. I always just seem to leave everything to the last minute, but just now I am setting my alarm to get up that bit earlier for work to make sure I straighten my hair and put on mascara just in case Dexter comes into the shop. I am not a girly girl. I am far from it. Girls would play with their dolls when they were younger. I played with the boys and cars. I hated dolls, in fact I hated most girls. They were too boring for me. I am more of a tom boy dare devil kind of person. Most of my friends are boys, although I do have a handful of girlfriends that are real friends. Real friends are the ones who are by your side when you have more up's and downs than a hooker's pants. The ones who are still standing by you when shit goes south or good goes north. That is what I call friends the rest are acquaintances.

I have my bestie Emma we both grew up in the sa1me scheme, but we did not know each other then. We met on fuck book (this is what I call Facebook – don't even get me started on that it's like a dating site for looneys and the obsession for likes – who cares how many likes your picture gets I should rename myself no one on face book then comment on a post so it says no one likes your post – people are obsessed with their pictures and likes omg go get a real job if you put as much effort into working as you do Facebook you'd be a millionaire) it was on a group page where everyone who grew up in that scheme all joins and chats crap basically, but that is how we met. Fate is a funny thing, I believe in fate and that everything happens for a reason, and the saying your granny always said, if it is for you it will not go by you. I believe that fate brought us together as I do not go on Facebook much, I get fed up looking at pictures of people's dinners. Just eat the fucking thing instead of taking pictures. Or it is a half post Oh I am so angry …… so everyone asks what is wrong? Oh nothing, well shut the fuck up then. So, I think it was fate that brought us together. Emma is in her forties; she is the total opposite of me. She is just a bit taller than me and she wears heels, hooker heels and then she cannot walk in them, it cracks me up. She has short blonde hair, she does like make up and girly things, she is soft and caring. She is the type of person that would cry at Bambi, wears her heart on her sleeve kind of person. She would do anything for you and would fall in love in the drop of a hat. One Of the nicest people you will meet. She knows everything about me. She is basically, the opposite of me looks and personality wise. I am loud, like loud, what I lack in height I make up for in noise. I have an attitude of I do not give a fuck. I am the kind of person if you said to me does my bum look big in this? I would say no your arse is just big full stop. I do not hold back; I think I just got worse with age. If I do not like you, I do not put up with you. You know that way if you cannot be bothered with someone you try and put up with them, well I do not. Maybe that is why I only have a handful of friends lol. They call me the Ice Queen, I like it, I think they thought it would annoy me, but it does not. I just do not give a shit. If I do not like you then I am not going to waste my time getting to know you. It is pointless. If I have something to say, then I will say it directly to your face and not behind your back. I call a spade a spade and I am honest and open. Maybe a little too honest at times. I might not give a dam about a lot of things, but I am the kind of person if I had five pounds and you needed five pounds, I would give it to you and do without. My kindness is not a weakness it is just part of who I am.

Then there is Demi, omg what can I say about Demi. She is a nightmare, an absolute nightmare. We are a year apart so that would make her 42. See that £5 she would take it then ask for another £5. Give her an inch and she would take a mile. We are the same height; the same red hair and we both have the same temper. We have been friends/cousins all our lives. Her mum is my godmother. We are not blood cousins we all just grew up together. Her mum and dad were friends with my mum and dad when we were young and still to this day, we class each other as cousins. She is like thrush; you just cannot get rid of her no matter how many times you try. We grew up together, we peed the bed together (yes, I peed the bed when I was younger – so did Demi) and blamed each other we have laughed together been through everything together in life and we are still together. She is probably the only person who knows everything about me and does not judge me, and vice versa.

My lifelong friends Claire and her husband Richard. I have known them for 20 odd years, we all met at a dog show one year in Clarkston and we have been friends ever since. It is the kind of friendship where you both have work and other things, so you do not get to see each other all the time but when you do it is just like yesterday. Claire is the kind of friend if you murdered someone you could tell her; you could tell her anything and you can trust her 1 million percent, the same applies to Richard. In fact, he would probably murder the person for you ha-ha.

Chapter 3

Its Saturday and the shop is heaving. It is always busy at the weekends. People come from miles because we are the only shop who sells a huge range of exotic pets. We have skinny pigs (hairless guinea pigs) African pygmy hedgehogs, various snakes, chameleons, water dragons, Bosc monitors and much more so there is always two or three of us working at the weekend. By this point I am clued up. I have researched a lot of stuff; Matty knows everything, and my friend Claire works at the weekend. She has kept snakes and reptiles for years, so she knows her stuff. So, we are all working away, and the chime goes, my back is to the door so I cannot see who came in, but I get a funny feeling and I turn around and there he is. OMG there he is and Jesus he looks amazing. The two times I have seen him previously he had his working gear on. This time he has tight fitted jeans on and a black jumper with a light brown leather jacket and he just looks amazing. I knew I was doing it, but I could not stop myself and there I was again staring. Just standing and staring I must have looked like a Flamen goldfish in a bowl just staring, gob opened and staring. Matty comes up to me and says Oh Murrin I will let you get this one. Matty then goes over to Claire and the two of them are giggling. There it is again like school, oh so and so fancies so and so and everyone gathers and laughs. I may as well have had a big board on me saying enter the vagina. I go over to talk to him and he smells amazing. Omg he smells amazing. Looks amazing, smells amazing and he is talking to me and I am just thinking strip. Have your wicked way with me do what you want to be but just take me here and now. I do not do one-night stands but for you I will make an exception. I can hear they two giggling and laughing and I do not care, the only thing I care about is standing right in front of me. When I finally get myself together and listen to what he was saying he wants to leave his number so I can try and get him a nosey faley. Oh, my fucken god. Ding, dong, merrily on high. All my birthdays and Christmas have come at once. He wants to give me his number, and you know what that means when he wants to give you his number. He is thinking the same as me. It is not one sided, if he were not interested, he would not want to give me his number. It is like the 4th of July going on in my head fireworks are going off all over the place, bells are ringing, and I just want to burst but I played it cool. I took his number and said I would try and source one for him and a set up to go with it. How the hell was I going to do that. I could not get another one for someone else, but he has given me his number and said to text or call him and then leaves.

Matty and Claire are howling. They think it is funny because I am never like this with a guy, I play hard to get, what is the saying treat them mean and keep them keen. That was my moto, I never get all gooey over a guy, and I never go for guys that look like they have just stepped out of a boy band. It is not my thing and yet I am drawn to this guy who probably takes longer than me to get ready. I am a 5-minute wonder. Run the straighteners through my hair put on mascara maybe lipstick sometimes and I am done. This guy is like preened to perfection. He has left the shop and that is my brain cells gone for the day. I imagine him kissing me, I wonder if he is a good kisser, or he is so good looking he kisses like a washing machine or a goldfish. I can still smell him even though he is away. His aftershave is lingering in the shop and my heart is beating faster than normal and I am all warm down there thinking about him. Do you ever get that feeling if you fancy the ass off someone and you look at them the vagina melts? I'd 1certainly let him melt me that is for sure. The rest of the day was worthless. I could not concentrate on anything else except Dexter and imagining what I would do to him or for him. People were coming in and out of the shop and Denise and Stephen had to deal with them. I was too busy dealing with my thoughts.

It was later Matty and Claire left, and I was closing the shop myself, I was sitting there thinking, will I? Will I not? Will I text him, will I not? I could use the excuse that I found the set up and how much it cost. It was him that gave me his number so did that mean the ball was in my court. I was not sure, so I did what I always do. I wrote no on one piece of paper and yes on the other piece of paper and I picked yes. So, fuck it, I will do it. So, I wrote, Hi Dexter its Murrin, just to let you know I have looked up the cost of the set up bla bla bla. When really, I wanted to text Hi Dexter, come and fuck my brains out please, but the first text was appropriate. I had just sent the text and he texted straight back saying thanks bla bla bla, then asked how the shop went afterwards and kept the chat going. We chatted for quite a while, not about anything much just general chat. Then it comes again, I'm thinking about him and I'm thinking about him kissing me about him touching me and that's me got myself Horney as anything and to the bedroom I go and visit my purple surprise (my vibrator) I've only just turned the bloody thing on and you are lucky if it vibrated for 10 seconds and I was gone like a gas explosion. What the hell is going on with me, what is this guy doing to me. As soon as I think about him the vagina needs a friend.

Chapter 4

We have been chatting by text all the time now, it has been a few days. We have not spoken about anything untoward. Just general chit chat. He texts me first thing in the morning and we carry the chat on all day until I go to sleep. This has been a good few days now. So, we have built up a friendship and I really like him as a person. I feel comfortable talking to him about anything and everything. We literally send about 100 texts a day from the minute I open my eyes until I close them. Do not get me wrong, I fancy the pants off him, but it is the look he gives me and that smile. Now I feel comfortable enough to ask him his age. He is 24, I told him I was almost double his age, he said he did not care. He enjoyed chatting to me and we did have a lot in common, but we also had a good laugh. This went on for weeks. I mean every morning when I woke up, I woke up to a text from him. We would send texts all day and night until I fell asleep. It is not as if he said oh I can only text during certain times or anything like that and we did text each other all day. The texts started going from normal chat to flirty chat you know when you cross the boundary from oh how's work to, I like your hair, I love your smile and your eyes. He thought the same as me we both loved each other smile and the way we looked at each other. He said that to me, when he sees me no matter how bad a day, he is having I always turn his frown upside down. When he looks at me he wants to kiss me and I felt the exact same, Jesus Christ this purple surprise has never been used so much in its life and then came the bombshell message, I need to tell you something he said I'm engaged. Jesus fucken Christ. You would have been as well shooting me in the gut. I was already hooked. He had me at Hello from that first day he walked into the shop. He had me. All these weeks we have been texting, but how can that be possible, how can he manage to send all they messages every day and not get caught. He must have been sitting beside his fiancé and texting me at the same time. I was devastated, totally devastated. All this time, so many personal things I had told him and the same from him to me. I had never been so open and honest about my feelings to anyone before. I did not know that I was even capable of such a thing. I should have known, from the minute he walked into the shop and looked at me with that look I should have known. I was gutted, totally gutted. I felt as if someone had ripped me open and took out my insides. So many texts, how could this be possible, how can someone be in the same house as someone and send that many texts. I did not text back for a while. In such a short period of time I was hooked, when my phone lit up, my face lit up because it was him. I still had that warm fuzzy feeling every time I spoke to him. I was gutted totally gutted. I did not answer his text. I did not know how to respond to it, and I did not want him knowing how badly the news had been for me. So, he texted back asking can we still be friends because there was a brilliant friendship there, and that there was an explanation as to why he was engaged but messaging me all day that he would explain. I could not answer him back, I knew it would have come out the wrong way and I did not know what to do. I had already fallen for this guy. It was the whole package. I was attracted to him, I fancied the pants off him, I had built a friendship with him. I looked forward to his texts and our banter together and it was all about to get ripped away before it even began.

The following day he texted in the morning the same as he always did. He said that he would come into the shop and explain. He was not happy in his relationship with Lorraine. It had broken down years ago. He worked for Lorraine's parents. They had a house together bla bla bla. It was an awkward situation. The same as what any other man would say who wants his cake and eat it. The problem was I had already fallen for him. It was too late. We had built a friendship first. He became the person that I could talk to about anything and everything and he never judged me. I woke up with a smile on my face when I saw his message in the morning and it would keep me going all day and we said good night to each other every night. In such a short space of time I had feelings for him. How could this be possible. I was never a feeling kind of person. I have previously been married and that is a whole other book. I went to hell and back with my husband and I swore to myself that I would never, ever let another man in. I was so young when my husband and I met, I did not really know what love was. I had never understood true love. I can hear myself shouting at me saying it is the same old chestnut. Walk away, just walk away now. They all say that. It is the cliché I am not happy in my relationship. So why not leave then? If you are not happy then leave. My head is saying one thing and my heart is saying another. How can this have happened to me. I do not do the whole feelings shit. I never let anyone in. I never let anyone know what I am really thinking or feeling inside so why have I fallen for this guy so quickly and it is about to get taken away before its even started.

Chapter 5

So, I am on fuck book and I get a friend request from a David Williams and I accept. Thought nothing else of it until he sent me a message. It only happens to be an ex from the past, great just what I need right now, or maybe that is exactly what I needed a distraction from Dexter. So, I start chatting away and one thing leads to another as it does, and we are going on a date. A date, bloody great I hate dates. I hate going out on dates to a restaurant the noise of other people eating food annoys the life out of me. I want to smash their faces in and tell them to shut the fuck up. Plus, I usually talk to Dexter all night. I will need to tell him I cannot text tonight I am going on a date. Did I do it to make him jealous, Of course I did. I wanted a reaction. I wanted to know if he felt the same about me as I did about him and it worked a treat. He was spitting feathers. Send me a picture of what you look like. Will you miss talking to me? I will miss talking to you. Will you text me when you get home? I did not even want to go on the date. I just wanted a distraction away from Dexter. David came up to the flat instead. We watched some TV he was going on about how great it was that we had found each other again after all this time, and all I could think about was Dexter. I could hear my phone pinging. I knew who it was. I took my phone into the toilet and it was a message from Dexter saying he misses me, text him when I get home. I told him I did not go on the date. He had come up to the flat instead and that I had come into the toilet to message him. I knew there and then this was not going to end well. I knew I had fallen for him and vice versa, but he was engaged to another woman. I cannot even say if he told me straight away it would have been any different. I had never felt like that before with anyone. It was instant, from the first time I saw him, and he looked at me the way he did I was hooked. There is no other way to say or put it. I was not interested in David, I only wanted Dexter. David stayed for a while and then left. I did not even kiss him good night when he left. I just let him go and went straight for my phone.

It is the weekend and one of the girls from class is 18. We have all been invited to her party. Again Dexter, will you send me a picture before you go out. Let me see you, do you think you will meet anyone tonight? I have still been seeing David, I am trying to distract myself away from Dexter. Nothing has happened yet. We still chat all day every day. I know at this point it is wrong. Its more than just friends. We have told each other a lot of personal stuff. He continues to text all day every day and comes into the shop after he finishes work. The girls come to my house for a few drinks before the party and we get ready I did my hair, put some lipstick and mascara on then sent him a picture. He replies saying I look very sexy and that he will miss me tonight, but can I text him and let him know I am ok, and I got home.

We all go out and have a great night. Everyone comes back to my flat after the party and we continue to drink into the early hours. Total disaster because I must get up and open the shop in the morning and Sunday is a busy day. When I get up, I am still drunk. Luckily, I only stay two minutes from the shop, so I walk to the shop and open it up. Dexter messages to see how I am. I told him I had not long gone to bed and that I was still blazing drunk. He says I will come into the shop and see you. I said no chance bad idea. Being sober and resisting each other was bad enough but adding alcohol to the mix would be a bad idea. You know what I it is like when your drunk. Your senses are all over the place. You dare to do stuff you would not normally do. Me, him and booze would not go together, and I told him that on the phone. Do not come into the shop it is a bad idea. What did he do? He came into the shop with a six pack of beer. A six pack of beer and that look. He knew what he was doing. I had already told him about the way he looks at me. It makes me go all gooey, it is the killer look. He comes over to me to give me the beer and it is too late. Our lips meet and we are kissing in the middle of the shop. His lips are so soft, he does not kiss like a washing machine or a goldfish. It is nice its tender, there is some tongue but not too much, its passion and lust at the same time. You can feel the force of the kiss, and I am thinking oh please do not touch me. I will go, I will go like a cylinder head gasket. I can feel him pressed against me and he is going hard. We are just getting into the kiss and the fucken chime goes. Oh, my fucken god. Bastards! Whoever it is they are bastards. Total bastards.

Its Les, he is in for rats for his snake. I could kill him. Cock blocking bastard. This has been a build up for weeks, months. Have you any idea what that kiss meant or how long it has taken, and you cock blocking bastard have just ruined it. Take your rats and shove them right up your arse. I look like Madonna in that video with they pointed tits, my nipples have gone hard and I have just looked over and Dexter's still hard and he is trying to hide it. I am crossing my arms and laughing at the same time. Why am I laughing? It is a nervous laugh, Its happened. After all this time it happened. I know It is wrong on so many levels, but I have fallen for this man hook, line and sinker. Well there is no going back now. Its officially started. I laugh at people when they say oh, I have fallen for a married man or a man who is involved with someone else. I laugh and tell them they will never change. Do not do it. Why would you even put yourself through that and now I am doing the exact same thing. I am the brunt of the joke now, I am that person, the one everyone laughs at and says what an idiot, but I don't care, I don't care because its him and the hold he has over me in such a short time is too strong. I have tried to fight it. But I just did not win.

Les eventually leaves the shop. It seems like he had been in for hours. Harping on about snakes and feeding and bla bla bla will you just get to fuck already. I want to go back to the kissing, I want to go back to feeling Dexter's lips against mine, that soft skin and feel the hardness against me. The minute his arse is out of the door I go and get the keys and lock the shop. Fuck the customers I do not care. All I care about is the kissing. He comes over to where I am and lifts me onto the counter. I can feel him pressing against me, he is hard, the kissing is passionate and I get the warmth again, my nipples are like boulders, we are just getting into it and chap chap, would you bloody believe it someone is at the door. Why didn't we go into the back shop? Why would we even do anything in the front shop. He is engaged for god sake. We could get caught. See, this is what happens with alcohol you lose all your senses you think your invincible. Someone is trying to tell us to stop. What we are doing is wrong. It is wrong on so many levels, but I just cannot fight it or stop it. I want him so bad. I want to be with him so bad. He is all I think about from I open my eyes in the morning until I go to sleep at night.

After the chap at the door, I said he had better leave. It was too dodgy, what if we had got caught. Anyone could have been at the door. It could have been Lorraine or David. I have still been seeing David. Nothing serious. It was more of a distraction hoping It would take my mind off Dexter but who was I kidding? He was the only one I wanted. After he left the shop, he began texting again, but the texting moved up a level from flirting to I did not want to leave the shop, I cannot believe we done that. I wanted it to go on longer. What do you think would have happened if someone had not come to the door? I dread to think what would have happened. I had played this scenario in my head for weeks. I had imagined how this would go for weeks what the kiss would be like. How it would feel if he held me if he touched me. How I would feel, how he would feel, and it was amazing. I can still smell him on me. His aftershave is lingering even although he has gone. I can still taste him.

Chapter 6

David has come up to the flat and making dinner. He has brought up the ingredients himself to make me dinner because he knows I am hung over from the night before and I have been working all day. Or so he thinks. I am still half drunk, and if you call kissing Dexter working then hell yeah, I have been working all day. I love my work. I run a bath while he is making dinner and I am lying in the bath thinking about Dexter. I have my phone in the bathroom with me and I am talking to him and having a bath at the same time. We are still reminiscing about today's events wondering what would have happened if the door did not go, how far do you think it would have gone. Him telling me he wanted to do that from the beginning, so did I. The messages have taken a different turning now. Is this what you call an affair. Omg it is. I am the other women. If you had known how many times, I have told people in the past that they are so stupid, they will never leave their wives, partners. Do not do it and I have just done the same thing. David is in the kitchen making me dinner and I am lying in the bath talking to another man. Wanting to be with this other man. It is so wrong. I know it is so wrong, but I cannot help it. I really cannot help it.

David and I have dinner and I am sitting here thinking. Oh, I cannot do this. I really cannot do this. It is like cheating. I have just not five minutes ago kissed another man. I wanted to be with another man. I have lay in that bath talking to another man while he has made my dinner. How selfish is that. How wrong is that. He is asking if he can stay the night so he can have a few beers. You know what that means, he wants sex. Can I stay the night? Why do men always say it as can I stay the night. It is not there the spark is not there the passion is not there the lust is not there. I would just as well lie like a sack of potatoes or you would need a set of jump leads to get me going. It is just not there. I know he was a distraction, but it has not worked, and it is not fair. He made the dinner though and it is only fair that he has a beer. Nothing needs to happen. Two people can share a bed and not have sex. I have shared a bed with a guy before and not had sex, but it is ruining my text time with Dexter.

22

Why did he have to ask if he could stay the night and have some beer. I am fuming, I will have to take my mobile back to the bathroom again to text Dexter. This is when I know it is so wrong. I am hiding the fact that I am texting someone. I am not in a serious relationship with someone, but it is still wrong. I am having to take my mobile to the toilet to text and that is when I start to wonder, well how is Dexter managing to constantly text me from 7am until whatever time I fall asleep every day. Does he spend the night in the toilet with his phone? Surely that is not what he does, but how can he get away with texting all day and night and Lorraine does not know. It must be true, their relationship must be over. So why does he not just leave. I am telling myself this. I can hear one me shouting at the other me. Do not do it, just do not do it.

David stayed the night, we did sleep in the same bed together, but we just did not have sex together. He did not question it, he probably just thought I was going to make him wait because we had only just started dating again. The second time that I went to the toilet was the last time I spoke to Dexter that night and I felt cheated. I felt as if I had been cheated out of my text time with Dexter. How dare he ask to spend the night and ruin my text time with Dexter.

Chapter 7

As usual we have been texting each other all day, he said he is coming into the shop after work. Oh god, this might be it. This might just be the day it happens. Oh god, I better run home and get sexy underwear on just in case. Make sure I am shaved and raring to go. I rush home, get my best underwear on, check the lady garden looks inviting and off back to the shop.

He walks in the door just after 4pm, he has his work trousers on, oh god I love these work trousers he has, they are like black combat trousers with grey pockets, he has a black t shirt on and of course his baseball cap. He looks at me and I am gone. He comes behind the counter and he pulls me towards him. He is hard already. I tell him to hang on and I go and lock the shop door. I take him by the hand, and we go into the back shop where no one can see us. If anyone comes to the door, they cannot get in. Let them chap It will look like I have gone out. There is a freezer in the back shop, he lifts me up against the freezer and we start to kiss, his lips are so soft, and I begin to bite them a little bit, I can feel he is hard already, I can feel him thrusting against me. Every part of me wants him. I want to feel him inside of me, but I know when I give myself to him then I will really give myself to him and that is what frightens me the most. Letting go. It is too late to turn back now, I jump off the freezer and take down his combats, he has white Calvin Klein boxer shorts on. I take them off and turn him around. You can tell he is not sure what is going on. He has obviously never had this before, I part the cheeks of his arse and run my tongue up and down, slowly circling the bum hole, it makes him twinge, it always does, men are so sensitive there they just don't know it. Some do not want to admit it. He keeps twitching, but you can tell he likes it. He is taking my clothes off, I am taking the rest of his clothes off and we are having sex, up against the freezer in the back shop. It is so wrong, but it feels so right, it feels like we were meant for each other. That our bodies have come together as one. We are moving in unison to each other and it feels amazing. It is not sex, it is making love, because I am in love with this man, very much in love with him. This is all going to go horribly wrong.

I do not understand this, I really do not get this, I am never like this with anyone. I do not let people in. I always keep people at arm's length. My friends, my family. I just do not let people in. I just cannot do it. I am so severely damaged inside. I thought I was dead inside, not capable of feeling anything. I carry a dark secret about with me and I tell no one. Only a handful of people know, and I do not let them in. I cannot it is the fear of being hurt, I am already so hurt and angry inside that there is not room for anything else. I cannot trust anyone else. If I become too friendly even with my friends, I take a step back. I love my friends; I do not tell them that. I do not even say it to my family. I cannot do it. I am scared, scared to let anyone in, scared to let anyone know what goes on inside my head. If you saw me in the street, or you know me. You would think I was the happiest person ever. It is a mask, I get up every morning and put that mask on. I walk out the door and that mask is like super man's cape kind of thing. The me that everyone else knows is like a superhero kind of me. It is like what I aspire to be, happy, funny, I do not give a shit about anything or anyone. I do not do feelings, emotions, I do not cry at bambi. If you saw me you would think, ah she just says it how it is, she is so funny and happy. It is all bull shit. It is a mask, the real me is dying inside, I am so damaged that there is no room for other feelings. I did not think I could have other feelings other than what I carry about with me every day, yet I know in my heart I have feelings other than hate and anger for this man. How can this be possible because the real me is dying, the superhero side of me does not give a shit about anything. So, which me has the feelings, I do not know. I just know that I feel something. I like it and I hate it at the same time because I am terrified, terrified of either part of me letting go and letting someone in.

25

Chapter 8

I have decided it is time to get another dog. I lost my dog over 10 years ago and replacing a dog is not an easy thing. People who do not have dogs do not understand that they are part of the family. If you lose your dog it is the exact same as losing a family member. I already have a sphynx cat (bald cat with no fur, they are hairless) called Thelma I just could not replace my dog. Dogs are so loyal, no matter what you do or say they never judge you. Maybe that is why I prefer animals to humans. I have been thinking about it for some time now and as god as my witness the postman has just came and delivered a magazine type thing with a bulldog on the front. Omg that is it, it is a sign. It is fate. I am meant to get another dog. I am one of these people if I get an idea or want something, I need to have it now. So, off I go onto the computer and look up for bulldog puppies for sale, low and behold there are some in Dunfermline. Phone the person up and he says he has both bitches and dogs. Happy Days I am going through tonight to see them and pick one.

Dexter said he would come with me, he was just as excited as I was. I was wishing the day away. I was going to get a new dog and we would get to spend a few hours together. I was buzzing. Nothing and no one were going to spoil today, I was on such a high. I love dogs, I love all animals. I love how they accept you for who you are, and they do not ask for anything in return except loving and getting fed. They would be the one standing beside you in battle, there in the good times and the bad times. There by your side until the end.

He comes to pick me up in the works van, we are both like teenagers laughing and giggling all the way to Dunfermline, just as we are about to get to where the person stays, Dexter pulls over and takes me into the back of the van. No one is going to come to the shop door, no chime is going to go, no one is going to chap the shop window. It is just us locked inside the back of a van with no one else. I had gone and got sexy underwear. It was black, black is his favourite colour. Its crotchless and a black bask top. As soon as he sees it, he immediately goes hard.

Underwear is his thing. He has a fetish for underwear, and I was all but too willing to feed his desire. I knew he would appreciate it. I knew he would think I had gone to some effort to please him and please him I did. It was amazing. Knowing that no one was going to interrupt us, you would think that the thrill of maybe getting caught would be more exciting but not this night. This night was the night that I could do anything and everything to him and no one would come. It was just me, him and dirty sex in the back of an old works van.

I picked my little girl after that. Omg this was a night to remember we had just had amazing sex and now I was faced with a room full of little balls of wrinkles running about. I was in my element. The saying is true, the dog chooses you. You do not choose it. She came up to me and immediately I knew I had fallen in love. I could love a dog; they were not going to hurt you. Not like humans it is a different kind of love. I picked my little girl. She was not ready to leave yet. I had to wait another 2 weeks to get her. I had already chosen a name for her before I even got her. Dexter said to me you do not know she might not look like a Levi but from the minute I clapped eyes on her I knew. I just knew.

Chapter 9

After the first time it got easier, or should I say it became a routine. We would text each other all day and night. Most days he would come into the shop and off we would go into the back shop and lock the door.

The texting started to take a different twist on things. It was as if the sex brought us closer together. Dexter started to open more. He had told me that he lost his brother when he was young, his brother had been killed by a bus when he was only 16. He felt cheated out of his childhood because his parents did not take it too well especially his mum, and why the hell would they. I could not even begin to imagine how that was for a family. He was close with his brother and he missed him so badly. I had a twinge of jealousy when he told me that because me and my sister are not close, in fact I am not close with anyone. Is that all my own doing. I never talk about what happened. I cannot do it. It is too painful. It is as if, if I say it out loud to anyone then I have to accept it, I have to deal with it so I keep it buried in the back of my head, but he has just told me his darkest secret about his brother and his feelings and I have felt jealous of how he has spoken about his brother and how close they were. What they used to talk about at night, what they got up to in their room when their parents went to bed. How is brother Kevin would sneak out at night and Dexter would cover for him. It was joy, it was happiness. Although it was so sad that he lost his brother, you could tell he really loved him. His mum took the death the worst, Jesus Christ I imagine she would, can you imagine your child going before you. The person that you nurtured all that time of pregnancy and after they are born. I could not imagine it. I have never had children. I never wanted them. I did not want to bring another human being into this world. I always said when the time was right, and my head was right I would foster children that needed help. So, I cannot begin to imagine how either of his parents felt. Dexter felt as if he was cheated out of his childhood, him and his sister Joanne. His friend Justin's mum Dianne brought him, and Joanne up took them holidays did things with them and he felt wronged by that. As an outsider looking in. I could see it from both angels. I can understand why he feels like that but then I can also see it from his mum's perspective even though I have never seen or met the woman I understand. Her insides must feel like mine. She must be as dead inside as I am. No mother should ever have to bury a child before her. It is not right. I am always honest with him, so I tell him I understand both sides. I explain how his parents feel inside, I have not yet said why but I have put a different spin on things and now he understands. I was in no way taking anything away from him. He lost his brother who was his best friend, his partner in crime. The one who told him stories about girls, and booze, the things most boys talk about. He missed that. His brother would never get to see him have his first car, his first proper girlfriend, his wedding, his first child or children. It was horribly taken away from him and the rest of his family. It is a horrible story.

He has just unloaded his secret and his true feelings about his brother and although it is sad, I am jealous. I am jealous of how he can freely talk about his brother and how much he loved him and misses him terribly I am jealous because I do not have that, I do not have they feelings. Sure, my sister and I are ok, she obviously knows my secret, she thinks I should just be able to deal with it. If only it was that easy. We have had fun together but not like what they have what they had. I cannot openly talk about my feelings. I do not tell my sister that I love her or vice versa. We never speak about what happened and I keep everything to myself and it is been hidden for so long, not spoken about for so long that the carpet is at the roof. You know the saying just sweep everything under the carpet, well I have swept everything under that carpet for so long that the carpet is at the roof and it has no place else to go.

Now it has got me thinking about it, him unloading his secret has brought jealousy, because I do not have that, I cannot have that, and the reason why I cannot have that has come to the surface and within minutes I have hit a dip. Jesus Fuck I have hit a dip. I have what I call dips, potholes and then your fucked. I have hit a dip, this has hit a nerve.

What am I going to do because I cannot speak to anyone about this when I am like this except one person? Steven. Steven and I met many years ago through work. We became good friends; I knew straight away that he was someone that I could trust. There is no point in asking why I knew I could trust him when I am not a trusting person, but I know Steven is like me. Do not ask me why I know, it's not as if we have a wee club together but you just know. So, one night out of the blue he sent me a message with a secret that he had been carrying about for years. After he told me. I said I already knew, when he asked why I knew I told him because the same happened to me. Please do not ask me how you know, you just know. The way the person carries themselves. We try too hard to be happy and funny because it is what we want to be inside. We put on a front as big as Brighton Pier so that the world does not know what is really going on inside. There is no middle ground. You are either up in the clouds or your down in the gutter. We never meet in the middle. There is no middle ground and I still to this day do not know why.

It is the stupid things that set you off, a noise, a smell something that someone says. Its stupid things, like what I have just been told. It is nothing to do with me, it is his story, but it has affected me in a way that I have hit a dip. Fuck, how do I get out of this because it is only the afternoon and we text each other right up until bedtime fuck, fuck, fuck. I cannot tell him, no chance. I am not ready to tell him I need to lie, what the fuck am I going to say. He will know, he will know by the way I am texting that something is wrong. I cannot lie. We have never lied to each other, what am I going to do. Before I know what, I have done I have texted him and told him the truth. I was abused as a child by my grans husband. Not my papa, well he was not my dad's real dad. Him and my gran had split, and she was with another man called Donald. I was abused as a child and I have just said it. Jesus Fucken Christ, I have just said it, even though I have not said it out loud. I have still said it. Why the hell did I do that. Why could I not have just kept my big mouth shut and had a bit of happiness for a while longer. Dexter had become a brilliant distraction from what I carry about every day. Every day is a struggle to get up, put the mask on and walk out the door. Every bloody day. Yet here was my chance of a little happiness, even though I knew it was wrong. It was happiness that I had never known before. I believed Dexter and that his relationship had ended. He was still there living in the same house and I knew, deep in my heart I knew it was wrong, but I wanted and craved that little bit of happiness for once in my life rather than misery, anger and emptiness.

I was dreading the returned messaged. I thought who will want to take on something so damaged, so empty and filled with so much anger and misery. He replied saying how brave I was, how do I manage to deal with this every day. No one has ever said that before. People think it happened so long ago why can you just not accept it and move on. I cannot, if I knew the answer to that then I would be a millionaire, or the best psychiatrist in the world. I cannot get past this. It haunts me every single day of my life. Sure, I am living, but it is not living its simply existing and making it through another day. If it has not happened to you then you cannot know what goes on in my head and why I cannot get past it. I just cannot. If you know me as a friend or an acquaintance you think oh, she is lovely, so happy and bubbly. Its bullshit. I am dying inside. I cannot feel emotions, I did not think it would be possible to love someone and let someone inside my head even just a little bit for the fear of getting even more damaged. Only 2 of my friends know outside my family and I cannot even let them in. I trust them with my life, I could not be without them, but I never tell them and when we start to get too close then I back off. Its instinct, it just happens naturally. I am even like that with my family. I do not tell any of them that I love them, I did not think I was capable of such a thing and yet I know I feel something for this man, and I do not like it because I am terrified. Terrified of being damaged even more than I am and feeling any kind of emotion at all.

I tell him that I just need a bit of time to myself tonight. I will text him goodnight, but I just need to straighten my head. I immediately go for my phone and speak to Steven.

Chapter 10

Oh god where do I start with this. Steven and I have remained friends since we met. We are each other's go to. If we hit a dip, we go to each other, if we hit a pothole, we go to each other and it is a relationship that no one will ever understand. He is exactly like me. Dead inside, totally dead and totally damaged. We are either great for each other or total toxic for each other. There is never an in between. Kind of like our moods, its either up in the clouds or in the gutter. Our relationship is the same. Really good or bad. Usually everyone will joke if you find one then you will find the other. Do I love this guy, yes of course I do? I have never told him that but yes, I love him for the way he is, for what he has overcome and is still here. It is a different kind of love though. It is a love that I cannot explain, a bit like our relationship but I know that no matter what, this man will always be in my life. We are bonded with something that is as horrible as it is good. Everyone I date hates him with a passion. It is a jealousy thing but none of them know or understand why we are the way we are and to be honest I really do not give a fuck. He is either my magic potion or bonfire night. That is how extreme it is. We think the same, we have so much in common apart from the obvious and we just work, or not sometimes. We are there for each other to help each other, or we take everything out on each other. Have a blazing row and then we are friends again. We have lived together, slept together, went into business together had laughed together, had enormous arguments together but it is always together. He dates people, I date people, we are not in a relationship as such we are just bonded together by something so horrid.

We are different by the way it affects us, Steven goes down the self-harm route, I go down the anger route, always lashing out at other people. I am the nicest person you will meet but if you do me wrong then I am your worst nightmare and I would fight to the death. It would not bother me. The only way you will get one over on me is if your prepared to kill me. It is the only way I am going down. Man or woman I just do not care. If you pick a fight with me then I will happily accept, if I am having a dip or a pothole, the thought of smashing someone's face off the pavement to hear the bones crack would be a huge relief for me. I have so much hurt and anger inside it must come out somehow. When I was younger, I was always getting into fights. If anyone got beat up by someone, they would come to me and I would happily accept the fight. Demi was always getting herself into trouble when she was younger. Usually stealing other girls' boyfriend's then the girls would want to kick her head in, and she would say that is fine. I will phone my cousin and off I would go. It was a way of channeling my anger. Was it wrong? Yes of course it was but at the time I did not care.

I did try kick boxing and martial arts as a way of channeling my anger, but I would always get carried away and get disqualified. I get too caught up. When I start, I do not want to stop? I just want to keep going. It was a relief for me. It was something that made me feel better, just not the other people at the other end of my fists. The bigger they were the more I wanted to smash their faces in.

I never went down the self-harming route like Steven did, I understand why he does it because you want to feel any other kind of pain other than the pain inside your head and your whole body. It might sound stupid to a normal person but no matter how much physical pain you endure it is not even a patch of the pain inside. Do not get me wrong, Steven also would argue black was white with anyone but 9 times out of 10 he came off the worst because he was so hammered.

That is another thing. Drink is not your friend. I learned that the hard way. You think at the end of a bottle there is a wee guy jumping about dancing like the tequila add. Is there fuck. It is your worst enemy. You drink to forget; you want to drink so much that you blank everything out. The only thing you black out is yourself at the end of the night with the amount of alcohol you have drank. You get up in the morning and it is still there. It is even worse now because you have a hangover and you are dealing with your demons, so what do you do? You simply start again and go on a bender for a few days until you physically cannot drink another drink.

It is a vicious circle, there is no right or wrong answer. People deal with things in different ways. We all find our own way of coping with things. I just chose to brush them under the carpet and forget about them until the carpet gets to the roof and you skip the dip and the pothole stage and go straight to your fucked stage. I have been there once, and I said never again. My answer was tablets, the chicken shit way out, but for me it seemed the easier way out. You get to a point where you just cannot take the pain any longer. It is so bad that you cannot breathe there is no room left inside for air, there is no room left for anything and all you can see is black. Nothing else just black, there is no light, there is no way of getting away from it. It follows you everywhere like the moon does. Every bloody day is a struggle to even get out of bed. If you do not face things and keep sweeping it under the carpet then it eventually has no place left to go except come out, but it all comes out at once with no letter saying eh hello I'm coming, it just comes and you are fucked. There is no place to run, no place to hide, there is no light, no hope, no nothing just pain, blackness and the feeling of no other way out except death. Death is your only option. It is your only friend, because if you die, it all dies with you. All that pain, anger, emptiness, hurt all the stuff that's swimming about your head like a fishbowl will die when you die. When you put it like that dying or death is a dream. It is a way out. It is a way to stop everything all in one go. People think that people who try and take their own lives are selfish. When you have walked in our shoes, dealt with the things that we deal with every single day in life, only then do you have the right to say its selfish. I would swap lives with someone who has not been sexually abused in an instant. I would give up everything I have, own or ever will own to know one day of peace in my head. Just one.

Chapter 11

David is coming up tonight and I need to tell him the truth. It is not fair, I know it has not been anything serious but there is no point in wasting his time. I only have eyes and a heart for one man and one man only, Dexter. When he comes up, I feel cheated out of my time with Dexter and I have now taken my mobile to the toilet on 2 occasions to speak to Dexter and it is wrong. It is simply wrong and its unfair. The only problem being he thinks everything is hunky dory and it is not. So why am I dreading doing this? What has happened to the I do not give a shit Murrin? It seems that more and more of her is going away day by day and it is this person with feeling and emotion that is left. I feel so bad. How can I not do this? The old me would just say, oh it is not working see you later, and not bat an eyelid. Where have I gone? I seem to be changing as the days go on. Do I like it? No not really. I feel exposed, I feel vulnerable. Is this what normal people feel like daily? Maybe being damaged is not so bad after all. I do not care about things or feelings or other people's feelings for that matter. I am dreading this. I know what I will do. I will go and get a bottle of wine and have a glass of wine for Dutch courage. Jesus are you even listening to yourself. What is wrong with you.

Just do what you would normally do and tell the guy to bolt. Simple. I am starting to change. I have not even realised myself until now that I have started to change. I go up to the flat, open the wine, have one glass, David has not arrived yet, 2 glasses, David arrives. I remember pouring the last glass and then Blackout. I wake up in the morning in bed. There is no David. I look around the bedroom and his stuff is not there. I go into the toilet for a pee and his toothbrush has gone. He insisted on leaving some toiletries the last time he was up, so it saved him bringing them up and down. Everything is gone. There is no sign of David, no sign of his belongings and I have no clue what I said for him to leave. Maybe I should have waited until after I told him before I opened the bottle of wine and then I think about my phone and Dexter, omg did I say goodnight to Dexter last night. I do not know.

After getting my phone and reading the messages from the night before it seems David and I got into argument and he left. I had only given Dexter a vague idea and description of how the night went but at least I said goodnight. I felt bad though, I felt bad for David. I felt awful about what happened. Maybe if we had met again before Dexter had walked into the shop it would have been a different scenario, who knows, but what I do know is nobody and nothing was going to come anywhere close to how I felt about this man. This man with the look. This man with the smile. This man who leaves his socks on when having sex for traction. This man who has walked into my life and began to melt the ice queen and make me feel something, anything other than blackness, hurt and anger. This man who has made me feel like a deer in amongst a pride of lions in a room, so very vulnerable and scared.

Chapter 12

The shop was starting to get quieter and quieter. The internet was killing it. I still had wages to pay and myself to pay but it got to the point I could not make everything meet. The electricity bill was through the roof with all the lights and heat lamps for the viv's, the water bills, it was just all bills, bills, bills and not enough money coming in to pay all the bills and wages. So, I did what I always do to make decisions I wrote close the shop in one piece of paper and keep it open on another. I picked close the shop and that was what I did. I started to sell everything off, my only worry was if I close the shop how to I get to see Dexter, because the shop was where we would always meet. He said he would work something out, so it was a win, win for me. It got to the point that I had no money left. Nothing. I had house rent to pay and no money, so I had to go and get a real job for a while. How the hell was I going to do that. I had not had a real job in like 15 years. I have always worked for myself or been self-employed. I was up shit creek without a paddle.

By the end of the day I have a job. I am one of these people who can sell sand to an Arab, or if I really want something, I will stop at nothing to get it. I phoned around all the local take away shops and found one willing to give me a chance. Great I can deliver food to people; it is not like working for someone. Its deliver and get paid. Happy days. I cannot stand the thought of having a boss to work for. I am far too, do not speak to me like that kind of person. I remember a job I had when I was younger. Omg it was a YTS way back then when you only got paid £29.50 a week. Can you imagine working for that these days? Imagine saying to teenagers these days you are working all week for not even thirty quid. They would tell you to bolt. Do not even start me on the young today. Soon we are going to have no policemen, no nurses or doctors because all everyone wants to do right now is be a social media star. Post pictures for likes and followers. It is beginning to feel like there never was a world before social media. We all played in the streets when we were younger and happy. Playing kick, the can, rounders. The kids these days will not go outside for the fear of missing a like on Facebook (or fuck book as I like to call it) or Instagram.

I was a trainee hairdresser; you will find I always flip from one thing to another. So, I am working away cleaning mirrors with newspaper (it works by the way) and one of the girls who started as a trainee the same as what I am now purposely knocks over the wee trolley thing with all the rollers on it and tells me to pick it up. Knowing fine well she did it on purpose and now she is telling me to pick it up. Get yourself to fuck, arsehole. Pick it up yourself and walked out the door.

Pretty much all the jobs I had after that were the same. I would flit from one job to another until I went to college and studied accounts. Oh yes, she is good with numbers. Not much else but numbers. I went to work in offices doing accounts and I hated it with a passion. Omg the people were so boring. They may as well have had sticks stuck up their arses because they were the most boring people ever. I loved math's and figures. I just could not stand the kind of people who worked in that sector except my last accounts job before going Self-employed. I was only there as a temp, waiting for the new girl to come. She had handed her notice in at her old work and there were a few weeks gap before she started so I was temping. It was a place that sold computers and stuff like that. It was all open plan, and everyone was on the same floor except the Directors, they have their own offices. Accounts was mixed with web design and sales. I loved it. There was a warehouse downstairs and I got on with everyone. Typical, just my luck. I got a job that I liked, and I was only there to temp until the new girl started, but I seemed to fit in. It was the first place where I seemed to fit in, and they embraced my madness. I do quizzes with all the employees after work and everyone puts in a pound. The person with the most correct answers wins the money. I love it here, it is great, instead of trying to calm me down, they embrace my madness. I do my work, of course I do my work, but the quiz is an after-work thing at 5pm when we all finish. I ended on a high. My last job for an employer was a great one. After that I became self-employed and I have been ever since, up until now.

Now I must go and deliver hot food from the takeaway shop to the people who order the food. Simple enough. Take the food, deliver it, get paid. Aye right, I did not get time to pee let alone anything else. As soon as I got a delivery then I am off to go and take it to the person waiting. The only problem is, by the time I get back there are more orders, sometimes 2 or 3 at the same time. I do not have time to pee, I do not have time to text Dexter. I have about 7 or 8 messages from him asking if I am ok. I have not replied, and I am thinking is it not obvious I am busy. He is missing me; he has not heard from me in a while. When I say we were constantly texting? I mean constantly texting. If I did not reply to his messages straight away, he would think something was wrong. Has he said something to upset me? Have I fallen out with him? Why have I not replied. I could hear my phone going ping, ping ping and I thought I need to pull over and send him a message before he has heart failure. I told him how busy it was, and he was not happy, he had become so used to me texting him back all the time when I was in the shop, but this was different. I cannot text and drive at the same time. I have a problem because I need the money to pay the bills, but I cannot do both at the same time. He is at work during the day, but he can text all day from work, right through to bedtime. I can reply during the day, but I cannot reply at night when I am doing the deliveries. We are not getting to see each other as much because I gave up the shop and it is starting to take its toll.

The messages yet again go in a different direction. It has gone from chatty, to flirty, to enjoying each other, to telling each other our darkest secrets to needing each other. He needs me and I needed him too, but I could not say that. I did not want to say that because there is that wee voice in my head saying this is not going to end well, you are going to get hurt and there is no more room in your head left for anymore hurt. It is not possible. Your head will just explode. I can tell by his response that he is not happy. He wanted me to say the same thing too, but I could not say it, I just could not say it. I felt it, I knew I felt it but if I said it then it was putting myself out there. It would be like putting a deer in a room with a hundred lions. He is asking me how I feel and at this point

I just cannot say it. I am sure he knows how I feel, it must be written all over my face when I see him. He must feel it in the kiss when I am kissing him, when I am touching him, when both of our bodies become as one. It's different. The sex is different from other people, I feel different. I feel as if I am giving him my whole sole when we are together. I have not had the shop for a while now so he comes to the flat when he can, now the sex has taken a different direction. We are not on the freezer in the shop, or in the van it is in a bed. We have never had sex on a bed before, it is weird, but there is another twist to it because I can dress differently. I love underwear. What woman does not feel sexy in nice underwear. We all do. It gives you that edge, that knowing the person you are doing it for will be turned on by it. You know they are going to be looking at you are thinking I cannot wait to take that off or keep it on. We have not been able to do this before. It has gone through so many stages, and with each stage new feelings and emotions develop and there I am a deer in headlights again because the more I want it, the more scared I become and I just know it is not going to end well.

Chapter 13

I have been doing the deliveries for a while now, although I am not just doing them for the takeaway place, I am doing them for a catalogue company too delivering clothes to people. This is not sitting well with Dexter. Two driving jobs and I cannot keep up with the texts and the driving. Something must give. I am missing out on text time with Dexter but also, I have been working so we have not physically seen each other face to face for a few days and like a junkie needs heroin we needed each other. That is how strong it feels, you cannot do without him or you go into withdrawal. He is telling me this, I really want to say the same, but he knows. He knows how damaged and frightened I am to let go. When I finish work at night and we get time to chat, he is telling me how much he has missed me, and it is not the same now during the day. We cannot constantly text each other and see each other and he asks me for a picture, but not a normal picture. He wants a picture of me with underwear on. Oh my god are you fucking joking me? I have never done anything like this before. Why the hell would I want to send anyone a picture of myself in my underwear you hear stories that things end up on the net when you post something its always there. No, I cannot do it. He is asking again, he said he misses me and misses looking at me can I just send one picture. He will send one to me. The next minute I get a picture message and I thought it would be him in his boxers but oh no it is the penis. The penis in all its glory standing to attention and I do not know what to do. He has done it. He says do you trust me. You know I would never show it to anyone else and I think oh fuck it. I take a picture of myself and send it. Then after I have sent it, I regret it. I start to panic in case it ends up in the wrong hands or someone else sees it. I know people do it all the time but that is them not me, but it is too late I have sent it. It has gone and that is that.

He texts me and said see that wasn't so bad, and I think about it and say well, actually it wasn't that bad and it is not as if he can show it to anyone else, by the end of the night it wasn't a good night text. It was good night phone sex.

Chapter 14

I got a new job, I ended up working for a courier company. I had saw an advert on gumtree and I thought well it is like what I do just now, but I will only need this one job. I went to see about the job, and I got it. I never really understand why people keep saying, oh there is no jobs out there. There is it is just you cannot be bothered to look.

So, the guys is asking me if I have had previous experience and I tell him I am doing the same kind of thing just now but for a take away place and a catalogue place. Exact same thing. He said have you driven a van before? Oh yes of course I have driven a van before. My fucken arse. Of course, I have not driven a van before, but I was not about to tell him that and not get the job, so I do what I always do and wing it. Brilliant then, you have got the job. Come to the depot and get your uniform. Pick up your van tomorrow when you start. You can take it home with you. Bob's your uncle, fanny is your aunt and your raring to go. So, I am telling Dexter and he says. I did not know you could drive a van. I know me either but Ill soon find out.

What did I do first day on the job? Smashed the bloody van. Oh, Jesus what am I going to do. I have only just started the Flippen job. Great start this is. I will just go back to the depot and say I was delivering a parcel, and someone hit the van while I was at the persons door. I will be fucked if I am saying it was me first day on the job. So, true to my thoughts I went back to the depot after my shift, put that sweet innocent face on and lied through my back teeth and they believed me. I was the only female in the depot. It was all men, but I seem to fit in better with men anyway rather than women. I am not really a girly girl. The thought of talking about hair, nails and make up bore the knickers off me.

I like this job in fact, I love it. I go into the depot in the morning get my parcels and away I go. No one telling me what to do, just driving about delivering parcels and meeting new people.

It has not been sitting exceptionally good with Dexter though. He is missing me every day. The delivery slots for the parcels are every couple of minutes so every second counts and I cannot get behind or it fucks the whole system up. Dexter is being more open and honest about his feelings and I am still scared, I am absolutely shitting myself because if I let go it is only going to end in heartache and so I take the plunge. I text him and say, I cannot do it anymore. I know for a fact that I am so in love with this man that I would die for him. I would literally stand in front of a loaded gun and give my life for his, but I cannot tell him that. I cannot put myself out there and tell him. He replies to me can we talk, can he please come up to the flat. No, I am literally in floods of tears because I want this man with every ounce of my being and I know I cannot have him. To end this now is bad enough but if it went on any longer and I got more attached than I already was I do not know what would happen.

The next minute the door is open, and he walks in. Bloody great, I look like I have golf balls in my eyes. I do not cry. I cannot remember the last time I cried. I did not even think I was capable of crying. He takes one look at me, kisses me on the top of the head and walks out the door. The minute the door closes, I find myself on the hall floor crying, as in really crying floods of tears. I feel as if someone has come into the house, got a Stanley knife ripped me open from my head to my toes and taken all my organs out. All that is left is a shell. I have gone from feeling nothing, to feeling something to feeling like everything has been ripped out of my body and here I am lying on the hall floor crying like a baby and I think to myself, this is why I have never truly loved anyone. This is why because this pain is almost as bad as the pain, I endure every single day. Although this is the first time it has happened. If it was something you went through every day in life it does not get easier the body just adapts to it. The body is a weird and wonderful thing. If it cannot cope with something it can shut it down or blank it out. If you are in constant pain, it does not go away the body just learns how to adapt to it and deal with it. I never ever want my body to adapt and feel like this ever again. If this is what love is, then I do not want it, because when it gets ripped away it is the second worse feeling in the world, and I cannot take any more pain. I have enough pain and hurt as it is. There is no room for anymore. The body cannot take anymore. I lie on that hall floor and I wonder to myself why did I put myself in a position like that when I knew it was going to end in misery. He had me from the get-go. Why didn't I listen to my head? It was screaming at you do not do this, and yet you still did it anyway. The want and desire far outweighed the walk away, and now this is what it has come to. You are on the floor crying and feeling as if your whole insides have been ripped out with a Stanley knife.

My phone goes, and I know its him. I cannot answer the phone because he will know I am crying. I do not want him to think he has had such an effect on me, so I do not answer the phone. He calls again, I still do not answer and then he messages saying please answer the phone I need to tell you something. I answer the phone, he stupidly asks if I am ok, and then he says. I need to tell you something but if I say it, I cannot take it back. I do not know what you mean by that. What do you mean? So, he repeats himself, I need to tell you something but if I say it, I cannot take it back after I have said it. Ok what is it. He says I love you. It is you, I love you. I want to be with you. I will give up my life, my house, my job everything to be with you. Oh, my fucken god. Really are you being real it is going to be me and you just us together. Yes, just us together forever. I love you; you are my best friend and I love you. I love everything about you. I want to be with you. Oh god what do I do? What do I say? Do I say it back to him? I have never said it. Am I capable of saying those 3 words and before I knew it, it was out my mouth and over the phone? I love you too

Chapter 15

As true to his word he went home and told Lorraine that he was leaving, he said that their relationship had been dead for many years but they had the house together, he worked for her parents, she did her thing and he did his. It did not sound like a relationship and there could not have been a relationship because no woman would let her partner sit there all night and message someone else. It just could not happen. He said that she had a male friend that she had met at the stable as her family had horses, she was more interested in the horses and her male friend and I never questioned it. Why would I? We did not lie to each other. We were open and honest with each other. I told him my darkest secret, in fact I told him everything. It was the one thing I always said from the start. The minute you lie to me, that will be it. No matter what. I already have huge trust issues and there is hell way and no way I was ever going to let anyone lie to me again. I said no matter how big or bad the truth is, I would rather know the truth. It was the one and only thing that I was adamant about. He was my best friend, my lover, my everything and that was what I saved him under in my phone. My Everything.

The split did not go as well as I thought it would, as far as I was concerned there was not a relationship, there was a bit of toing and froing in the beginning. A few arguments about the house, money the usual things. Dexter went to stay with his friends at first until things blew over and then he would move into the flat. Lorraine would call, there would be a huge argument and that went on for a little while, but it was money. They argued over money. Not why did you leave me because there was no relationship, but the arguments were always over money and who was getting what Dexter was staying with his friends for the time being, but they were also Lorraine's friends and Lorraine would turn up at the house to start arguments he said. So, he moved into the flat sooner than expected and it was to be the beginning of our happy ever after.

Chapter 16

I still had my job with the courier company and because Dexter worked for Lorraine's parents, he lost his job. So, I got him a job in beside me. He was to start work the following week, but he could come out and shadow me this week and I would show him the ropes for work. As always, we had a laugh. We always made everything into a laugh. No matter how bad it was we would always see the funny side of things and turn it around. We were like a pair of school kids getting up to naughty stuff and giggling away about it. I was changing. I could tell I was changing. That huge wall that I always had up was starting to come down brick by brick. A softer side of me started to appear. I was getting used to this love word and I was starting to show love which as something I had never done. We were in love; everyone could see we were happy and in love. The age gap never bothered us. We embraced it. We laughed about it. Age was nothing but a number. We loved each other; he was my best friend he was my everything and I was his soulmate.

His induction was to start in work the following week. Although I had started to soften the old Murrin was still there too. I am like mouth almighty. I could start an argument in an empty house if you pissed me off. I was in the depo arguing over parcels. The shift manager was being an absolute dick, and I was having none of it. He was trying to take the piss and I snapped. I am a red head with the worst temper ever. I can be your best friend one minute and your worst nightmare the next and you just do not see it coming. It is like a switch going on or off its that quick. I can go from zero to a hundred in nano seconds. So, I am standing in the middle of the depo, screaming at the top of my voice arguing with the shift manager and all these new starts appear for their induction. All eyes are on the midget with red head and one of the newbies say, oh my god who is that and Dexter says, it is my Mrs. Great way for him to start work but he did not care. That was the thing. He embraced my soft side and my other side. It was as if there was two different Murrin's. The one that Dexter knew, and the one that everyone else knew. I better make that three different Murrin's because there was the only that only Steven saw.

Steven is the only person who has seen me at the very top but also the very bottom. The one where I am in the gutter and it is not a nice place to be or to see. Dexter has not seen a hint of this side yet. I only had that little dip when he was telling me about his brother that was nothing. No one apart from Steven has seen me go from a hundred to a zero. Dexter knows about it but knowing about it and seeing it are two different things. Right now, the past few months have been a whirl wind. It is like Dorothy when she goes to bed in her aunt's house and then next minute the tornado comes and swishes the house away and she ends up in the wizard of oz. That is how life has been lately. I have not had time to dip, too much has gone on lately for me to dip. Therefore, I always work long hours. The minute your alone with your thoughts then you can go from ok, pass a dip and head straight for the pothole. Potholes are bad enough, when the your fucked comes, there is no guarantee you are going to make it out the other side. You just do not know, and if you are going through it alone then do not expect to come back out at the other side. Both Steven and I have been there all too often and it is not a pretty sight and for someone who has no clue what is going on inside your head and how it feels they can only help you the way they think they should help you. It is a vicious circle. It is practically impossible because If I could tell you what is going on inside my head and how to fix it then I would not wake up every day and put that mask on. I would not feel the hurt, anger and pain.

People think if everything else in your life is going good then surely you do not think about it or it is not there. It does not work like that. It is not as if you can write your brain a letter and say oh today is going to be a good day, can you please forget you have been abused until tomorrow. Thanks xxx

It is always there, it does not go away, the fucker unfortunately does not go on vacation and you get time out. It is there when you are happy. It is there when you are sad. It is worse when you are sad, but it is always there. It moves to a new house when you move to a new house. It becomes like a limb of your body. There is just no way of getting away from it, you just must learn to live with it. Some people do it better than others. Some people can speak openly about it straight away. I am not one of those people. For example, I went to get a tattoo one day. The worst mistake of my life, a day I will never forget. I had my periods (do not go for a tattoo when you have your periods bad ass idea it hurts like fuck the pain was almost unbearable) I sat there for over 4 fucking hours listening to this person telling me about how her mother passed her about to men like sweeties for sex. I have not met this person before, I do not know her from Adam and yet she is telling me all about what happened. My first instinct is to get to fuck but she has the tattoo gun and I am thinking, she will shut up in a minute. Did she fuck, she started to get more graphic about it, I do not know what worse, listening to her or the pain in my back it was my worst tattoo experience ever and I have more than a few. In a way though I was jealous. See there is that jealous thing again, I was jealous that she could just sit there and talk about it in a way that sounded like she was going to the shops for a packet of crisps. The worst thing she has probably ever been through in her life and she is talking about it as if, oh the crisps were salt and vinegar flavour. Inside I am screaming will you please shut the fuck up. It was a small room. There was myself and one other person being tattooed at the same time by another girl and she is there sitting telling 3 strangers that she was abused several times by several men and it was her mother that passed her about, and yet I thought she was casually talking about different flavour's of crisps. I could see the other woman's face, I do not think she could believe her ears either, but that must just be her way of dealing with it. We all deal with it in different ways. There is no right or wrong way to deal with it. You just deal with it as best as you can.

I have tried several different ways. The 2 most popular ones are drink or drugs. Thankfully, I have never gone down the road of drugs, but I never judge anyone who has. No one can ever judge anyone until they have walked in that person's shoes. Joe Bloggs down the street with the fancy big detached house and sports car may be a part time druggie, you never know. Some people are functioning drug users. Never judge a book by its cover until you have read it. People in glass houses should not throw stones, there are so many sayings, but they all mean the same dam thing. The junkie sitting in the street right now that you have just looked down your nose at could become you in a few years' time. You just do not know what is going to happen and you do not know what turned them to drink or drugs in the first place.

I had been to see a psychiatrist many years ago, a waste of bloody time. I started peeing the bed again. Remember from my childhood. It was always the same dream. A tiger would jump through the bathroom door and I would pee the bed. The tiger dream was my nightmare. Do not ask me what it means the psychiatrist said it was what I associated my abuser with. You will never guess what my favourite animal is, and I have tattooed on me. How fucked up is that. Not to take anything away from psychiatrists they study hard and must be clever, but I always say, and I still say no one except someone who has been through it can understand you. They can try, but they will just never be on the same page or wavelength as you.

I also tried the safe place therapy, they basically make you think of a safe place. Somewhere you enjoy being that is your safe place. Well where the fuck is mine? I do not have a safe place, there is nowhere that makes me feel safe and happy. This was only a few years ago I did this. It was part of my diversion. My other way of dealing with things was to steal things. Do not even ask me why. I would steal fucken stock cubes. I had cupboards full of fucken stock cubes. All different kinds of stock cubes. It was not like I stole things to benefit me like food or anything like that, oh no I stole fucken stock cubes. The worse the day I was having, the more stuff I would steal. Stock cubes, tick repellent when I had no dog. it was pointless things, things that would not do me any good or benefit. I was not even sly about it, I was literally picking it from the shelf, not even looking to see if anyone was watching me and put it in my bag. I eventually got caught in Tesco. The security guard took me into the back room and called the police. Now any clever person that was going to steal something would know do not shit on your own doorstep. If you are having one of those days then go somewhere else and do it, Oh no not me. I went to my local Tesco. I got to the point that I was not even hiding the fact I was stealing. I was doing it right at the checkout bit before putting the shopping through that I was going to pay for. I have money, I have plenty money yet here I am taking items from a shop, putting them in my bag and not even batting an eyelid or having any sort of remorse or regret. Nothing, I feel nothing. So, when the security guard caught me and asked me to go through to the back shop with him off, I went. Now most people would be totally mortified. Its where they stay, people might see them. Me, I do not give a fuck. I just do not care.

When the police officer came into the back room, he took one look at what I had taken and what I had paid for and immediately said to me. Oh, hen you need help not jail. I had already been in trouble for fighting. I got slapped with a social worker all of my own and a rehabilitation program thing and this was part of the process.

To be fair Sandra was lovely. Sandra was my social worker. She looks sweet and pretty, like what a step ford wife would look like. The husband, the 2 kids, white picket fence, has the dinner made for him coming home from work bla bla bla. You know the kind of person I mean. She is very softly spoken and so calming and assuring. I would have to go and see her every Monday. I would sit there for an hour and she would ask me questions about how I feel and why I did what I did and so forth. It was her job to ask me they questions and try and work out what was going on in my head. No one knows what is going on in my head, not even me. Everything just swirls about like a washing machine on a hot wash, but you have fucked up and put coloured clothes in with white. The wash that takes forever to get the white clothes thoroughly clean, but the dark clothes are in there too and it is all spinning about together. It is so mixed up with the dye from the dark clothes running into the white clothes and that is how my head feels. An absolute fucken mess. However, I tell Sandra what she wants to hear. I am sorry for what I did, I feel awful when really, I do not. It was a terrible thing that I did, and I will never do it again. My fucken arse I will not. The minute my head goes fucked then you know I am going to either hit the bottle, start an argument with someone, fight with someone or go to the shops. Take your pick. It is going to be one of the following just to feel something anything other than what I feel inside.

Every week I go and see Sandra and every week I hit her with the same bullshit story that she wants to hear and now I am rehabilitated. Does she believe me? I do not know, I think she wants to believe me. She is the kind of person that wants to think she had made a bit of a difference in your life. She is most definitely in the right job. She has most likely helped so many people. Just not me. I do not think anyone will ever fix me. I am way too damaged. I am beyond repair.

The safe place therapy was almost just as bad. The only place that I can think of to feel happy is in bed with Thelma when she decides she wants a bit of attention. I do not know what is worse, the fact I do not seem to have a happy place or the fact the only thing I can think of is with Thelma and she is as bad as me. She does not give a fuck. It was doomed before it even began. My happy place was with a cat who does not give a rat's ass about me. Would she help me in my happy safe place? Would she fuck. She would put the final nail in the coffin given half the chance, so I was fucked. before I even started the program.

Tap tap find your happy safe place? My happy safe place has fucked off and left me because she does not give a rat's ass. It failed. It was a failure even before it started. It was pointless.

The social worker was pointless, and the therapy was pointless but yes, I am so rehabilitated happy fucken days. You have both done your jobs so well.

Chapter 17

We have been working for the courier company for a few weeks now, it is starting to get boring. It is the same thing day after day. Load the van, deliver the parcels, go back to the depo then home. See I told you I get bored easy and flip from one thing to the next. Dexter says let us go to Blackpool. Are you fucking joking? I hate Blackpool. Oh, come on it will be a laugh. Ok let us go to Blackpool.

We get to Blackpool but us pair of idiots have not booked anything. So, we arrive, and the only place we can get is this shithole, and I mean a shithole. Dumb and dumber did not think this through. I have got him as bad as me now, I always do things on impulse. Our first holiday together and we are in a shithole. It is a smoking room. Dexter smokes, I do not, and I do not mind him smoking. I used to smoke. I just do not anymore. I have been off the fags for 10 years, but I vape. This vape is like my dummy. I cannot live without the bloody thing. We get to the room and omg its worse than the bit at the front where we have just been. The wallpaper is hanging off the walls, there is big brown marks on the ceiling, a smoking room by god. Fifty men have lived in this room and smoked 50 fags a day each and never opened the window. Its howling. We turn to each other and burst out laughing. I do not care that this place is a shit hole, I do not care the wallpaper is hanging off. I do not care about the state of the place I only care that we are there together, and we are going to make memories even if the room is horrendous. We are still together and that is all that matters. I would still fuck you on the bed the dirtier the better. We laugh and then we are as one on the minging bed, in the rank hotel, in the smoke-filled room.

Right come on let us get ready and go out. Where do you fancy going, he said? I know, let us go to a strip club. He has not ever been to a strip club. He cannot believe I want to take him to a strip club. Why not? I am comfortable in my relationship, it is something you have never done and we always said we would do as much stuff as we possibly could together and I want to take you to your first strip club. When we got there the bouncers were not going to let me in. Eh? What do you mean I cannot get in. Apparently, they do not let females in because it always ends up in a fight. Why would you want to take your partner up to a strip club if you are a jealous person and you knew you were going to go off on one. I was at the point I was just about to say, he is my son and I am taking him for his first lap dance, but the bouncer must have thought we didn't look the type to cause trouble and they let us in. It is like any other strip club (hell yeah I have been to a strip club before it's a great night out if your with friends if you do not want chatted up, the guys are too busy with the girls so they leave you alone) its dark its dingy, it smells of sweat and sex, but Dexter has never been before and we are making memories. I asked him if he wanted to pick a girl for a dance. I do not think he totally knows how to take me yet. Murrin texting on the phone or seeing for an hour here and there is a different thing. Now we are together, and I want to make the most of it. I am happy. For the first time in a long time I am happy. I have always believed that you should make the most out of life. If there is something that you want to do then god dam do it, do not just talk about it, get up and do it. To try something and like it or not like it is better than to not try at all. I am a firm believer in that. He didn't want to choose a girl, I would have been happy for him to get a lap dance for the experience, he would have still been coming home with me at the end of the night and that was all that mattered. I offered and he refused. He was simply happy with the fact that we were there that his girlfriend (because that is what I am now) took him to a lap dancing club. We went back to the dirty hotel, in the stinking room and had sex on the dirty bed till the early hours of the following morning.

Wake up, wake up, I am a nightmare, I have always been an early riser and I am beginning to realise that Dexter is not an early riser. Extremely far from it. This fucker would sleep till the cows came home. We are only here for a few days and I want to fit in as much as we possibly can. I hated Blackpool. I really did, but this time it is different, this time it is with Dexter, is it just because we are together or am, I just finally finding out what happiness really is. I do not know and to be perfectly honest I do not care. I am having a great time, even although we are in the worst room, in the worst hotel ever. The only thing I do remember about Blackpool is I like to play the 2p machine and the Arabian Derby (the game where you throw the balls into the holes and whatever number it goes through your horse moves that many spaces and it's a race to the end) let's do that today. Or at least let us make that one of the things we do today. I am excited. I am like a kid in a sweetie shop. I like the 2p machine that you win tickets and the more tickets you win the better the prize you will get. I am thinking about all of this and getting excited and Dexter still is not fully awake. It takes him about an hour or so to wake up in the morning. He needs the green monster energy drink a few fags and then that is him half awake. Only another green monster drink and more fags to go.

We Have been up and down the sea front with all she shops that sell all the shit of the day. All the shit and all the shops that sell the same things they did before when I hated Blackpool but this time, I love it. Although it is the same shops, selling the same shit as before I do not care. I want to go into every shop, we are laughing about all the shit and its funny. Everything is just funny. Why have I never felt this before. Why have I never felt any other emotion rather than anger, hurt and emptiness. Did I never allow myself to be genuinely happy? Was my previous marriage and my past so different that I am now seeing everything a different way? It is like looking through sunglasses. You put sunglasses on, and the world is dark, you take them off and everything is so bright. This is how I feel, as if I have taken sunglasses off and I see the world and everything in it a different way.

I enjoy going into all the tacky shops selling novelty Blackpool shite, I love it, but why do I love it? I love it because I am with Dexter, Dexter makes me feel safe, nothing bad will happen when I am with Dexter. I see things differently because of Dexter, he has let me see this other different side to life, its bright, its happy, I am enjoying myself. For once in my god dam life I am genuinely happy. I have not thought about my past as much, it is still there of course it is still there but instead of dreading getting up every morning I look forward to getting up, I still get up and put my mask on but Dexter is there beside me and I look forward to putting the mask on and having a happy day, because that is what I am now, happy.

We spent the whole day up and down the piers, in and out all the shops. I played my 2p machine. I remember I liked it but this time I love it, the more excited I got the happier Dexter looked. I am thrilled and excited when I win tickets and I am shouting with joy, other people would walk away and say they are embarrassed but not Dexter. He embraces my madness, he says that is what he loves about me and he loves all of me. The good, the bad and the ugly.

When we get back to the stinking hotel, I go into the bathroom and I get changed. Dexter loves underwear, underwear is his thing and I bought it before we came as a surprise. I walk out of the bathroom and I have all black leather on. You can see the excitement in his face. You do not need to look at him you know he is going to be excited. In this stinking room with the horrible smell, the fallen off wallpaper and we did not care, we did not care because we were together. Again our 2 bodies become as one and go in unison together on the stinking bed.

At night we walked along the pier and into a few bars, had a few beers and then Dexter wants to go on this ball like thing along the pier, ok I will do it, I will go on anything that does not spin. I cannot stand anything that spins because it makes me feel sick. Sick is my worst enemy. Give me pain actual bodily pain any day of the week over being sick. I cannot stand being sick. I do not know why but I always cry for my mum when I feel sick. We arrive at the ball, it is at the far end of the pier, it just looks like a normal ball. The guy straps us in, it is only me and Dexter, it only has 2 spaces. The guy said, now hold on. Eh? What do you mean hold on? He says it shoots you into the air, just as his mouth had finished the word air off, we went omfg I have lost my whole insides in a split second. All my insides have gone arse from elbow out my mouth. Jesus mother Mary of god. Dexter is laughing, he knew what it did, my brain is still trying to process what has happened it was so quick. Everything has just fell out my arse now. It shot us up but now we are spinning in the air. Oh, Jesus fucken Christ I am shouting I have been shouting since the guy finished saying the word air. There are people waiting to get on. They are listening to me screaming and I am thinking why the fuck are you not running for the hills. I never knew what was going to happen I just went on it and woosh up I go but if I was standing at the bottom listening to me shouting. I would have been off like a shot. Dexter is still laughing; I am still screaming, and everyone is laughing. When we finally got off, the guy gave us a DVD of the events. Another memory. A memory for the memory box. We have a memory box. Its every time we do something, we keep part of it and put it in a memory box so we can keep it and always look back on all the fun stuff we have done together.

We had to head home the following morning. We were both back to work. I went there hating Blackpool I left loving it. I loved it. Did I love it because I was there with Dexter and everything just seamed better, brighter? It was the exact same place with the exact same stuff although this time I loved it even the stinking room in the horrible hotel that we just laughed at.

Chapter 18

We are still working at the courier company and Dexter is saying he wants a dog. I already have Levi, my next door neighbour watches her while I am at work. Although we went and picked her together Dexter wants a French Bulldog. Levi is our dog now, but Dexter wants to add another one to the mix. Why the hell not? I love dogs. So, we see an advert for this Frenchie. The first thing I said to him was do not go in all guns blazing and say oh I want the dog bla bla bla play it cool. What happened when we saw the puppy? After saying to Dexter do not go in all guns blazing. I am the one that pics him up and says we will take him. I saw him, I wanted him and everything else went out the window. Dexter named him Salem.

What are we going to do with another dog though because Jean downstairs watches Levi when I am at work? Jean is in her early 70's, when I first met her, I instantly liked and respected her. I cannot even remember what the argument was about. Probably the Shute always being blocked. We lived in a close with six flats. Each level had a Shute where you would put your rubbish and it would all lead to a big skip at the bottom. The only thing was if you put too much in then it would block the Shute, and this always happened. I was always out working so if it blocked it was Jean or Reggie who would need to unblock it. Reggie stayed directly across from Jean him and his partner Samantha. they were both on drugs. You knew they were on drugs. Samantha would go out and sell her body so that they could keep up their habit. Something I will always remember Dexter saying. I would have judged them before. Before I met you, I would have judged them for taking drugs because you do not think, why are they on drugs in the first place? Not all drug addicts chose drugs for the hell of it. Some of them felt as if they had no other option. They could have something in their past that is so horrific that they cannot deal with it. The brain just cannot deal with it. They could have been in that dark place that I once was and saw no other way out, only death. Death becomes a dream. Some people dream of nice holidays and cars, expensive shoes, but some people dream about death. They are so caught up in the hurt, the anger, the misery, the emptiness that it crushes you. It crushes you from the inside until you cannot breathe anymore, and you just want to die. You just want to die. Dying is a dream, it is something that you would welcome with open arms. All that pain, all the hurt, the anger the emptiness everything gone in an instant. Let me put a different spin on it. Your mum or someone you love has a terminal illness, you can see that they are in awful pain, terrible pain. You see that the pain is so bad that it is crushing them. Literally crushing them from the inside and you are sitting there watching this with your own eyes. The doctor comes in and says, we can give your mum a little injection and it will take everything away in an instant. What do you do? You are not going to sit there and say oh no just let her suffer. You are going to choose the miracle injection aren't you. Of course, you are. That is what death is like to me and other people. A miracle injection that would take all that pain and suffering away. Yet we all get up out of our god dam beds every day, put on whatever the hell it is you need to get on with the day and you do it. For some people its drugs, for some it is the bottom of a bottle of booze waiting for the wee tequila man singing, but there is no singing. The happy cheery tequila guy is not there is it just even more misery and although you drink to forget. It does not make you forget; it only makes you worse. Some people get up in the morning and they cut themselves. You might think to yourself what the fuck are they doing that for? Why would someone want to take a knife or a razor to themselves and start cutting? It is easy, it is another way out. What you feel inside is far worse, so feeling actual physical pain is a diversion from what is going on inside your head. It sounds stupid to you, but to me it sounds like going to the shop for a packet of crisps. Its normal. They are just dealing with their demons the way they know how. You find your way of dealing with it and you stick to it.

I am sure that is what the argument was about the Shute being blocked. I opened the door to this tiny little woman; she was smaller than me and that is saying a lot. She was maybe 4 foot 9 or 10. She is thin with an old-fashioned hair style and milk bottle glasses. As soon as I opened the door, she had opened her mouth. Oh, she was giving me dogs abuse. She was pointing her finger at me and shouting at the top of her voice and I Instantly liked and respected her. It is strange because usually anyone who starts an argument with me, I do not argue, I just lunge at you. It is as simple as that, but she was an older woman and she reminded me of my gran. My gran was about the same age as Jean when she died. She was the same height, she wore the same milk bottle glasses and if that were her in the situation that Jean was in, she would have done the exact same thing so instead of arguing with her. I embraced her and after that we became good friends and neighbours and I always unblocked the bloody Shute, no matter who blocked it.

Dexter is going to take Salem to work with him in the van. You just know this is not going to go down well. Van full of over 100 parcels, over 100 parcels to deliver with a minute and a half stop gap. This is never going to be possible. He is a puppy; puppies need the toilet all the time. They need fed all the time but oh no, Dexter was adamant that he was going to take Salem to work in the van. We took him home to the house and immediately Levi loved him. Oh, she loved him. You would have thought all her Christmases had come at once. She was so excited she peed the floor. Thelma hates him, Thelma hates everyone except Dexter. Thelma is a typical cat, I will come to you if it suits me, if it does not then fuck off and it was a fuck off look you got. She hated Levi, she tolerated me at times, she absolutely hated kids and other people, yet she loves Dexter. Everyone loves Dexter. Dexter with the smile, Dexter with the eyes. Do cats think the same way we do? Was Thelma like that with me because that was the way I used to be with other people. If you get too close to me then I back off. Are pets like their owners? Levi loved everybody. I still had the shop when I got her. She would come to work with me all day, she would play with the skinny pigs, she was loved and clapped by everyone who walked through the door. She loved to see and play with other dogs on our travels. She is a happy dog. Is she a happy dog because when I got her, I was happy? Dexter was still in his other life, but he was also in ours too. Have I made Thelma stand offish with other people because that is how I was? I would have been as well walking about with a sandwich board saying do not come near me or I will smash your bloody face in. If I want, you then I will come to you when it suits me. If I want sex then I will let you know, if I do not then stay the fuck away from me. It is exactly how Thelma is but not with sex with food and attention. I will allow you to come to me if it is for food, I will come up onto you for a rub if it suits me. If it does not suit me human, then stay the fuck away from me. Did I choose Thelma, or did Thelma choose me? I do not know. All I know is Thelma hates the world and anyone in it except for Dexter.

Dexter takes Salem to work, I know this, you are probably sitting there reading this thinking you know this. Everybody knows this is going to happen except Dexter. The first day at work what happens? Salem shits all over his new bed. All over Dexter's van. His van is full of parcels. He has if you are lucky a 1-minute stop gap per delivery and now he is out the van trying to clean up all the shit, his parcels are now running late. His timing is all out of the window and the only thing I want to say is I told you so but I never.

He did continue to take Salem to work and the same thing happened near enough every single day, but I will give him his due, he stuck to it. Salem had issues. Why am I not surprised? Everything runs out of him. His stomach is fucked, alarm bells should have gone off when his mother and father were not there to view. I should have stuck to what I told Dexter to do yet I picked him up and said we will take him. Now he has issues. We tried everything. The vets sell you the most expensive food on the shelf and it still does not work. Nothing works until finally one day it did just stop by itself.

He is not making as much money with the parcels, he is getting paid with every parcel he delivers and most of the time he is going back to the depo with more parcels than he has delivered, by the time he pays for his van, the insurance etc. it just was not worthwhile for him. Me? I was working for someone in the depo and I got paid regardless. I have not smashed the van again. I think once I did it the first time and got over it then I got used to driving the van. So, Dexter quits. I am still there for a short time afterwards because what is happening? Dexter and I are now separated, and he is at home alone. If we are not with each other then we are always texting each other but we are never apart. Only at work, he was in his van I was in mine. We finished work and went home together. Everything was always together.

Dexter is lonely because he is at home and I am working. We have bills to pay, the rent does not pay itself, but he has an idea. Let us buy our own van and do our own deliveries. Work for ourselves. Not for someone else. Fucken great idea. I was always used to being self-employed and working for myself. This would be different though, we would be a team. We would be together, we would make it a laugh. Brilliant idea. My stash of cash is no more. I used some of it to buy Dexter into the courier company and the rest went on Salem. Dexter got a pay out from Lorraine from his house. Although we are not long together there is not his money, my money. Everything goes into one pot. There is one other thing he wants though before the van. He wants a parrot. As in a parrot with wings that flaps and Oh my fucken god a parrot? Did I forget to mention I would go in a ring with Mike Tyson any day of the week, all day rather than have a parrot. I am shit scared of birds. It is the flapping. I hate the bloody flapping. It freaks me the fuck out. I did not tell him, but I did have a cockatiel thing years ago. My ex wanted a Flamen bird and I was shit scared of them. He went to work, and I opened the kitchen door and the wee fucker flew away. Cheerio!! See you later. I had to lie through my back teeth and say the bird let itself out the cage and it flew out of the window. Goodbye flapping bird. It was only a couple of quid. It was not the point. I was terrified of the thing and now he wants to pay thousands of pounds on a fucken bird with wings that flap. I do not have a back door in the flat. I would be as well getting bundles of twenty quid bills and flapping them out the window. No! I am not getting a bird. They hate me, I hate them it is the perfect relationship.

He is looking at me with that face, the face of a 3-year-old kid that has a shop full of sweeties in front of him and his mum comes along and ruins it by saying. You need to come home. You cannot have any of the sweets. Takes the poor child by the hand and drags him up the road with no sweets. This is how he looks. Can you not look at me like that? I am terrified of birds. I am only scared of 2 things in my life, birds and the bloody dentist. Even the word dentist gives me the heave. I need to get diazepam from the doctor just to get me in the dentist door, and then I need enough sedation to knock out an elephant before they can get anywhere near my teeth. I would need to be fed diazepam like smarties every day to have a fucken bird. Do not bother giving me food, just shovel me with tablets. It is the only way a bird is getting in this house. End of.

Where do I find myself the next day after no way end of? We are only going to a fucken pet shop to look at parrots. Jesus fucken Christ. I am outside the shop and I know there are going to be birds in here and I swear my arse has just fell out of my trousers, can I go in. My heart is racing my hands are sweating like a pig in the butchers and Dexter is standing there with that same look again and I think oh fuck it have the bloody sweets. I go into the shop and its full of birds. Heaving with birds. It looks like a bird sanctuary never mind a pet shop and I think I have peed myself. I am not joking. I have honestly dribbled. Get me the fuck out of here. They are flapping and squawking, and I know I have dribbled but if I literally shit myself then there is no hiding that. Dexter please get me the fuck out of here. Then I am drawn to a cage right at the very front. It is a white thing. I am not a bird person, but I think it is a cockatoo. I look at it and straight away I know it has issues. Why am I always drawn to things with issues? I am standing in this shop shit scared of birds and yet I am drawn to the one who has fucken issues. Ok that is enough for the day, get me out of here.

We continued to go to the shop, Dexter really wanted a parrot. I am thinking I can maybe get over my fear but to be honest. I want to go back and see the white bird with issues. The second visit was not as bad as the first. I still do not like birds, I still hate the flapping. If they would just not flap it would be ok. We meet a lovely lady called Sonia who works in the pet shop. She is roughly the same age as me. She is happy and bubbly. She has shoulder length dark hair and her voice is even a happy cheery voice. She knows everything about birds. Her knowledge is amazing, but it is just someone that I like from the beginning. You just know. People flight in and out your life like soapy bubbles. Some people make an impact, some do not. Some you would just like to kick to the kerb and not think twice about. Everyone is different and I like this woman. I like how she thinks and feels about animals and you can tell she cares. She spends a great deal of time with us, Dexter explains I am a total shite bag with birds, but we would love a parrot. Eh no, I do not think so. You want a parrot. I would rather swipe 20 quid bills out the window.

For weeks we went to this shop. Chatted with Sonia and I was still drawn to this bird with the issues that I called Meany. She was an evil bitch, but I liked that. She hated everyone. OMG a bit like Thelma. She hates everyone too. They would be a match made in heaven. Ok, I am ready to take a bird. Let us do this but I want Meany. I want the bird with issues. Not a new baby parrot, No, I want the nut case. Unfortunately, by the time I had decided I was ok with birds, someone had just taken Meany. All this time this poor bird was in the shop and no one wanted her because she had issues. All this time, now I gear myself up to take a parrot and someone has just beaten us to it. Just my Donald Duck. Sonia had told us that she could get us a baby Macaw. She knew someone who had just had 2 baby green wing macaws and they were both available. Ok, we will take the baby.

She arrives, we go to collect her. Eh? Where is the baby? This thing is fucken huge. Where is our parrot. This is her. Eh? This is her a baby. She is huge, she is massive. Her colouring is electric. I must admit her colours are amazing, but this is not a baby. Babies are nice and cute, and this is a monster. A monster with monster size wings. I am not taking that bloody thing home. Dexter has already bought the cage and built it. This cage takes up half the bloody living room. Alarm bells should have gone off then. The cages in the pet shop were tiny. This cage can fit a family of 6. Mum, Dad and 4 kids. The flat is becoming a Flamen zoo. I still have reptiles in the house from the shop. I kept some of the reptiles and the tarantulas. One whole room of the house is full of vivarium's. We now have the ever so torn faced Thelma, Levi, Salem and now a monster who Dexter has named Pricilla. Let me just say. The kitchen window is not big enough for her to fly throw. I am going to have to get used to this bird.

Chapter 19

Dexter buys a van, a white transit van. Eh? Do you not remember the first day in the courier company? I smashed the fucken van. It was not my van. This van is now going to be our only source of bread and butter. We are going to be man with a van. Well woman/man with a van. We place an advert in Gumtree and within days all these jobs start coming in. We would arrive and people would look at us both and think yeah like that is going to happen. She is a woman. Oh yes, she may be a woman, but I bet she has bigger balls than you mate! This woman can lift as much as most men.

Oh, we got some mental jobs through that. Jesus Christ. Some people have the cheek to phone for a man with a van to do a house removal and they have not even packed up their shit. It does not say man with a van and packaging company. Pack your stuff yourself and we will move it. Again, though we would turn it around and make it into a laugh. We always saw the funny side in everything. No matter how bad the situation was, we always turned it around.

There was this family. To this day I still do not know what the scam was, but I am telling you it was a scam. The same bloody family every week. Not exaggerating every week. Literally every week. We called them the tinkers because they moved about so much. They would move from one street to another every bloody week. You would go to one house and it was different furniture and take it to another house. The following week a different house, different furniture but always the same people. I still wonder to this day what the hell the scam was. I guess I will never know.

Some houses were howling. Oh, my mother of god. If you know someone is coming to your house to move stuff at least try and tidy up. Some people really did not care. I have an absolute cheek to say anything because I have gone through most of my life not giving a fuck about anything but if someone was coming to my house to do something I would at least try and tidy up. I am talking dirty shitty nappies lying about. I do not do children. Well babies, I have never had that urge or want for a baby. I would not know what to do with it. It cries, what do you do? How do you know what it wants oh my Jesus no. I have nieces and nephews I never once looked after them when they were babies not a Flamen chance? If you can talk and tell me what you want, that is ok. I can tolerate that, for a while but then you need to go back. I have seen you, I have played with you now go back. Is that because of what I am and what I carry around. I do not know. I just know I have never wanted one and when I get one its ok for a day or so but then it must go back. Do not get me wrong. I am the favourite aunty when you are a child. I have a screw loose and I am so much fun and then you must go back. Is it a defensive thing? I do not know, I really do not know the answer to that, but I know when someone gets too close to me then I back off. I always back off. I know I would ever be able to cope with a baby. I am the nightmare person on the airplane. Your child is crying, and I just really want to tell you to shut the baby up. Please just make it stop crying. I cannot cope with a baby crying. I would never ever harm a child but, I cannot stand babies crying. I just cannot take it and I would never know what to do with it so no I have never had or wanted one.

We have been doing the removals for a while and we are wanting a wee holiday. We have booked this Villa type place with a hot tub and 4 or 5 bedrooms and it is only us 2 and the dogs. Jean will come and feed Thelma and we are going to meet Dexter's parents because they need to watch Pricilla. I have met his dad. I picked them up from a works night out previously and I instantly liked him. He had the same fucked up sense of humor as me. We are practically the same age. Well not a kick in the arse off it. This is another thing. I do not think his mum has taken the news too well. I am one of those people if I do not like you. You know I do not like you and Dexter knows this. I think this is why I have not met his mum yet or his sister.

I get to their house. I am one of these people I see you I hug you and kiss you. None of his family are like this. I am so fuck it, I am not changing. I walk over to hug his mum and omg she is frosty. She is just a bit taller than me, she has short blonde hair, some make up but not a lot her face looks like she has just chewed a wasp. You can just tell she does not like me. The dad is ok. He too is not that much taller than me. Greyish hair with glasses. He is sound as a pound, but the mum is very stand offish. The sister walks in and as soon as I see her, I know I am not going to get on with her. I can just tell. You just know. She acknowledges me but at the same time she is kind of looking down on me. Do not get me wrong, she said hello accepted the hug, but I just knew, there and then I knew.

Thankfully, it was a short visit, Dexter asked me what I thought when we left and I thought shit, I do not lie to him. So, I say it fast. Ok your dads nice, your mum is like frosty the snowman and I think your sister might be a bitch.

Chapter 20

The cottage is amazing. Omg it is so nice. The place is decked out in all the mod cons and I love it. There are housecoats in each room with matching slippers. There should be it cost a fortune, but we did not care. It was making more memories. I think we bought enough booze to sink the titanic. I do not drink anymore to forget. It is different. The drinking is different. I can take it or leave it whereas I would drink until I blacked out.

Oh, I love it Dexter, I love it. It is amazing. It is just us and the dogs and it is just brilliant. Our clothes were off, and we were in the hot tub. I do not even think we looked around the whole place yet or even unpacked we were straight in the hot tub. Making love and memories in the hot tub. It was amazing, everything was perfect. We were in the hot tub drinking beer, having a laugh. Not a care in the world. Just us. The stars were in the sky and we just looked up at the stars and the moment was magical and he asked to marry me. Will you marry me? Oh fuck, there is that wee voice again. Say no! You have been here before. It was a total disaster and you swore you would never marry anyone again unless it was Simon Cowell. Oh god yeah, I have a thing for Simon Cowell. I just love the way he says things like it is. Not so much anymore since Eric was born, but nevertheless there was hell way and no way I was ever going to get married again.

Yes! I have got foot and mouth again. I did not even think about it and the yes was out my mouth and I could not take it back. Did I want to take it back? One part of me did and the other part did not.

After the initial shock set in the first thing, I said without thinking. Well this will go down well in your house. Frosty the snowman and the bitch will love this. We both just laughed and lay under the stars for the rest of the night in the hot tub laughing like we always did.

My sister Fiona, her man Greg, my niece Lucy and nephew Lee were coming to stay. My sister and I are opposites. I am a red head, she has blonde hair. I am loud as fuck, she is as quiet as a mouse. I am out there with planet Pluto. She is reserved and normal. She is all about her family and providing for them, saving her money. I would swipe 20 quid bills out the window. We are just opposite. The only thing we have in common is our height. We are the same height as each other, and roughly the same build but she is always that bit slimmer. We are 2 years apart in age so she would be 41. Greg is tall and very slim. He is about 6 foot. He is the kind of person you want to smash his face in. He can eat anything, drink like a fish and stays the exact same weight. Greg is one or the other. If he is at work or during the week, he fits in with my sister and the whole happily reserved family. Then he gets a drink, and everything goes to hell and he is the funniest person ever. It annoys the life out of my sister and the kids but to other people It is funny. It is always the same though. If you are married to someone and you think they are the biggest arse hole drunk, someone else always finds them funny. Greg is 2 or 3 years older than my sister. Lucy is 15, she takes her dads height, she is almost as tall as Greg with long blonde hair, stunning girl with no makeup just natural beauty. Lee is the same, tall like his dad, the same blonde hair and like myself and my sister. They are 2 years apart. The place was big enough for loads of people everyone could have had their own room, it was a brilliant night. Dexter and I had already been in the hot tub. I think we spent the whole week in there, we should have just hired a hot tub. My niece and nephew are just in their teens, they do not drink, so I had got some kids cocktails as well as adults' ones.

Dexter, Greg and Lee are in the hot tub. The 2 men are drinking, and I say its ok I got kids cocktails, so they feel like adults and not left out. My sister is not in the hot tub yet. She is drinking tea. Before the kids came along my sister was like me a loose cannon. She drank, she smoked, she tried recreational drugs as we all have, but the minute the kids were born she stopped. It was only every now and then. If you met her you would think she was the most reserved human being ever and where the fuck did, I come from. How can these two be sisters. I give her an alcoholic drink, she does not want it. I tell her to just drink it. It is her holidays. After drink number one, hello! Here comes my old sister. The sensible mum, the one who saves money and is so reserved has gone. Now she wants to join in.

I got outside to see the boys, Lee's eyes look sparkled. He looks drunk. I asked Dexter did you give him some beer, he looks pissed. I am not so drunk yet or I would not have noticed. I am on my sisters' level just now not theirs. Dexter comes inside and looks. Oh, I had only given him the adults cocktails. Not the kids. Omg, I am blind as a bat. I am long sighted and short sighted. My sister will kill me. Shit hurry up, just get her drunk.

It ended up a brilliant night we were all laughing and joking my sister was in the hot tub, we were up till late the kids went to bed, my sister stayed up. She was having a whale of a time. In fact, the last 2 standing were Dexter and my sister. I get to the point I know I am drunk I know my limit and I just do a disappearing act. No matter where I am, I always head for home and bed, and for this week. This place was home.

My sister, Greg and the kids left the following day. We were all hanging like a bag of washing from the night before. I think we consumed some amount of alcohol. This time though I am not drinking to black out, it is a different drinking. It is social drinking. I did not drink until I blacked out, no I knew when I was drunk, and I went to bed. It is hard to explain. Everything is still there. It is all still swimming about in that bloody washing machine but as well as hurt, anger and emptiness, happiness has gone into the washing machine too. So, there is white clothes, dark clothes and bright happy clothes and they are all swimming about together. Although the dark clothes are there happy clothes are there too and it does not make the dark clothes so dark anymore. My sunglasses are off, and I see the world differently. Like 2 superheroes fighting. One part of my head is batman and the other part is the Joker. They are constantly at war with each other. They hate each other. They despise each other. They fight to the death, so right now one part of me is constantly fighting with the other part. It is not giving me a break, but I have batman in my head helping me. The joker is still there that bastard is never going away but right now I have batman and batman is helping to make my life that little bit easier just now. I wish he would hurry up and kill the Joker, but the Jokers powers are far stronger than batman's. Am I still struggling, hell yeah, but there are also happy bits? Batman must be kicking the joker's ass at some point because I am still struggling and happy at the same time.

We spent the rest of the week together just us with Levi and Salem. Our little family. We had spoken about this many time. Before the whole I love you thing. I did not want children I just did not want them. I do not do babies and they only thing I have ever wanted to do was to one day be able to Foster Children, what do I want to Foster? The kids with issues. I always pick everything with issues. There are so many children out there who are the same as me. They have been through the same thing and someone who has not been through what we have will never understand. God, I know they try, and they really do want to think they have made your life a little bit easier. I cannot say for everyone else, but I do the, yes, you have helped me. Like my social worker. As lovely as she was, and I know she really did want to think that she had helped me. I could see it in her face. She is most definitely in the right job because she really does care. It just did not help me and so I lied. I bare faced lied to her and said I was grateful for everything she done, that she made a difference in my life and I would be forever grateful. Her face lit up like a Christmas tree. That is how I know that woman is most definitely in the right job it just did not help me. Nothing seems to help me.

There are so many kids out there like me that are severely damaged, and no one wants, and I know this. When I worked for the courier company. I was shadowing this guy for the day. He was telling me he Is going down the fostering process just now. Him and his wife, I was just about to do the whole foot and mouth thing again and something stopped me. He continued to tell me how the whole process works and then he gets to the bit that says. You can basically choose your child. There is that bloody packet of crisps thing again. Its kids not fucken crisps. Tick if you want this, tick if you want that and then he says is. We are not going to accept a damaged child with abuse issues. Right there and then I wanted to take the hammer to the front of the face and smash his face in with it, and I really mean smash his face in until there is nothing left. Or until all the lights flash in a fruit machine. You know when you put money in, and you hit the jackpot and all the lights are flashing. This is how badly I want to smash his face in until all the lights are flashing, and everything is ringing and happy and then I would stop. Only then I would stop. Get me to fuck out this van. I have had enough. He continues to say, how do you even deal with someone like that. Someone like that? What the fuck do you mean someone like that. It is not as if that child went up to an adult and said stick it in me. Wait to I part my legs like margarine. It is not the child's fault. Is the word child not even ringing alarm bells mate? I simply just said I knew enough about the route I would make my own way home.

So yes, one day that is what I would like to do. Either foster children who need help or help in some sort of way. I have always known this. I had always been open and honest with Dexter about everything. After the I love you, I did say to him again. I will not have children. He was 19 years younger than me, maybe one day he would feel different and want children of his own, but then my dream also became his dream. We would both do it together.

Chapter 21

We are still doing man with a van and removals. We have now
accumulated even more bloody reptiles. Pricilla has issues. Why the fuck
am I not surprised. Of course, the monster flappy bird has issues. She
has started plucking her feathers and she looks like a scrawny beanpole
with a few feathers here and there. She is not exactly my favourite pet,
but I would never harm her, and she is part of our fucked-up family. We
have an understanding. We love to hate each other. She loves Dexter.
Of course, she loves Dexter. Everyone loves Dexter.

We call Sonia from the pet shop. She comes up to the house. Ah she is
plucking her feathers and snapping them. This can happen when she
gets taken away from her sister. Here comes that jealousy thing again.
Would my sister pluck her feathers if I were not there? I do not think so.
Great Pricilla has issues, what happens? I begin to like Pricilla. Pricilla
the bird with issues. We had to take her to the vets she needs sedation
medicine for a while and a white-collar thing that can only be described
as an upside-down lamp shade. I continued to do the love hate thing
with her. It became a standing joke. I concluded she did not like the
cage and let us get her a java stand. She should be out all day and
maybe she would not be to be fucked in the head. We would not go to
work as much just now, only take enough jobs to pay the bills and make
sure Pricilla was ok. I did not think I liked this bird, but the minute Sonia
said she missed her sister and we did not know that ourselves, I felt as if
we had let her down. I began to cry. Like real water running down my
eyes. What is wrong with me? I do not cry. Was it because Pricilla had
issues and I did not know? Was it because I was now starting to feel
emotions like normal human beings? I was not sure, did I like the fact I
was crying. No, it was freaking me out. There were 2 different sides to
this new world. It seemed brighter, yet I was starting to feel emotions
like any other person. This I did not like, this is where I feel like that deer
again in the room with lions and I do not like it. It is scary. I feel
vulnerable and open and scared but happy at the same time.

We got her a Java Stand, when we got up, we let Pricilla out the cage and on the Java stand and she seemed happy. Really happy. We only took enough jobs to pay the bills or something that Dexter could do by himself and someone was home for Pricilla. She seemed happy on the java stand and open and free. If both of us were going out, we would put her back in her cage until we got back. She did not like it she would scream. It reminds me of a screaming baby, and I do not like screaming babies. We stayed in a flat with 5 other people in the same bit. If I cannot stand her screaming and she is mine, then what are other people going to think. We go out leave her on the java stand and no noise. Problem solved. Happy fucken days. We come home, we are coming up the stairs and I cannot hear her screaming. Brilliant it has worked. Walk into the flat and she has managed to go from the Java stand up the curtains and she has chewed a big huge hole right through the wall. As in right through the wall. She can crack a walnut in 2 seconds flat can you imagine what she has done to the wall. It is a rental flat. Jesus fucken Christ. Dexter is raging and for some strange reason I am laughing inside. I know it is wrong. It is so wrong. It is not our flat and yet I think this is hysterical. She may have chewed a hole through the wall, but she has been quiet.

Ok, we need to find something else to do. She is a bird with issues, but we took on that responsibility and when I am in, I am all in. If your broken it is just more of a challenge to help you. I am keeping this bird. Dexter thinks we have made a mistake maybe someone else would be better off with her. No! It is not happening. Me, the one who hated her and was frightened of her is now the one in her corner backing her to stay. There must be another way. She is our problem we need to fix it. We need to find a way to either not work so much or someone needs to be in the house with Pricilla.

What do we do? Dexter has an idea. We can start growing cannabis. Eh? How the fuck does someone go from van removals to growing drugs. This is why we got on so well. His head is surely as fucked as mine. I flight through life moving from one thing to the next, but I have never grown cannabis. I cannot even keep a house plant. I always kill the bloody things. It is the perfect idea. No one comes to the flat. It is just us. We are the top flat, Its Reggie downstairs who is always sparked out on drugs if a smell arose everyone would think it was him. My family do not come and visit neither does Dexter's.

I have seen his mum and dad a few times now and frosty the snowman is starting to melt. She is slowly but surely starting to like me. I think I understand why she is so stand offish, but I am not sure yet. So, I just do baby steps. The sister, my opinion has not changed. Something just is not sitting right, her boyfriend is a total roaster. There is just no getting away from it. He is a roaster. All he does is moan. From the minute you go in until you leave. I always give Dexter this look, and he knows I have had enough. The old me would have just walked out the door and never even batted an eyelid, but this was Dexter's family. They are soon going to be my family and is it me, or is it the sister, something is not sitting right with the sister. Dexter has told me all about her, but I am the kind of person that I will judge for myself. I listen to what you say but I will judge for myself. You might not like someone, and I gel with them straight away. I listen to what other people say but I make up my own mind. I know that Dexter and Joanne are not close, he has told me why they are not close, but I will make up my own mind.

So, we go to a shop to buy everything we need to start growing the cannabis. We must have had this huge sandwich board on us saying we are thick as fuck. We do not have a clue what we are doing or how to grow the stuff and the man inside was amazing. He told us from stage 1 to the end. We were in the shop for hours.

Come home, set it all up in the cupboard and away we go. Nothing ventured nothing gained. Hopefully, it works. In the meantime, though we need money. We have bills to pay. They do not just pay themselves. So, the takeaway shop that I used to do deliveries for I go back to and they hire us straight away. How are we going to work this because Pricilla still needs attention, we still have Levi, Salem and all the reptiles? We always do everything together. It is always together. I do not even take a bath myself. Dexter will sit on the toilet and talk to me in the bath. We are together all the time. It literally is like we are joined together and any time we are apart it feels wrong. It does not feel right.

We start it as Dexter would go out and start when it was quiet. I would then join him in a few hours, and we would do it together. In between him leaving and me starting he is constantly texting me. He can text and drive. I cannot. If we are not together then we must be speaking to each other. It is like one cannot exist without the other. So, we either need to be together or speak to each other. This is the way it has been since the beginning. Even way back before we were properly together. We would text from I opened my eyes until I closed them. I would always fall asleep first.

We were the best god dam delivery people ever. We had previously worked for the courier company and now we are delivering take away food to the same area. We know this area like the back of our hand. Dexter drives, I get out drop the food off, he turns the car and we are good to go. We smash the hell out of this. In the beginning like everything else it is great. It is like a race between the other drivers to see who can deliver the most food and get the best tips. We always smashed it. Totally smashed it. Everyone hated being on with us. We made the most money and we were miles in front of everyone else.

The only thing was the streets are tiny, we have a bloody transit van. Ok, we need a car a small car to throw it about quicker. We need the van too. Anytime we go anywhere we need to take half the bloody house with us. So, we go and buy a little run around car. It will make its money back in no time, plus Dexter's plants are growing. He has managed to turn little seeds into growing plants. You cannot smell anything yet, we bought the fan the whole proper set up from start to finish. We are growing drugs and delivering food.

Like everything else the novelty starts to wear off. We are still the best, there is no doubt about that, but the shop has just taken on this just eat thing. It totally ruined the arse out of our tips. We only get £1.50 to

£2.00 per delivery. You count on they tips to boost your money up at the end of the night. With just eat people pay online, so when you get to their door most of them are not giving you a tip anymore or saying keep the change. You get to know the ones who do tip regardless and the ones who do not. If you are going out with 5 deliveries in one go. You always take the person who you know is going to tip first and the rest can go cold. If we really didn't like you Dexter would drive and I would sit with the bag in my hand, open the window, put the food outside the window and leave it there until Dexter made it to your door, so by the time we got there your dinner was freezing. Or if it were something, we liked I would open the bags see what was inside eat some of it and then give you the rest. Moral of the story. Always tip your delivery driver. It is something they all do. Maybe not to the extent we did but if you do not tip then your dinner is coming last in the queue you can bet your life on that.

Chapter 22

We have still been doing deliveries, I only go in the busy period. Pricilla is getting better; she is not plucking her feathers. The dogs are great, Thelma is still just Thelma. Dexter has managed to grow, harvest and sell all the cannabis to his uncle Ted up in Aviemore. He is on his second grow. We have even more reptiles now. We have been up and down to Blackpool on several occasions to get more exotic reptiles from the Reptile Room in Blackpool. The house is full, and the food bill is enormous.

Frosty the snowman has melted, it was not overnight. It was a gradual thing. From the minute I saw her, I knew how much pain she was in. Although Dexter had already told me about his brother, saying one thing and seeing another is something totally different. Its written all over her face. You can see it in her eyes, her whole demeanor. She is dying inside, and why would she not be. I cannot imagine for a minute what any of them are going through. His mum does not keep well at the best of times but every time I see her, I am thinking she is getting worse and worse. Now I know just by looking at her how much pain she is in mentally. I can tell her head is fucked. Can she tell mine is the same? Its 2 different kinds of pain, hers is a pain of losing a child. Mine is from my childhood. Does she feel the exact same as me on the inside? Is this what is bringing us closer together. Her first reception of me was frosty as fuck. We have since became good friends. I have become the person she talks to and confides in. I have not told her about me, but I wonder does she know. I mean I could see it in her from day one. She may as well have had a sandwich board saying. You might be fucking my son, but I have no interest in you whatsoever. I am only meeting you because they have made me do it. That was what the look on her face said, but I could see past her face, I can see the pain in her eyes. Did she see mine?

I still love his dad Bert, he has just the same sick sense of humor as me. I liked him instantly, the first time I saw him I just knew we would get on. My opinion has not changed about his sister or her boyfriend. If anything, it has gotten worse. She is the most self-obsessed selfish bastard ever. She just takes, takes, takes and never gives back. She has a son to her previous relationship called Jack who is 3. He is a lovely wee boy. He has a wee cute button face light brown hair and he is small but cute. See I do not mind toddlers they can tell you what is wrong with them. I really do not know why she had a child. Dexter told me that his parents brought him up. She had him then she would be out partying with her friends while Agnes and Bert looked after Jack. I knew all this previously, but I always make my own mind up about people. Some people over exaggerate things. In this instance Dexter under exaggerated. This is what pisses me off. There are so many people out there who would literally give you everything they have and will ever have just to be able to have a child. Then you get the kind of people who just need to sit on a toilet pan to get pregnant and they hand their child about like smarties. It riles the life out of me. I totally get that a 2-parent family and single parents need to work, of course you need to work, but when you finish work then look after your child. It is your child. You brought him or her into this world. If you did not want to reproduce a child, then you should have stopped at Paisley or put something on the end of it. The responsibility of sex is a 2-way thing. Both people should take protection.

Nigel just moans about everything and he is always tired. It is all you ever hear. I am tired. When he karks it, that is what they will have on his tombstone if he gets one. Here lies Nigel who is tired. Everyone is sick fed up listening to him moaning. Everyone cannot stand Nigel, but they have no option but to put up with him I do not. I just give Dexter that look, and we go. He feels the same way I do so he is glad to leave too.

We still have the van and the car. Enough reptiles to open another shop but now are going to start back up the mini zoos. Before I had the shop and while I had the shop, I would do mini zoos to schools' nurseries, kids parties. Dexter came with me one time and he loved it. Ok, we have more than enough reptiles, it is something we can do together. This was the bit I hated about it. Great yeah £100 for an hour work but it is packing the animals, taking them there and unloading them again. This time though there is 2 of us, everything is better when there is 2 of you. It is easier, and no matter what, we turn everything into a laugh. It is always a laugh. If things go tits up. We laugh about it. We always see the funny side in everything. Any job we do we always see the funny side, if there is not one, we make one.

Chapter 23

Dexter loves doing the zoos. He knew nothing about reptiles until he met me and then he became fascinated with them. When I fell asleep at night he would read up on things. We never watched much television. We never really had time, we would always just lie in bed at night with a wood wick candle for noise and talk. Even though we have been together all day. We never ran out of things to talk about. We talked about everything and anything, but I always fell asleep first. I fell asleep and he would read up on reptiles and other various things and then we would talk about it the following day. We never really watched television at all unless we went away to the caravan and it was DVDs.

We would do a kid's party and Dexter would be in his element talking to the kids about all the reptiles. He has totally come out of his shell. When we first met, he would never have done that. He did not have the confidence to do it. I do not know why. He knew a lot of stuff. He was a clever guy who knew a lot of things about general stuff and history. He had a fountain of knowledge and we would lie in bed every night and he would tell me about things he knew or read. He took my sunglasses off and I gave him confidence. We were perfect for each other. It just worked. He was one part of the jigsaw and I was the other but when we came together you could see the whole picture. That is just how it felt. He was my missing bit and I was his.

We have lots of things all on the go at one time now. Dexter is still growing cannabis, we are still doing the deliveries for the takeaway place, some man with a van jobs. We pick the ones we want, and we are doing the zoos. Life is wonderful, everything is fantastic. Pricilla is still an arsehole, but she is not snapping her feathers, Salem has no tummy issues, Levi still loves everyone. Thelma is still a torn face sod, but we are one big happy family. I have not had a dip in ages and now I am just waiting for the butt. Things are never this good. Agnes and I have become good friends, she confides in me. Bert is still the same jovial person. I still do not like the Joanne and Nigel, but it does not bother me. In fact, I put up with them at his parent's house if they are there, if it is only for a short period of time.

We have decided that we are going to get married on Valentine's day. I am going to try with his sister for Dexter's sake even although he feels the same as about her, but I ask her to be one of my bridesmaids. My niece Lucy will be the other one and Emma my maid of honor. Emma was the only one who knew about us from day one. In fact, Emma has seen Dexter in all his glory. We were in the back shop one day and there was a chap at the door. I was going to ignore it, but I could hear Emma's voice, so I ran to open the door. Before I could say to her Dexter was in the back, she opened the door to use the toilet. While I had answered the door, Dexter had stripped off and was lying sprawled out on the freezer as in a surprise way, but it was him and Emma that got the surprise because he was on the freezer, she opened the door and he was lying there bollock naked.

Chapter 24

We need to move to a new house. We need a bigger house, we have a room full of reptiles, the 2 dogs, Pricilla and Thelma. It is time to jump ship. Our landlord has a new house that is becoming empty. Brilliant, we will take the bigger house. No need for a man with a van we can do it ourselves.

It was the move from hell. I have an absolute cheek to moan about the other people's removals we done but we are the top bloody flat. We always dissed the removals that were in flats. We did it once and never again and yet here we are doing it for ourselves. We have 2 retics with their vivs, a blue tree monitor and her viv, a flared dragon with his viv, about 5 chameleons with their vivs, snakes, uromastics, and much more. Its unplugging all the vivs trying to get them set up again quickly and move all the reptiles. That is before we have even thought about moving anything else. What did we do, we turned it into a laugh? Somehow, we always turned it into a laugh. No matter how bad the situation was we would always put a different spin on it. It is the part I loved the most. I wondered if the next time I took a dip or hit a pothole we would be able to turn that into a laugh. I have only had 3 dips. The stupid one when he told me about his brother, the one after the tattoo shop and the one about fostering. I was caught off guard. Some people think a trigger will be you watching something on tv that is the same thing. For some strange fucked up reason it is not. Well for me anyway I can sit and watch special victims' unit and be ok about it. Well not ok but you know what I mean. For me, it is the stupid things, smells, being caught off guard like the time in the tattoo shop and the convo in the van. If I am going to watch tv then I know I am going to watch TV if that makes sense. It can be the way someone says something or the way they do something. Or just nothing. Most times there is no warning. It just comes, it is there before you know it and by then it is too late. The easiest one is when you have nothing to do. If you have nothing to do then your brain is not occupied and that is when pandoras box opens and you cannot close it. Doing nothing is your worst enemy. I always keep myself busy. Even before Dexter came into my life I would work constantly or have stuff to do. I cannot sit for longer than an hour doing nothing. I cannot do it. Well I could do it but then the box opens so I get up and do something. Anything. Time is not your friend. Time is your worst enemy.

From the minute Dexter walked in that door my life has been a whirl wind. A total world wind. My head does not know if its New Year or New York. It is so mixed up processing all this new stuff it has never felt before its farting skittles. Right now, my head is as fucked up as I am, but I think it is a few months behind in reality. It has not caught up yet. The thing that scares me the most. I have had 3 shitty little dips, that is all I have had in over a year I just know that by the time my head catches up then no magic red shoes are taking me back to Kansas. The wicked witch will be like a fairy princess. I will be heading straight for hell.

Chapter 25

We have a new house with a garden, well a postage stamp but it is a garden. It is much bigger than the flat, although the flat was a huge flat. So, you walk in the door the kitchen is to your right, you go up one level to the living room. A huge living room come dining room, up another level to the bathroom and 1 bedroom, up another level to another 2 bedrooms. There is a veranda off the living room and a garage under the house. Masses of room. We are happy as pigs in shit. It is not our own house, but it is a house. We love it. The décor is hellish, and I mean hellish, but this is our fault. The landlord said she would do it but no, we wanted in quicker and we would do it ourselves. The carpets are an orange brown with flowers. The walls have that woodchip paper. It is all dark wood or varnished in dark wood. It is a big house it just looks smaller and narrow with all these dark colours. It is not a problem, we will make this house our home. We will put our own twist on it and have fun doing it. Just like we always do.

It is a new house, what do we do. We must christen all the bedroom it would be rude not to. Our sex life is still amazing. We have an amazing sex life. I like nice underwear; Dexter loves nice underwear we are a match made in heaven. Everything just fits so nicely into place. Life is great, life is wonderful, I am happy. This is something I thought I could never be. Genuinely happy with my best friend, my fiancé, my everything but most of all the man that I trust more than anything in this world. The person who makes the impossible possible. I am about to marry this man. Something I swore I would never do again, but I loved him so very much that I was prepared to put myself in the room full of lions, I believed in him. I believed in us, and why wouldn't I. he was my best friend.

We did the house up one room at a time. We had just moved to a new house; we had all new stuff to buy for the house. Our wedding would be soon. We have not even started planning anything. I am one of these people who leave everything to the last minute and I mean the last minute. I work better under stress. I love stress, Stress is your best friend. If you are working under stress all the time, then you do not have time to think about other things. Maybe that is why I fly by the seat of my pants and literally do everything last minute.

Dexter has never had a dog that has had puppies. I have been down this road. It does not end well. I am an animal person. Give me 100 puppies any day over 1 baby. I have never let any of my bulldogs have pups because they are a bastard to breed. Too many complications. I have never done it. I had a bullmastiff who had pups and it was heart breaking handing the puppies over. It broke my heart. It is something we have not done together. Everything is about making memories, taking old memories but making new ones. Our memories, like Blackpool. I hated Blackpool, now we are never away from the place. Let us have a baby together, it is the only baby we are ever going to have together. When Levi comes into season, we will get a mate for her. Or a stud rather. Better go make money then because it will be the most expensive shag you will ever pay for. It will probably cost you about a grand.

Chapter 26

We are going camping. I have always wanted to go camping and fishing. So, we buy the tent, the sleeping bags the whole shebang. Fishing rods bait we have everything. We even went and bought blow up canoes I am so excited. I have never been camping. I cannot wait to go camping and make more memories. See this is why we have the van. We are going camping and the van is full from one end to the other. Jesus Christ half the house is in the van. The only thing missing is the bloody kitchen sink.

We go to the perfect place, right on the loch. We pitch the tent up and the loch is right there only meters away. It is perfect, the water is so still, the place is beautiful and its quiet and oh my god just kill me now and I would die a happy person. Its bliss. It is what I wish my head would be like for one day, just one day. If I were to paint a picture of how peace would look. This is it. If I could have bottled it, it would have been priceless, totally priceless. If I could choose a place to die, then this would be it. If the doctor said you have a few hours left to live, this is where I would come. It is perfect.

Jesus it takes ages to build the tent, I have the patience of a bloody goldfish. Dexter thinks he knows what he is doing. I have never pitched a tent, the dogs would have probably done a better job, but we get there in the end. We unpack the van and half the house. Get the dogs out and the angels decide they want to wash their clothes and its pissing from the heavens. We just looked at each other and burst out laughing. Its only rain. We had a few beers laughed and played games till the place was pitch black. We sat under the stars laughing and joking until we went to bed.

I wake up in the morning and I start having a flap attack. I can hear the water. I wake Dexter I think we are getting washed into the Loch. The water had come right up to where the tent was. I had visions of half the house in the loch. I would not have bothered so much about the house, but bulldogs cannot swim.

Dexter is not a morning person. I have always been the same since a child. I am up at the crack of dawn. I would drive my mum and dad up the wall. This is where we are total opposites. This is when we are only separated and not in contact with each other. From the time I wake up until Dexter wakes up, this is when I am alone. I cannot speak to him, I cannot text him. It is the only time I have on my own with my thoughts. Everything races through my head first thing in the morning, I have happy thoughts, I have sad thoughts, I still have so much hurt and anger inside but to even add happy thoughts to the mix is something I have never really done before. Sure, I have lied my ass off with previous relationships. A guy says I love you I am like yeah whatever. I will say it, but I do not mean it. I cannot mean it. It is just something you want to hear. You think our relationship is so great. We have fun together, we have sex together then I want to roll over and say goodnight thanks very much now get to fuck. Do not touch me, do not speak to me, just let me go to sleep. A bit like Thelma with her food. Do we have fun together? Yes. You meet me and you think I am the happiest person alive. I am the person in a room of 30 people being the entertainment. I will talk to anyone. You think our relationship is so great because we are having so much fun and inside, I am dying. Totally dying. I get up out of bed, put the mask on and I go out and be a superhero for the day. I am such a happy person until you piss me off and I become your worst fucken nightmare. I am already dead inside, I do not give a fuck if I die on the outside. I am a walking time bomb just waiting to go off. If you are the one on the other end, then you my friend better run because there is only one way I am going down and that is to die. So, you better be prepared to kill me. I welcome death. Death is a dream to me so what do I care? I would stand in front of a loaded gun and say I dare you to shoot me. You would be doing me a favour and putting me out of my misery. If you could kill me then hold off for a second so I can shake your hand for doing it. This is how I used to be. Do not get me wrong, that is still there, that is never going to go away, but right now there is light and happiness in the mix. So even although most of the time you still feel all of that there is also happiness there and it is something I have never had. It is just making it that bit better to get through another day. This is how I live. I live from one day to the next. I am not even really living. I am simply just existing, and yet you would never know it.

Dexter is lying there beside me snoring like a pig and I love it, snoring helps me sleep. I need noise to go to sleep. I have always needed noise to sleep. I cannot lie in a quiet room and go to sleep. I cannot be in a quiet room anywhere I need noise, or it freaks me the fuck out. Silence is not your friend either. As soon as there is silence, that box opens because the head does not have anything else to listen to. So, I have always gone to sleep with noise. Before Dexter started living with us, I would take the laptop into bed put something on Netflix, you would be lucky if I saw 5 minutes and I would crash out. I never left the lead in the laptop so it would eventually cut off when the battery ran out when I fell asleep. Dexter is the same. He cannot sleep without noise. He must be the same as me. He cannot go to sleep with silence, or he starts to think about his brother, who was his best friend. He too needs noise to sleep. This is how it is so weird and yet we fit together. At home we burn a wood wick candle that crackles, and Dexter tells me stories until I fall asleep. I would fall asleep and Dexter would watch something on his phone or iPad, and he would eventually fall asleep. This is the only time we are not with each other or in communication with each other. This is the only time that we are alone and separated from each other. This is the only time I have to myself with my thoughts. My head and I are still at war with each other but now I have a backup army on the battlefield, whereas before I was standing there with a few men and the bastard had a whole squad of people. It is still not an equal battle, far from it but sometimes my army does win. Whether I win or I lose I still get up out of bed and head straight for my mask and I am good to go.

I immediately wake him up, the water is coming we are going to end up in the loch. I have not even got myself out of the tent yet to see. The tent has like 3 bedrooms and a living area. We are in one bedroom, the dogs are in one bedroom and all our clothes food and half the house is in the other. It is the dogs, I am flapping about the dogs because they cannot swim. Fuck the clothes and half the house. I do not care about the clothes and the stuff, but I care about my dogs. I have actual fear in my heart about my dogs. I have never been camping before. I know the minute I arrived I said I would have happily died and gone to heaven but not like this. I do not want my dogs to drown.

Dexter is the worst person in the world to wake up. I swear to god Northern Ireland and Sothern Ireland could be in all-out war with each other throwing bombs and Dexter would sleep right through it. The bomb could go off right beside him and he would not even flinch. I am at the inside bit of the bed. Do not even ask me why we did this in the first place because I am always up first.

I am shaking and screaming at him to get up. We are going to drown, the dogs are going to drown. Wake the fuck up. He kind of semi woke up and said it would just be the water against the stones. That we would be fine. I got up stood on him to get out and sure as anything it was the water against the stones. We were not going to end up in the loch. Dexter went back to sleep and me? I am up. I am excited. Its new memories and something I have never done before. I want to make the most of this. I have never been camping before. I have never had genuine emotions before. I am happy, I am seeing the world through a whole different light. The sunglasses are off, and it is wonderful. Life is just wonderful.

Dexter had shown me the night before how to fish. I had bought myself a pink fishing rod and I was going to catch a fish. I was determined I was going to catch a fish. I took the dogs a walk and then I go and get my fishing rod. I just sat there looking at the loch, the scenery and how still the water was. My head does not like quiet. I need noise or my head is off galivanting looking for the worst memory ever to give you and then says take that bitch. If it does not send you in a total spin the bastard goes back, looks for something else and says here try this one. This is how my head works. Yet I am sitting here at this loch, it is so peaceful and still and the bastard is not throwing me all the shit of the day until I keel over. Has he died, I wish to fuck he had, nothing in this world would give me more pleasure than for this bastard to die? If I could have picked my time to die. It would have been right at this very minute. I would have died so happy and peaceful, but you know that is not going to happen. Get real Murrin, your death is most likely going to be a your fucked. I want it to be something else. God, I dream of it being something else, anything other than a your fucked so yes. I am a walking ticking time bomb 24 hours of every day. I can go from 0 to a 100 in a split second. Like the flick of a switch that is how fast my mood changes, I do not have time to process what has been said and I am already on you. Goading you to kill me.

I sat at that loch and just looked at the world for hours. Do not even ask me where the bastard was, I do not know, all I know is I have never felt so at peace. I was not even thinking about anything, I was just sitting watching the water, looking at the trees and a wee man on a boat fishing. Oh god I forgot about the fishing. I was so caught up in the peace and quiet I forgot my fishing rod. I have remembered from the night before what to do so I take my rod and I am trying to catch a fish. I am having the time of my life. My head is peaceful, Dexter is here even though he is asleep the dogs are beside me and everything is amazing. I can see the world differently and I never want it to end. God please just take me now. If there is such a thing as god, then do me a favour and take me right now. Right here and now. It did not happen. Either there is no god, he just did not listen, or I am going to be doomed for the rest of my life.

I do not know how long I was at the loch with my pink rod. It could have been minutes or hours, I do not know. All I know is something is on the other end of the line and I am so excited I have dribbled again. This is how excited I am. I have caught a fish. Oh, my fucken god I have caught a fish. I am screaming for Dexter, if you were someone walking by you would think I was being murdered this is how loud I am when I am excited. This is the 2nd time this morning I have woke Dexter, but I do not care. I have caught a fish. I am so excited I have peed myself. Dexter hates being woken up. It is our understanding. I always fall asleep first, so he is left with himself and his thoughts. He lets me fall asleep first and I let him sleep in the morning. It is something we have always done. I do not care though. I am so excited, Dexter wakes up and instead of being crabbit for getting woke up he looks at me and bursts out laughing. I have caught an eel not a fish. I do not care, he is buckled laughing. Dexter is so not a morning person it takes him 2 energy drinks and about 5 fags to wake up and yet he is buckled laughing. He can see the excitement in my face about catching something and I do not care that it is an eel I still caught something. We laughed about it the whole day. We always laughed about everything.

We bought these blow up canoe things from the car boot sale. Yip, we are taking our chances into a loch with something that we have bought from the car boot sale. I love the car boot sale. This is one of my happy places. Maybe this should have been my happy place in therapy instead of Thelma and it might have worked. I am the female version of Del Boy. I will buy and sell anything. The first time I took Dexter to the car boot sale he was in shock. More like shock horror. He would not speak to anyone, he did not interact with anyone, he looked like the deer in the bedroom with all these lions. Dexter and I talk and laugh but he cannot do it with other people. He is shy around other people. This is where I am as good for him as he is for me. I give him confidence. So much confidence. He does not know how to interact with other people. If I am honest, he looked down on the people I love to be with at first. This was totally new to him. In his previous relationship money was not an issue. Lorraine's parents had money, they had the best of everything. Designer clothes, shoes bags etc. I have never been a materialistic person. If I like it, I will buy it. If it is in the shop for a tenner and I can get it for a quid at the car boot, then I am buying it from the car boot. I am not paying shit loads of money for someone else's name. Why the fuck would I want to do that. Same clothes, same design, same everything except the label. People are paying hundreds of extra pounds on a label. Not me, I would rather dish the money out of the window and get a better experience than paying for a label. Do not get me wrong, I am shite with money. I never save money. I do not see the point. Why save money all your life, buy the necessities and leave the money for someone else to spend. Are you joking? I could have all these great experiences with money but instead I save it and leave it for someone else to spend. Hell no. Money burns a hole in my pocket. If I have it, I spend it. I do not care what I spend it on but it sure as hell is not a label with some other fucker's name that I do not even know.

Me, I am not shy. I will talk to everyone and anyone at the car boot. I love these people, but at arm's length. You put me in a room with other people and I am in my element. I will talk and laugh tell stories about adventures I have been on I will talk about anything. These are what I call acquaintances. You see them, you laugh with them, they think you are funny, they do not know that inside I am dying. They think I am the happiest person alive. I see these same people every single week and no one knows who I really am. All they see is a happy Murrin. If you were to say to everyone that amongst all of you, one of you is dying inside. None of them would pick me. They would not even consider it being me. That is how good I am at hiding things. There are hundreds of people at the car boot, yet I have a handful of friends. Patricia and Dale, talk about chalk and cheese. Patricia is like me; she is a wheeler and dealer. If anything were falling off the back of a van, she would be inside the fucken van emptying it. Dale, he would be the one to stick her in. Dale is so honest and straight laced, and Patricia would sell her knickers. I genuinely love these people. Patricia is taller than me she is in her 60's. she has like darkish blonde hair, glasses and come rain hail or snow she always has sandals on. It could be knee deep in snow and she would have sandals on. Dale is really tall and slim, he would do anything for anyone. Do not get me wrong Patricia would too. She just has the dodgyness in her like me. They are farmers. They live on a farm. Dale looks like he belongs in a farm. Patricia, she looks like she belongs in Cotton Vale Prison in the cell next to me. Then there is Rebecca, now at first, I did not like Rebecca. I hate anyone touching my stuff. I would go to the car to get my stuff and she would be in my bags. That pisses me off, anyone touching my bags is in for a bollocking. Do not touch my bags unless you want to die. We got off on the wrong foot and yet she became one of the people I class as friends. This usually does not happen with me. Usually my first impression is the right impression but not with Rebecca. She is the same height as me, short blonde hair, nicely spoken, she works in a lawyer's office. She is about the same build as me about a 10. Then its Mary and Lyla, well if I have never met 2 nicer ladies. Mother and daughter. Would you believe it they are the same height as me? Mary, she is like your typical gran, she has her gran hair style, she has a wee shopping trolley that holds her up and she is just so sweet. I swear that trolley is like a part of her, I often wonder does she take it to bed with her. You never see her without the trolley. Her daughter Lyla is roughly the same age as me, in her 40's she is the same height as me, blonde hair and maybe a 14. She is in the perfect job. This woman would take the clothes off her back and give them to you. She works in a like family Center kind of thing where the kids have nothing. This woman comes to the car boot sale every week and I swear she spends all her wages on other people. She is always buying for other people never herself. She buys for her family, or she buys stuff to take into the kids at work. This is how this woman rolls. I really like these 2 ladies. I have become that good of a friend and I know I can trust this woman more than anything. This woman knows my secret. This is how much I trust her. She works with kids like me. This woman could see it in me. She saw the hurt in me like I saw the hurt in Agnes. We really must all have sandwich boards and flashing lights saying we are fucked in the head. Out of hundreds of people and I mean hundreds maybe in the thousands I have 5 people I class as friends. Do not get me wrong I like all the people. I chat away to everyone, unless you piss me off or touch my stuff then I am on you even before your hand comes off what you touched. That is how my temper works. It is as fast as a switch, the switch flicks and I am gone.

The car boot is my go-to place. I love it, I love the banter, I love the arguing over prices, I just love the people and the atmosphere. As time went on it became Dexter's go to place. He started interacting with other people. These people are no less of a person because they want a bargain. Joe Bloggs in his mansion gets two quotes for a new marble worktop. One company say they will do it for five grand, the other company says four grand. Joe Bloggs does not turn around and say, I will pay the five grand for the same thing. No, is he hell he is going with the company at four grand? Joe Bloggs might be up his own arse and think he is better than everyone else with his flashy house and car but deep down inside Joe Bloggs still loves a bargain. No matter what way you want to paint it. This is how I feel about the car boot and the people in it. These are my kind of people. A bit of wheeling and dealing, ducking and diving, everyone has their own story and their own way of working and where they get their stock. I love it. No two days are ever the same. The place is a shite hole, I mean a shite hole, there is never toilet paper in the toilet. The refugees come in first thing and steal all the toilet roll out of the toilets. You know if you need a pee you need to take your own or you are fucked. The toilets stink to high heavens, if you cannot squat then do not go to the toilet. The car park is always massing of puddles the roof leaks, its dark, its cold its horrible and yet I love it. I really love it and the people. It is always the same people week in and week out. You get the odd stranger every now and then but most weeks its always the same people and I know everyone. I talk to everyone.

So, we are in the middle of the loch in these canoes that we have bought off of blue van man (I do not know his name, I only ever call him blue van man) we are taking a god dam chance that they do not have holes in them and we are right out in the middle of the loch. One dog each. I have Levi and Dexter has Salem. We are happy as pigs in shit. We are laughing, the dogs are happy, we are happy and right there and then in the middle of this loch I am happier than I have ever been before. Maybe the bastard does not like water. I do not know but I know right here and right now all I feel is peace. Total peace in my head except joy. There I go again. I am wishing my life away. Just take me now. Please just take me now and I will die happy. I know I will die happy. I have never been in a position or place like this where I knew if I died right here right now it would be a happy death.

The rest of our time there was much the same, we laughed, we fished, I caught another bloody eel, we played in the water, the dogs played in the water. It was amazing. Absolutely amazing. It was one of my favourite places to go. Here and the beach. I did not want to go home. Levi did not want to go home. She refused to leave. It was that bad Dexter had to physically lift her up and put her in the van.

We have been to a friend's caravan umpteen times with the dogs. We always like going away and making memories together. This memory box is full. We have had to upgrade it to a bigger box. I love the beach. I do not care if its pissing of rain, windy whatever the weather I love the beach, again I feel at ease on the beach. The bastard fears water. Why have I never thought of this before? The loch, the beech. The two things they have in common are water. Yet if I go in a bath and lie too long then he is away galivanting again looking for something to hit me with, here bitch try this with your bath. I always revert to him being he. I do not know why I do this. I have no clue who or what is in my head I always just revert to him as a he.

Chapter 27

Our life has just been a constant whirl wind. We have done so much together in such a short period of time. We have been up and down to Blackpool numerous times. A weekend here, a weekend there all the time making memories and laughing. Nothing else matters. Levi is pregnant. I do not have a good feeling about this. I really do not but it is something that we are going to share together. It is all about making memories together. I have experienced this before with someone else but not with me and Dexter, so it is something that we are going to share together.

Agnes and I have become good friends. Her health is starting to take a turn for the worse and I can see this woman shrinking right in front of my eyes. I know just by looking at this woman she is dead inside. She has given up. She has other children, a grandchild and a husband but she is still dying inside. Its written all over her face. She may as well have one of the sandwich boards saying, do not come near me, I do not want to care for you, I do not want to let you in in case anything happens to you and it hurts me. She carried a child for nine months, she nurtured this child for nine months, she gave this child life and some bastard took him away. That is a pain someone could not even begin to imagine. It is there written all over her face and I am the only one who sees it. What is wrong with these people. Dexter will say, she gave up that is it. Me and Joanne were still there, and she gave up on us. We felt cheated. It is not as simple as that. Is this why they are so selfish? Is it a vendetta against their mother? Before I came into his life, Dexter would take his family or leave them. It was as simple as that. He was not close to his sister, he thought she was selfish boot. The exact same as my first impression, they are not a hugging kind of family. They do not say I love you to each other either. Before I met him, he was that selfish person like his sister. I just gave him a different perspective on life. He saw life through my eyes now. My feelings and the hurt that I carried I shared that with him. Life is not all black and white. Like our old neighbours, Dexter would have judged them before. They took drugs. So, what, you do not know what has happened to them in their lives for them to do that. Who are you to judge anyone until you have walked in their shoes or gone through what they have? You just cannot do it. You might think you know what your mum is feeling inside but I bet it is not even a fraction of what goes on inside her head. I bet she does not even know what is going on inside her head although I know she is damaged and of course I care for this woman. She has issues. It is always the one with issues.

Chapter 28

Levi's time is getting nearer she is due about Christmas Day. Perfect. I fucken hate Christmas with a passion. Absolutely hate it. Do not ask me why but it is the worst time of the year possible for me. It sucks. Fuck you Father Christmas and your fucken elves. You can all kiss my happy jack ass. Dexter hates Christmas too. We both hate Christmas. I hate bloody Christmas trees, I hate the fucken things. Everything about Christmas I hate. Christmas movies, Christmas dinner, Christmas day, Boxing day the whole shebang I hate it from start to finish I wish it would just fuck off in the tornado in Dorothy's house and fuck off to the wizard of oz and never come back.

This Christmas would be different though because Levi would have her puppies and it was going to be a memory that we would share together but a brilliant distraction from Christmas. We could not have timed it better if we tried. It is our 2nd Christmas together. The first one was a half ass one. Frosty the snow queen, the bitch and the moaning boyfriend was not somewhere I wanted to spend Christmas. Christmas is bad enough for me never mind spending it with them. I was going to my sisters to spend Christmas with my family. The deal was Dexter would go and see his family for dinner. Exchange presents and then come to my sisters.

It was as good as Christmas was going to get. My mum was there my mum is tiny, she is about 4 foot 8 or 9 she takes a child size 13 or an adult size 1 in a shoe. She has dark coloured short hair and glasses. Am I close to this woman? No, she is my mother, I love her and yet again I keep her at arm's length. I keep everyone at arm's length. My sister is obviously there it is at her house, Greg and the kids. I had my dinner, exchanged presents and left. I just hate Christmas.

Christmas day came and went, she never had her puppies. It was great though because it was our excuse to miss Christmas. It was as if it was meant to be. No shuffling about from one house to the next for food exchanging gifts and kidding on we were happy. It was Christmas our way with a Chinese and shit tv. Waiting for Levi to have her puppies.

As the days went on, I started to panic, I knew something was wrong. I should have listened to my gut. I knew this was going to be bad. We had to take Levi to the vets. She had taken an infection in the womb and we nearly lost my baby and her baby at the same time. If we had not taken her that day, there and then we would have lost them both.

As we get to the vets to see Levi's baby, the vet nurse hands her over. Dexter looks at her and asks if there are more. I am saying have you seen her. She is a fat bastard. If there were any more puppies this fucker has ate them. No wonder she did not want to come out. I have been through this before. Dexter has not. Puppies do not come out this size. This is like a human giving birth to a fucken toddler. No wonder she could not get her out. I do not even think a humans vaginia would dilate as much for this little fucker. I loved her instantly.

Now I thought Levi was going to be a brilliant mum, this dog loved everyone. She would allow anyone to clap her, she played with any dog, rabbit, any other animal. She was the sweetest and happiest dog ever. As soon as we brought her and the baby home, she went into the hall cupboard. We had the whelping box ready, everything was ready, and she choose to ignore her baby and go into a cupboard. It was Salem who became mother. We still had no name for her, but we had to bottle feed her and raise her ourselves. Levi continued to stay in the cupboard and take fuck all to do with her child and I knew there and then we had fucked up. Was Levi like me. Was she a happy go lucky bubbly dog but she just did not want children the same way I did not want children and we got her pregnant? Did she want this baby? Did she fuck. She just wanted to hide in a cupboard for peace and quiet. This thing squealed when it wanted fed, squealed when it needed its arse licked and squealed at any given time. I do not like babies crying yet I am ok with this little thing squealing every two flamen minutes. Was the squealing to Levi like a crying baby was to me? We fucked it. I knew we fucked it. Right there and then I lost my little girl and it was all my own fault because I accepted to choose a new memory with Dexter over what she wanted. I never asked her if she wanted a baby. I just assumed she would be a brilliant mother because she was such a loving and caring dog. Right there and then I knew I had lost her, and she hated me. She fucken hated me. I could see it in her eyes. You have just done to me exactly what you do not want to do yourself. How dare you get me pregnant when you will not do it yourself, and off to the cupboard she went.

Now Salem was a totally different kettle of fish, ah he was in his element. He is like a dad that has been on an IVF program all his life and this is his last chance to have a baby. He loves this little thing, this little fat ball of wrinkles. You can see it in his eyes in everything he does. He is so in love. He is like super dad. He cleaned her, he licked her to make her go to the toilet, he lay beside her, he did practically everything except hold the bottle of goat's milk for her. He was so excited, when he went out, he delivered his messages quick. This is what I call them reading and receiving messages. They go out sniff the pee this is them reading the message from their friends then pee the reply. Salem was peeing all over the place. It was as if he was so proud of being a dad, he had to tell everyone. He was leaving bits of pee everywhere. Levi? She is still in the cupboard. She does not give a fuck about this ball of wrinkles. She wants to put red shoes on the fucker and send it to Kansas herself with no wizard of oz to find her way back. She hated her. She hated us. She had turned into a dog version of Thelma. God Thelma paid the ball of wrinkles more attention than Levi and that is saying a lot. Thelma is a cat version of me, and her only happiness is Dexter. It is a fucked-up family, but it is my family.

We called the ball of wrinkles Doris. She came out fat, she continued to be fat, she gulped goats' milk like it was going out of fashion. This thing was getting bigger by the day. Usually you have a puppy next minute you look, and it is an adult dog, you do not see the difference daily. With this thing you do. She looks as if her belly is going to explode at any given minute. She squeals, she gets fed, Salem licks her arse, she sleeps. It starts again.

Chapter 29

We are getting married in a few weeks and I have done nothing I mean nothing. Doris takes up most of the day with feeding etc., I have no wedding dress, no cake no fuck all and I am getting married in a few weeks. Future brides plan their wedding for years. Not me, I am a two-minute wonder.

Me and Emma went and picked my dress. I am not a materialistic person. I do not give a fuck about fancy dresses and labels. I picked my wedding shoes up at the car boot sale for a fiver. Brand new shoes, I am never going to wear them again. Why do I want to pay hundreds of pounds on something I am never going to wear again? I got my dress in Debenhams in the sale, a black dress. I am not being a normal bride If I am getting married it is going to be my way. Black wedding dress, a skull wedding cake and as least fuss possible. I hate weddings. You go to a wedding and it is like going to the bloody dentist, and you know I hate the dentist. It is the whole Flippen palaver. It is the longest god dam day of your life that feels as if it is never going to end. From the church service to the food to the speeches to the dancing. Most people are absolutely pissed by the dancing because the day was so bloody boring drink was the only thing that made it that bit easier to get through the day. I am not having a wedding like that. We are going to the registry office, say I do, go get fed have a drink and then home. The only part that really matters is that you love each other. Not how much money you can blow on one day. Like Christmas. Everyone forgets that Christmas is about baby Flamen Jesus not spending thousands of pounds. The wise men brought Frankincense and Murre not fucken Ipads.

I took the girls to go and pick their bridesmaids dresses. They can wear whatever the fuck they want. I do not care. The only thing that matters to me is I am going to marry the man I love. I would have turned up in a bin bag. I just do not care about things like that. So, if the girls want to wear rara skirts then that is fine, as long as they are happy with what they are wearing even Joanne. They all chose blue dresses from quiz.

Happy days job done. No faffing about. I hate shopping. I bloody hate it. I am one of these people you need to know what you are going for and out again. I am not arsing about the shops all day. Fuck that. In and out with at least damage possible.

Dexter was wearing his kilt all that was left to do was the invitations and flowers. I did them themself. I think we had the whole wedding palaver sorted in a few days. All that was left to do was turn up.

Dexter stayed with his parents the night before and Emma stayed with me.

Chapter 30

It is the morning. Oh, my fucken god, why did I say Emma could stay. We are opposites. If Emma were to get a parking ticket, she would fart skittles. She would not sleep until she had paid the fine and the traffic warden knew that she had paid the ticket. This is the kind of person she is. Me? I would take the parking ticket shove it right up his arse in broad daylight and get in my car. Emma is having kittens, she is not an animal person in any way shape or form, but she is having kittens. You would think she was the one getting married and I am the one trying to calm her down. It was kind of like what you would imagine if you were joining the army. You have the drill sergeant who is a total dick, but he has everything written down from crossing the t and dotting the I, and it is all on a clipboard. This is Emma. She has that clipboard today, she is the drill sergeant without being a dick but a drill sergeant all the same. Stage 1, stage 2 and so forth. This is just how she is as a person. I do not know why her house is not full of lists and post it notes. She is a worrier, I do not give a fuck. She is nice and caring. I am your worst nightmare, yet she sticks with me. She must see something, or she is a gluten for punishment, but she is my friend. She is my best friend, and today my best friend is the drill sergeant.

She makes me go to Asda for breakfast, ah we are just so opposite of each other it works. If I were her best maid, I would be awful. I would have probably given her enough booze while getting ready that she would forget she got married. I am that bad influence friend. I am the one who gets you into trouble. I am the friend you do not want to take home to your parents when you are at school. I am the kind of friend that leads you into temptation and then delivers you to evil and skips past the holy ghost, by the end of it your praying for Amen. I am that friend and yet this loving caring soft worrier of a person puts up with me.

My mum, sister, Greg and the kids come. Lee is giving me away, Lucy is my bridesmaid, we will meet Joanne there. She is not the person I want in the house before I get married. This is my day. She can be a bridesmaid but today is all about me and Dexter. That is the only thing I care about.

After all the slagging and moaning at Emma about flapping today what happens? I get into the car to take us two minutes up the road and I start to cry. Jesus fuck, Emma has already been crying. I have been fine. I am the one comforting her earlier. I swear I thought it was her wedding. She was the one with the screw loose and I was the screwdriver putting her back together, and now look at me. I have got mascara on as well. I tried. I put mascara on for my wedding. Nothing else, just mascara and now it is all going to be off. This is Emma's fault. She is rubbing off on me.

We get there and I gather myself together. I tell her, do not look at me. If you are going to cry, then cry yourself. Just do not look over to me and do it and we start laughing, then laughing turns her to tears again but they are happy tears. She is my best friend, she knows. She is the only person outside my family that knows. Of all the other friends that I have had in and out of my life for some reason I have never told any of them. Demi knows. Of course, Demi knows she is like thrush, you just cannot get rid of her and I never would want to. I knew she was happy for me. She did not need to tell me, I can see it in her face, and I know why she is crying but we never say it. I just know what she is thinking, and I think that is why I am crying because I am finally getting my happy ever after.

We go inside and there is Joanne well if anything was going to pull me back from sympathy it was her, although she does look genuinely happy, maybe I have read all this wrong. Maybe I have been the problem because I do tend to choose my own friends. As in Demi, Jesus fuck I am never going to get rid of her ever, not even when I die. I think that bastard would jump in the coffin beside me just to have the last word. That is just the kind of person she is. She never shuts up, but I know, If I had a bad secret or done something wrong. She is not going to be the one to sail me down the Clyde. She might stand at the side and wave, but she would never in a million years do anything like that. We love to hate each other but if she needed me, she has not even hung up the phone and I am there. It is the same with her as it is with me. We have been together our whole lives. I do have other people that I class as friends that I do genuinely like I just have not told them the truth. So, maybe it is me I have read it wrong with Joanne and I will see where the land lies after we wedding, but right now I want in that ceremony to marry the man I love.

The door opens I see Dexter standing there waiting for me. I see his face, it is that same look on his face that always gets me and I am buckled. That is, it I am gone. I am laughing I am walking over to where my soon to be husband was and all I can do is laugh, then that starts him off laughing. The poor woman who was marrying us ended up laughing. All our guests were laughing. We got married our way by laughing. We always turned everything into a laugh. You are now husband and wife just laugh at your bride never mind kissing her. The woman said it was the funniest wedding she had ever done. Laugh, laugh, laugh and your married. All the guests have sat for about five to ten minutes and laughed. Not Flamen hours in a church listening to some guy in a white collar harping on about a load of shite that you do not care about, no hymns to sing, thankfully because I sound like a cat getting thrown about in a pillow case when I sing. Most of them do not sign the bloody hymns, their lips are moving but nothing is coming out, but Jessie beside you. Oh, Jessie is all about God, she loves god so much she is giving it big licks singing away. She thinks that her voice that sounds like pots clattering together is on the radio station in heaven and she is giving it everything she has from the tips of her toes to the top of her head. She is in her element and everyone else is bored shitless.

We are married we move onto the restaurant we have the place to ourselves. Everyone from the registry office joined us and then we met more people for the meal. We were only allowed 12 people plus me and Dexter. So, it was my mum, my sister, Greg, Lucy, Lee, Demi and Emma. From Dexter's side it was his mum and dad, Joanne, Jack, Greeting face Nigel, and his two grans.

Joining us as the registry office were immediate family and our friends Matilda, Garry and the boys Rory and Theo. This is where it gets like a wedding. I suppose it is like any wedding someone does not like someone else so myself and Emma went there this morning and wrote out name card things where everyone was to sit. Nightmare. His two aunts hate each other. Again, I heard all the stories from both sides, I will listen to what you say, but I will make my own mind up. The one they all hate the most is Alison, they hate her with a passion, they moan about her house, her dogs, her children, they hate her husband, she seems to think that she is better than everyone else. This is the kind of person I always take a sudden dislike to. If you think your better than other people. I just do not like you. It is the worst quality to have. No one person is better than any other person. Joe Bloggs in his multi mansion house and five cars is still the same as Jimmy the homeless guy on the street. They both bleed the same, they are both human, they feel pain the same, the walk the same talk the same. The only difference is that wee Jimmy's sleeping bag is not as flashy as Joes house. Yet they are the same people. Never look down on anyone unless you are doing it to pick them up!

Yet I met Alison and I liked her instantly. She is small like me, she has short dark hair and a pretty face, there is minimal make up on and she is naturally pretty. She has a happy looking face, she looks welcoming, she was chatting and lovely the first time I met her, not like frosty the snow queen. Alison and I instantly bonded. God It was me who invited them to my wedding. It was going to just be the people from the registry office but no I wanted Alison there I liked Alison. It was her who made our skull wedding cake. So, her, her husband Paul who no one liked either, Paul is tall, well taller than Alison, he is a slim build Alison is medium build they just look like they belong together. Hannah their daughter I think she is about 20 and their son Troy, Now they have to be away from Agnes and away from Veronica, this is the other aunty I have only met her briefly for short periods, the jury is still out on that one just now, again I have listened to what both sisters have said, but I will still make my own mind up. Veronica isn't too tall, she has dark hair longer than Alison's hair, she has the same skin condition as Dexter, although hers is more visible on her arms they both have eczema her husband Ted, I liked him immediately like I liked Dexter's dad. He is the kind of uncle you want. He would have let you drink booze smoke and get up to stupid things when you are a child. I just got that vibe off him when I first met him. This is the uncle that Dexter grows the cannabis for and takes it up to Aviemore. They have two girls Lisa and Gill. Not only do the sisters not like each other the whole cousin situation too. It is a small ass place and we tried our best to keep them all apart.

The two grans hate each other with a passion, Fuck, we are running out of spaces. I listened to the stories from everyone, but I was still going to make my own mind up, I liked them both. Its Agnes's mum Mary they all have issues with no one really likes her. She is like a gran, she has the gran hair style, the gran glasses, she wears gran clothes kind of thing. Now I know the whole family hate her and yet I liked her. I enjoyed chatting to her every time I saw her. Bert's Mum Harriet she looks like a gran looks too. I have seen a lot more of Harriet than I have of Mary and I really like her. She just says it like it is. She is as bad as me. She has got foot and mouth, she is just thinking about what to say but it is already out of her mouth. She does not hold back. I like this. She obviously sees things the same way as me. You know she thinks Joanne is a selfish bitch, she openly talks about it and she cannot stand Nigel either, when he comes in the house me and Harriet leave.

So, myself and Emma went up in the morning to try and mix people up so that everyone was happy. My aunty Gwen who is Demi's mum and not my blood aunty, but it is the aunty I have chosen. I still call her Aunty Gwen. I can go to this woman with everything and anything. This woman will always be in my life to the day I die. She has known me my whole life, she knows my secret, this is how much I trust this woman. Then there is Uncle Willy, the uncle who would frighten the shite out of me and Demi as kids. If we pissed the bed you would go and tell aunty Gwen not uncle Willie. God even I feared uncle Willy when I was younger and that is saying a hell of a lot. He is still a grumpy bastard, but he is my grumpy bastard and the uncle I chose. Then Demi's kids, my niece and nephew David and Susan. Both are tall with blonde hair; David's is darker than Susan's. David has what you could call issues he has demons of his own in his head, he chooses to take his out on doors, walls anything really. Do I love them all? Yes of course I do I have just never told them.

Then we have Dexter's other aunt and uncle from Bert's side and there is no point asking, yes, I like them, they have the same personality as Bert. Bert's brother Duncan, they look as if they have been cut from the same cloth. They look alike, they are the same height, they both wear glasses and they are both funny as fuck. Duncan's wife Rose, she is the same height as Duncan, just a bigger build but she has the personality to go with it, she has a giving nature. You can just see it in her eyes. Everyone else moans about her because she is always unwell, it is not her fault she has health issues, they say she makes up health issues for sympathy, it is her that has made her daughter the way she is. She creates illnesses for Fiona but again I listen to what people tell me, but I always make up my own mind and I like this woman. I enjoy her company, she does not need to get drunk to have a laugh that is just how she is. You can just tell that Duncan and Rose will always be together. When I met her after being warned about her previously, I liked her, I wanted her to come and share our special day.

Then its Fiona their daughter, again I am going to make my own mind up. These people all think that Fiona is slower at learning stuff because of her mother. Fiona is the most loving and caring person ever. Every time I have seen her, she is an adult, but she will play with Jack all day teach him to do things takes him to the park, picks him up from school. You can just see it in this girl's face, she loves to help people, its back to the sandwich board again. Come and look at me I am so loving and caring. I will do anything for you and ask for nothing in return, and she does not. She might be a little bit slower than people, but she has a heart of gold, and that is priceless. She is the opposite of Dexter and Joanne total opposite by a mile. If Fiona was Agnes's daughter, then she would have picked up on her mother straight away. She would be the person standing right beside her mother all the way through no matter what. You can just see this in this young woman and that is what she is a young caring woman.

Then my real Cousin Paul with his soon to be wife Grace, Ah Paul, the only way to describe him is sex, drugs and rock in roll just minus the drugs part. He is about 5 foot 7, wirey hair, like brillo pad hair, a cute squishy face and I love him. He is wired to the moon. Put him in a room for his whole life with records and he would die a happy man. He was raised in South Africa, so he still has a strong Afrikaans Accent. He is always simply happy; I swear if he had a pet and it passed away, he would most likely have a goodbye party for the pet with his music and his booze. That is just how he is, and I love him. Of course, I have not told him, but I do. His soon to be wife Grace has exactly what Paul needs a calmer side. She is naturally pretty, does not wear much make up almost the same height as Paul, with blonde hair. Her personality is the total opposite of Paul but that is probably makes them a great couple.

Eddie and his wife May. Again, I listen to the stories, but I make up my own mind. They think that Eddie is boring and stuck up his own arse Eddie is Bert's other brother. They do not fit like Bert and Duncan, they two would be the class clowns at a party and Eddie would be the one sitting in a corner. They are brothers but they just do not fit. Even polar opposites fit but I do not see it with Eddie, it is their brother they obviously love him, but I bet it was Bert and Duncan that always got them all into trouble when they were young. The only thing that they all have in common is residing hairlines. His wife May again, I am going to make up my own mind because everyone thinks she is stuck up her own arse. She is pretty, really pretty, she has natural beauty, she is tall maybe 5 foot 7ish, blonde hair and she has makeup on, she is the kind of woman who looks after herself, gets her nails done kind of thing. That is not me, far from me but I instantly like this woman. It always seems to be if everyone hates someone, I end up loving them.

Then we have Matilda although she is our landlord, she has always been a friend first, she is like me in a way. She is not a girly girl. She a mix of me and my cousin Paul. She likes like rock and roll kind of things. She is naturally pretty. She does not need makeup, she does not use it every day but she has some on today and its subtle and lovely, again the same kind of height maybe a few extra inches with long dark hair, her husband Gary, lovely guy, would do anything to help you kind of guy, he is just taller than Mathilda is and his hair is going grey and he is embracing it. The two boys Rory and Theo. I think its roughly a year or year and a half age gap, but they are so funny. They call me aunty Murrin, again we are not blood related, so it is someone I chose as a good friend and they call me aunty. She should have called them Ronnie and Reggie because they are always up to something. Most kids are. They are funny and happy just like kids should be.

With Emma and I going up in the morning and placing all the names in the right places everyone was not seated anywhere near the person they did not like, and there was no awkward silence thing or people not talking. Everyone was talking and Agnes used her sticks for the day and she literally walked down the aisle. Everyone was told wear what you feel comfortable in. I do not care if it is a bin bag or jeans, just come and share our special day.

But these are the people we chose to spend our special day with, and it was the best day ever. I loved my wedding day. Loved it and yet I hate weddings, but it was not that all hanging about all day shit. We arrived, we were given drinks, had our food, more drinks. Handed out gifts, cut the cake and all went back to our house for a party. My idea of a great wedding. Each to their own.

Chapter 31

We are married now, I am so happy that I am married I want to walk about with a sandwich board telling the world I was happy. I was a happily married woman to my best friend, my everything, the other half of me. We are as one now. You walk different, you talk different, the world is bright now. Omg it is so bright. Is this because I am happy? Has the world always been like this and I have just never noticed because I never allowed myself to be happy?

Do not get me wrong the bastard is still there but he is all mixed up, there is happy feelings and happy memories in my head now, so he is not as fast at handing them out. He is in my head running about like a two-bob rocket trying to separate the happy thoughts from the bad ones. My head is like soup and he is drowning like a sack of shit with a brick in it.

Life is wonderful, Life is great, I have my best friend, the person I can trust, the person I tell everything to. We share everything. We even share the same toothbrush. This is how our relationship was.

Levi has come out of the cupboard, you can tell she still does not give a shit about Doris, she still wants to kick her ass to the land that never was. Salem is still Super dad he is besotted with her and I immediately see a bond between Salem and Doris much stronger than it was with Levi. I swear he thought he was the virgin Mary and god chose him to take care of the baby Jesus. I have had dogs all my life, I have never seen two dogs so bonded like this. If she even let out a yawn or anything. Salem was there in nano seconds. Levi? She would just fuck off and say fuck you.

So, now what is next? Our lives have just been one huge roller coaster for just over 2 years. I am one of these people I do not think about things I want to do and then hover about. No, I decide I want to do it and that is it. Full steam ahead. Dexter is the same, its brilliant. So, when we went to Blackpool and I previously hated it, when I went with

Dexter, I loved the place. We go all the time. Dexter has always wanted to go to Vegas. I have been. I hated the fucken place, but I was not with Dexter. Would it be different if it were with Dexter? Right Murrin think think, how can I pull something like this off in a couple of months. We do not do Christmas. I bloody hate it. I like my birthday. So does Dexter. We always make our birthdays special. We push the boat out for birthdays because we do not do Christmas. I am going to book Vegas but how I can I pull off working extra hours and getting that amount of cash without Dexter knowing. We practically live in each other's pockets. How the fuck Am I going to do this. We have got everything on the go just now. I am making stuff and selling it. I did this many years ago, I made hampers and flowers and shit sold it on Facebook, I made a lot of my own stuff for the wedding and I enjoyed doing it. So, I went back to it but as a side-line thing just while Dexter was doing deliveries. We have more than enough space in this house for everything. We rehomed all the reptiles. It was not fair, before we were always about, but things have changed now. It really is a fulltime job if you look after them properly. If anyone has reptiles, you will know what I mean. So, the reptile room now became my work room.

Dexter is growing more cannabis; he is still doing the takeaway place, but I am so busy now with my own work he needs to do the deliveries himself. Everything is ticking along nicely. I only work when Dexter is at work and we spend the rest of our time together.

Dexter would be texting while doing deliveries and I would text back. It was as if we needed each other that bad when we were apart it was like an addiction. We literally were addicted to each other. If I cannot physically see him then he is on the phone. It is like one cannot live without the other. If I do not text Dexter back in 5 minutes, he thinks there is an issue. This is how he has always been. His confidence is going through the roof now, but he is still a worrier.

Ok, I do not have a long time to get all this money he knows it will be his birthday soon and I would say, the birthday fairy will need to keep money from hampers and the car boot sale just now can we tighten our belts. Now he knew that it was his birthday coming up and we always went that bit above and beyond for birthday but how the fuck was I going to make thousands instead of hundreds

I was putting up hampers people were buying the hell out of them and the money was flying in. I would make it Dexter would deliver them before work then I would continue to work until he got home and then we were together. Always together. As the weeks went by something just did not feel right. Nothing had changed. I just knew it was not right. I felt it. Our routine had not changed but something just did not feel right. If it had been any other man. I would have said I had a gut feeling he was cheating on me. But this is Dexter, my Dexter, the person I trust more than anyone in this world. The minute the bastard sent the thought to me I threw it straight back, but instead of sending me something else he hit me straight back with the same thing and he never does that. If he sends you something and he does not get the reaction he wants he just looks for something better. He is a bastard. A complete bastard.

As the days were going by the thought kept coming, and I would send it back. There was no way that my best friend, my husband, my everything that man I trusted more than anything in this world would lie to me. It just would not happen, but it never went away. It just kept coming. Our routine has not changed. It is not as if its years down the road the honeymoon period is over, and it is a case of just pull my nightie down afterwards. No, we are just married. We are in love; everyone can see we are in love. If you were to write our relation down on paper with the age gap you would think no chance, but then if you met us and spent even a day with us, you know we belong together. This man knows everything I have been through and my true feelings. Not just feelings I thought he wanted to hear. No, I told him my true feelings. This was something I had never done before with anyone. Not with anyone. I did not even know I could do this.

He has not stopped telling me that he loves me, he has not stopped writing texts saying he cannot wait to get home to be with his fucked-up family. There was no dramatic change. I just knew my husband and best friend inside out and I knew something was not right.

I have been having irregular bleeding. My body is so fucked up inside I am a surgeon's worst nightmare, and a psychiatrist wet dream I think the only organ I have left that has not been damaged is my heart. Tablets have not worked so now it is an injection. They are going to give me a hormone injection to fool my body into thinking it is going through the change of life. Now I have been warned about this. Some people say it makes you go mad. It makes you go mad I think? You have no idea what goes on in my head every fucken day. Just give me the fucken jag. Happy Days just give me the needle so I can get home and finish these orders.

Chapter 32

Things still feel the same, that feeling is still there, and the pothole has not come yet. It is worse than watching paint dry. I am thinking will you just hurry up already so I can get it over and done with and get on with it. Things are still the same with Dexter, he says he loves me, he messages. In fact, he thinks we should buy our own home together. Now my credit history is fucked beyond fucked. There is no coming back from that, my ex-husband was a constant spender and had to keep up with everyone else. If the guy two doors down got a new car, that idiot would go buy a better car. We were so far up our arses in debt it was beyond believe. One of us had to be the responsible one and get a real job with real wage slips to be able to get a mortgage. Dexter's credit rating is perfect. He pays his bills, so it made more sense for him to get the job and I would keep things going at home and my orders. I still have that feeling, it will not go away, and no pothole has come. I needed a distraction or something different because I can start to feel myself dip but it is a different dip. It is not a smell or anything like that, it is simply different. I could feel myself going more into myself. What am I going to do because if I go too low, I am fucked? Dexter is saying all the right things, still texting and phoning on his break. Something just is not right. It just is not right. I feel it. I can feel I am going down, it is a different down though. Instead of boom here is your dip, that not enough ok hold on and he goes back for something else, but it is different. Everything is different it is like your hovering about the sky and looking down on your own life, it looks like your life you just see it from a different perspective. I am looking down on my life looking at my life, but it is not my life. Ok, what am I going to do?

I have to ask him, I need to do it because we are always honest with each other and although I am having these feelings, I do not think my best friend would do this to me, but I need to ask him and be honest with him. So, I tell him how I am feeling. See that look, the look that always made me go all gooey. It has just turned into how fucken dare you even ask me that or tell me that. Why the fuck would you do that.

You are my soulmate and we are always honest with each other. You are letting what happened to you in the past into our marriage now and you are losing the plot. You must be having a dip and you are blaming me and taking it out on me. I knew I fucked up. Right there and then I knew I fucked up. I had just turned around to the only person that I have ever been totally honest with and threw a bolt of lightning at him. This is how it felt. If there was ever a time, I wanted the ground to open and swallow me. It was now. Like the feeling at the Loch when I wanted to die. Now I want the bedroom floor to fall away and I go down with it. The look on his face. I fucked it, I know I have, it is written all over his face. I have just fucked up the only decent thing I have ever had in my life. He thinks that I am having a dip and that my abuse is now affecting our relationship and marriage. This was my worst fear. I told him this from the beginning. It has affected my whole life. It affected every relationship that I had because they did not know. I do not let people in enough to tell them. This is the most heinous thing that has ever happened to me and you did not want people to know. You feel embarrassed and ashamed even though you were a child this is how you feel. Do not ask me why. If I knew that I would have been a physiatrist You do not want people to look at you differently and feel pity for you. That is even worse. Now the thing that I dreaded the most has happened. I have let my past fuck this up. It is all my fault. I should have just kept my mouth shut, but this man was my husband and best friend. This is the man I shared all my feelings with. I was telling him what I was feeling even though I did not think it was possible I was still being honest with him and now I have fucked it. Well and truly fucked it. The thing I feared the most to destroy our relationship has just happened and again I am dreaming of death.

I am smashing fuck out of work between making the hampers and the car boot. I am sliding though, I know I am going down. I can feel it. I am literally working myself into the ground to stop my head from thinking. I need some sort of release I need it. Like really need it like a junkie needs heroin. I do not have Steven, my husband who is my best friend must see it in me. This man knows me better than anyone. I am a mess. I know I am a mess, that is when you know it is bad. I cannot drink, Dexter already thinks I am losing the plot. I can still see that how dare you even ask me that question face. My past is dictating my future. This bastard is never going to let me be happy. Not in a million years. I must do something. I go to the shops, this time it is not stock cubes. Its anything and everything I do not care what it is. I am not hiding this I am casually walking in the shop and just putting stuff in my bag and did not care if anyone was watching me. I just do not care. It is not working, it is not even touching the sides and I know I am heading for your fucked. I skipped the dip and went straight for the pothole. I am spiraling too fast too quick. It is too quick, and I cannot bring it back. I head for home. I am just going to have to be honest with Dexter even if he gives me that look because I am going down so fast all I can see is darkness.

I get home into the house, I do not even remember driving home. This is how bad it is. This is a different dip entirely. I have never had it like this before. It went too dark too quick. I can hear the shower, I know he is in the shower, but I need help. I am going too fast. I burst through the bathroom door and oh my fucken god. Are you for real? This fucken bastard my best friend is in the shower with his phone skelping one out with his phone in his hand. Oh, my fucken god. I did not walk out the bathroom a shell did, everything that was inside me fell out and it lay on that bathroom floor. Everything, just lying there on the floor. I was destroyed. The only god dam organ I had left that was undamaged and this lying sack of shit has just broken it into a million pieces My best friend, my husband, the person I trusted more than anyone in this world.

He gets out of the shower I can explain. Explain what that you are a dirty, lying, cheating face cunt. There is no explaining that, no matter what way you say it or dress it up. We are just fucken married. Not 50 years down the line the sex is shit and I am taking my false teeth out and giving you a gummy. No is it fuck. We are just fucken married, we should still be in the honeymoon period. Not the I just put up with you now period where the novelty has worn off and you are just too comfortable with each other. You are not trying. No, we are just married and happily married or so I thought so what the fuck is your excuse. Its porn. I was watching porn. My fucken arse you were watching porn. I remember a video something like that with us. Do not tell me your watching porn. Did you forget I am the wife who took you to your first strip club? Why the fuck would you hide porn from me? You are full of shit. He bare faced lied right to me. He swore on my life, the dogs lives and his dead brothers' life he was only watching porn. I have had this feeling for weeks. You bastard let me think it was all in my head because of my past. You took something that is so heinous to me and you twisted it back around on me. You knew exactly what you were doing you piece of shit. Of all the people that could have done something so bad was the person I thought I could trust the most. You took the worst part of my life, spun it around and let me think I was losing the plot. You had the audacity to give me that look knowing fine well it was true, and you gave me that look. You dared to lie to my face, My best friend. My everything I have been here falling apart by myself because your too busy trying to get into someone's knickers. Even if you wanted someone else you could have at least helped me to get through this your fucked, but you chose another woman over me and you just left me to spiral by myself,

This was the straw that broke the camel's back. I told him to get to fuck. I knew even before coming through the door today. I knew I would be lucky if I could get over the pot hole but I was heading for the you are fucked and now I have walked in on this piece of shit skelping one out with someone else while they were video watching each other. What a fucken idiot I have been. All these weeks, I knew I just knew something was not right, and away at the very beginning when the thought first entered my head, I threw it back. I bloody threw it back. Thinking there is no way Dexter would do that to me. Dexter who gave me brightness, Dexter who gave me happiness Dexter who showed me the world in a different way, Dexter who better not have given me the clap. I had to try and hold myself together until he left. This sack of shit knew I was starting to spiral, he fucken knew it. He knew I did not have Steven. I had nothing and no one to talk to and I went too far down. The minute he walked out the door I collapsed in a heap. I had to hold all of that in because I did not want the bastard to see what he had done to me. I was devasted. Everything just collapsed, I knew on the way home there was only a little bit of light left. This is when I knew I was heading for a you are fucked. I knew it. Even if Dexter the lying sack of shit had helped me, I knew this time I may not have made it. This is a different dip, pothole, you are fucked. It is different. I cannot explain to you why it is different I just knew it is different. I could feel myself going down, whereas before it just comes. It was kind of like this time it was warning me, hey I am coming soon and its never happened like that before. You are in the garden pulling up weeds and then the bastard is on you. That is how fast it comes. This was a gradual one though. I knew it was coming. He warned me it was coming as if he was doing me a favour. Did he like Dexter too and this was why he was warning me because he has never done this before. I know I am fucked. I can feel my chest tighten up. Everything has gone so dark, there is no light. There is no light at the end of the tunnel and all you see is dark. It feels dark, it looks dark, everything is just so dark. The tightening of your chest is the emotional pain. It takes over your whole body and you cannot breathe, you are crushed inside, and you are in so much pain, you are in that much pain that you want that miracle injection. You pray for death. You beg for death because death is the only thing that is going to take this away. A fully-grown man is standing on your chest doing a fucken rain dance to the Indian gods. This is what it feels like, but you cannot see light. There is no light, all you see is dark and you want to go towards the light. Where is the light? It has gone. It has packed his bags and left. It is not coming back and all you are left with is the darkness and the gut-wrenching pain. The pain that is so bad you want the injection. You want that injection so bad you would give everything and anything for it.

I know I am not coming back from this, before Dexter came into my life, I had only ever been this bad one other time. My whole life has been dips and potholes. Sure, I have had good days and bad days like everyone else, but the bad days always outweighed the good days, but this had been a different journey. I had opened the only organ I had left and allowed someone into my life and what goes on in my head. I had been honest with Dexter; this is why the pain is so much worse. He knows what I went through. It is not some random guy I am having a kid on relationship with. I trusted this man. I trusted this man so much I told him my darkest secret and I shared my feelings with him. I told him about the dips, the potholes and the you are fucked. So, this man knew exactly what I was going through. This man watched me spiral out of control and instead of being my husband and my best friend and helping me, this bastard has been trying to get into someone else's knickers and he has just given me the final nail for my coffin. This bastard is like Thelma sailing me down the Clyde. It has been written all over my face. I have asked him to his face, and he lied. The garage is full of stolen shite. Alarm bells should have been ringing like someone has just won the jackpot on a fruit machine, but it did not. He did not care, he just wanted to go back into the shower and finish his wank. That is how it felt, it was an inconvenience for him. I am right in front of you spiraling out of control and all you want to do is go back into that bathroom and finish your video wank. All this time, all the texts, the letters, the happy memories everything gone in an instant. It must have been all lies. The past two and a half years of my life has been nothing but lies. The man that I trusted with my life would rather finish a wank than save his wife. The man that I trusted more than anything has lied to my face and made me think it was because of my past. He has turned something so heinous to me on me. He turned my worst nightmare around to cover his lies. My best friend, my husband, my everything.

I lay on that floor and I knew, I knew there was no coming back from this. I am dealing with a different you are fucked and the person I trusted the most has just sold me down the Clyde like Thelma would have. I am lying on that floor and I cannot breathe, that guy is praying the fuck out of his rain dance on my chest and I cannot breathe. The pain cripples you to a point when you cannot take it anymore. You really cannot take it anymore. You want to die. Death is your best friend.

Death becomes that dream you crave so much. Death is like that day at the loch, this is what you think death is like. Its peaceful and quiet and it is amazing, and you want it so bad you go and get a bottle of vodka and enough pills to knock out and elephant and you are going to die. You want to die so bad to feel so at peace. I have never known a day of peace in my head so much as the day at the loch. This is what I want. Dying is going to be peaceful. Your head is so peaceful and quiet. That bastard dies when you die so he cannot throw shit at you all the time. He is at peace when you are. If nothing else, it will give me satisfaction of killing this bastard who has fucked my life up for so long. He dies when I die. I drink the vodka and take the pills and I am going to die. It is my dream. I just want to die and be at peace. It is all I have ever wanted. To be at peace. To live every single day at the loch and be at peace.

Chapter 33

Dexter's mum does not have a good feeling. Not Dexter who knows I have spiraled into oblivion no, Dexter's mum Agnes, who does not know about my past. Remember the first day I met her, and I knew what she was feeling inside, she must have seen it in me too. Simple as that. She makes Dexter go back to the house to check on me. Not Dexter thinks I better go and check on her. No, Dexter is away to his mum and dads to go and finish skelping one out in the fucken shower. I ruined his wank. How dare I spiral out of control and ruin his wank. What a bitch I am. Dexter comes back to the house and I am on the floor. I am surprised he phoned the ambulance and did not go back into the shower where I interrupted his wank.

I was spaced out for days in high dependency. I had taken enough amitriptyline to knock out a horse I had no intention of coming back. They fuck your head up apparently. No more than its fucked already. I was a step away from being a cabbage. Why could they just not have left me to be a fucken cabbage. A cabbage would not have a bastard stuck in their head all the time. I could have killed Agnes myself. If it had been left to Dexter, I would have been dead. I wanted to be dead. I wanted that peace at the loch. That is what I want more than anything in this world. I just want peace. I craved peace so bad, and now frosty the snowman has saved my fucken life. I saw what was in her head, so she has saw what is in mine. She will know what I am going through. Just let me go. It Is all I wanted to do. I know some people do it for attention I know that. Do I want attention? No. I just hurt so badly inside that every single day is an effort to get up, put on my mask and walk out the door. Every day is a living hell. I just want what I had that day at the Loch. This is all I want, That peace and quiet. Not this bastard, the one who runs about my head looking for stuff to keep throwing at me. I want this fucker dead more than I have ever wanted anything dead in its life. He dies and I get peace. My head and I are at war every single day. We are on that battlefield every single morning and it is a question of who wins today. If its him then I am in for a shit day. If it Is me? I get a half decent day, but this is what happens every day in my head. I open my eyes and Its straight to the battlefield. I have not even peed yet and I am at war. I was almost at peace for the first time ever and she has fucken saved me. Why the fuck would she do that? Dexter? He is not even caught up yet, he is still in that shower finishing his wank. My best friend. The person I trusted more than anyone. The one I shared my true feelings and fears with, and he would have just as well turned around and given me the nail and said, I would hammer it in, but I have a wank to finish.

It took days for the tablets to leave my system, It was my head that I fucked more than anything, I was seeing squirrels running up and down the walls (I found this out much later) I would have happily stayed at that stage. Give me running squirrels over this fucker any day. I would have even rather lived out the rest of whatever life I had left in a funny farm doped up to the eyeballs that this fucker couldn't get up and run about my head with shit to throw at me. He would be too zonked to do anything. Leave me with the fucken squirrels, but oh no. They pumped that much stuff into me to get the tablets and the side effects out of my system. Fucken bastards. They are all bastards, frosty the snowman is a bastard, everyone is a bastard. Just let me go and be at peace for once.

Once the tablets wore off and I started to get back to normal (whatever normal is) I was spitting feathers. Like the time when I was with David and I felt cheated out of my time with Dexter. I felt as if I was cheated out of death. I was fuming. I would have happily died and been at peace. The fucken idiot should have just gone into his mum and dads shower and wanked away until there was nothing left. I felt cheated out of death. I was raging. Absolutely raging. Now this man, my so-called best friend, the person I married until death do us part. He cheated me out of the death bit. The fucken bastard. He cheated on me with another woman and death. I hated him with a passion. I can see him looking at me but now I do not see the look, I see this face looking at me saying. You should have let me finish the wank. Why did you not just let me finish the wank?

Everything is racing through my head at the one time. It is all been lies, all of it. Two and a half god dam years of lies. My best friend lied to me. My best friend lied to me and not only that to cover his tracks he picked the worst thing ever and turned it round on me. He allowed me to think that I was losing the plot because I had been abused and it was affecting my life. My secret was messing about with my head and taking it out on Dexter. My abuse was the reason I was spiraling. I knew something was not right and I asked him. My best friend, the person I loved and told the truth to. The person who made me feel like how dared I even ask him such a thing. My best friend who turned my abuse around to suit him and let me think I was losing my mind. That is what my best friend and my husband did to me. I begged him to tell me the truth and he swore on all our lives, he swore on his dead brothers' life. The dead brother that I got jealous of because their relationship sounded so close and so wonderful. This man, my husband would not do that. Why would he do that. I have seen him cry over his brother on his anniversary, birthday etc., this man would not stoop so low that he would swear on his life, this man would not stoop so low that he would use the thing that hurts me the most against me and yet he did both. My best friend, my so-called husband, the person I trusted more than anything in this world and he has just shattered the only organ I had left that I had not damaged. This man would have been as well ripping my chest open with a Stanley knife, find out where the heart was and cut round about it, take it out and stand on it, reverse over it and that still would not have been a fraction of what this man had done to me. My best friend. He is standing over me and instead of that look that made me go all gooey had become I want to smash your fucken face in.

The switch had tripped within seconds. All that love, all that happiness all that bright light, all they texts, letters and the I love you's were all lies. This man is still lying to me saying it was porn. This man who is supposed to be my best friend is still lying to my face. This man has wasted two and a half years of my life. This man has bare faced lied to me and he is still lying to me now. Even now he still does not have the decency to tell me the truth and that minute is when I knew I was never going to let him away with what he had done. If this lying sack of shit had grew a pair of balls and been honest with me from the beginning not only would this not have happened, but he could have gone and wanked all over the place. I would have been heartbroken, but I would have rather known the truth. I would have rather he said. I am speaking to someone else it might go somewhere so cheerio.

He should not have even been speaking to anyone behind my back in the first place. Like with the time I took my phone to the toilet to text Dexter. I knew it was wrong. I had to be honest with the guy. He was not my best friend. He was not the person I confided in but I knew it was wrong and so I told him. Maybe I did not go the best way about it, but I still did it. The minute you are hiding something then you are doing something wrong. It is as simple as that and yet this lying cheating sack of shit is still lying to me. He still does not have the decency to tell me the truth. He is blaming it on the injection. I am in hospital and they have a note of my medical records, so they knew I had a hormone injection. This is why the dip was different. I knew it was a different kind of dip I knew that myself. So, any normal person who does not have a bastard inside their head already could have spiraled. This fucker thinks he has got away with it, this fucker forgets all this started before they even injected me. This fucker still thinks that much of me he is lying through his back teeth and just wants to go home, into the shower and have another wank to the other person on the end of the phone. This fucker knows that even if I got a hormone injection I had already starting to dip, I already had they feelings before the needle went in me. This fucker is looking me straight into my face and still lying to me, this is when I know you are fucked. You will reap what you sow mate. The switch has flicked. If he had even just have been honest with me then the following two and a half years would not have happened.

Chapter 34

I have gone home. After his looking right into my face and lying to me in hospital the bitch switch has tripped. All that love, all that brightness all those happy memories shattered in an instant. The new and improved Murrin has gone. The Murrin with feelings and hope is gone and all that is left is a shell, vengeance and hate. There is an exceptionally fine line between love and hate. If you hate someone then you must still have some sort of feelings for them otherwise you would not hate them. Love still had to be there or was it just I had that much vengeance inside. All I know it this lying sack of shit has lied to me. He has not even respected me enough to tell me the truth and all I want to do the smash the living daylights out of his face, but that is not good enough. I am going to do exactly what he did to me. He has wasted two and a half years of my life. So, I am going to waste two and a half years of his. I swore to myself I would never let any man or human being take me for granted again. Ever, and I was sticking to it. Had he been honest and told me he was speaking to someone then of course my heart would have been broken but I would have respected him for telling me the truth. Instead he twisted it around on me and used my past the thing I cannot deal with against me to suit him. I wanted to kill him but killing him would have been too easy. It would have been over and done with. No, I was going to do to this fucker exactly what he did to me, but I was not going to give him two and a half years of happy memories, was I fuck. I was going to make it as miserable as possible without getting caught. You reap what you sow.

Vegas has already been paid. I had more than enough spending money. I have been to Vegas, I know it is expensive. I had already prepared for that but was I going to allow this sack of shit to enjoy the holiday I spent months bursting my ass off for to give him while he was firing into someone else. Was I fuck? We always had one pot in the household. Not his and hers money. That is not how I roll. If I am in, then I am all in. You can have anything you want of mine. I do not care. Money has never meant anything to me. Materialistic stuff is something I have never wanted or craved I am not a selfish person. I would give you my last five pounds and go without. I do not care about things like that. I had saved more than enough money for Vegas. Dexter makes roughly £230 a week with his new job. The money is crap, but it was going to get us our house. I was working from the minute I opened my eyes until the minute I shut them. I had shit loads of money for spending, but I was not going to let him know that. I was going to make this holiday his worst fucken nightmare.

We are at the airport and this fucker is happy. Oh, he is so happy. He is going to Vegas. I am sitting there thinking, yeah mate just you wait. Ill soon wipe that smile off your face, however I got a beer with him and said cheers. Here is to our holiday when I really meant is welcome to hell. That happy look on his face, I could not believe it, this fucker still thinks I am stupid. This lying sack of shit thinks he is so very clever, and I am thick as fuck. He thinks the wife believes the shite I spun her about porn and I still get to go on my holiday. This fucker thinks he is having his cake and eating it at the same time. The man I went all gooey over when he looked at me has turned from all nice and gooey to, I want to smash your face in. I cannot stand to look at him. I hate him. I want nothing more than for him to feel a fraction of what he has done to me, and he thinks he is on cloud nine. He thinks he has got away with it and he still gets to go his holiday. Yeah, we will see about that. The thought of sitting next to him on the plane for hours upon hours is like a nightmare. From wanting to be together every minute of the day has gone to I need to spend as little time with you as possible. I am obviously still at the hurting stage. I cannot hurt in front of this man. When you love someone that much and they do that to you it must be like grieving because I know that inside I am shattered, I have all these emotions inside and I need to bury them just now because this fucker thinks he has won the fucken lottery. I have buried stuff my whole life. If I can get through life knowing I have been abused but I have the ability to hide it then hiding this should be a piece of cake. Nothing even comes close to what I have buried in my head. Nothing. I do not need to face my abuser every day, but I have to look at this piece of shit every day and hold back all my emotions and the want of smashing his face in.

It is not so bad at home because he is out working all day. Things have changed at home. I know they have changed. I will work from the sun comes up until it goes down. My excuse was the money for Vegas. The harder I work the more money we have. Oh, how fun it will be. My ass. So, I work and sleep. Work and sleep, but what am I going to do after Vegas? I will need to think about that as I know I cannot spend all my time with this piece of shit, or I will kill him. I will have a think in Vegas.

I bought a book. The only thing I like to read is Martina Cole. I do not know this woman, but I love her. I think her head is as fucked as mine. I cannot stand they books where people harp on about oh the sky was so blue, the clouds were like this the street looked like that. Who gives a fuck, just get to the point, by the time I have finished reading what the scenery looks like I am bored, and I have given up? I needed something to do because I am still fuming. I am raging inside. I have nothing but absolute venom for this man. This man who was my whole world has become my worst nightmare. He is sitting right next to me on the plane and I know I am stuck beside him for hours.

We get to the hotel. Now I already know this. I booked the thing. We had to pay a resort fee thing to the hotel on arrival it was like £40 a night. This covers your pool, Wi-Fi etc. Every hotel on the strip does it. I knew this, not only that we must pay a £400 deposit that we do not get back until we leave. I knew we had all this to pay upfront, but I act stupid. This did not happen the last time I was here. That is almost half our spending money gone, because I have not brought all the money I saved. Oh no, there was hell way and no way I was letting him enjoy this holiday. We are here for a week and now we are almost down to £1000 spending money. It is a fiver for a bottle of water in Vegas. Anyone who has been to Vegas knows that, anyone who has been to Vegas knows there is hell way and no way you are having a good holiday in Vegas for just over £1000 not a chance.

We put our stuff in our room and the atmosphere is crap already, we are so much money down off our spending money and it is only the start of the holiday. How are we going to manage all week with just over £1000? People spend that in 5 minutes in Vegas. Its ok I said we have a telly in our room. I could just see the look of disappointment in his face. He has been looking forward to this and its doomed before its even started. He is miserable and I am on cloud nine. Let us go for a walk. Just wait to he sees how much it is for a bottle of water then the disappointment is going to turn to misery. I cannot wait.

I need juice or something, it is even worse in the hotel. The front lobby had water and it was £10 for a bottle of water. When I booked it, because I knew I would never come back again after this I purposely went all out and booked The Vdara hotel. One of the main hotels on the strip. If we were going to do it then we were going to do it in Style. He saw the price for a bottle of water and near had heart failure. How are we going to manage all week with just over a grand? Oh god I wish I knew this. It was never like this the last time. I cannot believe it is so expensive for water. I had got myself a bottle of Snow Queen Vodka in duty free. I knew it was going to be expensive. He never got any booze. I had mine, I did not give a fuck. We went for a walk to find our bearings. Now it is June, Vegas in June is roasting. The heat is unbearable. You need water every two minutes. By the time you buy a bottle of water and walk down two or three hotels the water is like soup. Every hotel or shop is a different price for water. You can start at one shop and its £4 the next few shops down its £6 and you have no option but to buy it or you are going to pass out with the heat. We are only out a few hours if you are lucky. We have spent a fortune on water and energy drinks, and he is wondering how the hell we are going to make it through the week and inside I am howling. Dexter drinks green monster energy drinks like they are going out of fashion. He needs two of these and half a dozen fags before he can get out of bed, between two energy drinks and six fags your talking £15 before he is even up. Yeah, this week is going to go great. It is going to be a toss-up of water or food because you do not get breakfast and dinner in the hotel unless you have a platinum credit card. Its £10 for a tiny half bottle of beer. A cocktail is £50, and it is a tenner for a mars bar. God, if I had known all this, I would have brought more money.

This is my husband who is so clever. He is so clever, and I am so stupid, yet he knows I have been to Las Vegas before. The prices do not change that dramatically. If the shoe were on the other foot, I would have picked up on this because I knew my husband. I knew something was wrong and there was no change in routine. Yet this idiot knows I have been here, and he thinks I am so stupid.

We are not going to be able to gamble. The tables are a minimum bet of five pounds. You do not get free booze in the casino anymore. They used to do it years ago, but they stopped it. I already knew this. We will be lucky to get one drink a night in the casino. What are we going to do all week? We are not even a day in the place and his mood has gone a bit like my temper does. He has gone from a 100% to 0%. He has got a face like a well skelped arse and I have a silent disco going on.

We go for a walk and all I do is moan about the heat. I cannot take the heat. I need to stop every five minutes because the heat is unbearable. This idiot has not put two and two together. I grew up in South Africa. That is what you call heat. I was in South Africa from the age of 10 to 15. I lived in heat for years. I can take the heat, this idiot does not pick up on that though and all I do is moan. It is too warm I need a seat, it is too warm I need a drink. I cannot drink that water because it is too warm now. I need cold water. If we need to keep buying water every 5 minutes, we are not going to last a day never mind a week. Ok I say well let us just go back to the room and watch TV. Watch TV? We are in Vegas, I know but it is too warm to walk about so let us just go back to the room and watch TV till it cools down, but I know It is not going to cool down. It stays warm at night too. Yet I am the stupid one.

We are stuck in a place with intense heat, hardly any money, he has been looking forward to this holiday and I am spoiling it. Too right I am spoiling it. I am going to make this week as miserable as possible. I am not letting him enjoy it. I burst my arse working for the money to go and what was he doing? Trying to get his leg over someone else. Not a fucken chance was I going to let him enjoy this holiday. The whole week went much the same. I moaned about the heat. I moaned I could not walk, I moaned about moaning. Everything we did I moaned about.

I got drunk one night, I nearly gave the game away the minute the vodka hit me what I was feeling inside started to come out and we had a big argument about what had happened at home. Now that is something we never did. We never argued. We did not even bicker about things. That time at home was the first proper argument we had. It was something we never done. This is why I did not expect him to be talking to someone else. I would see the point if it were Joanne and Nigel because all they do is argue constantly, but we did not. It just did not happen. Right up until I started to get that feeling everything was great, or so I thought anyway. I just did not see it coming. I was still trying to wrap my head around the fact my husband and best friend fucked me over.

The rest of the holiday was shit, we sat by the pool or watched tv at night because we did not have enough money to go out every night and I knew I could not get drunk or drink again in case I gave the game away. The thing that we were looking forward to the most was going to a Vegas strip club, we had been to the one in Blackpool that time, but then we were happy. I was happy going to the strip club, this time I did not even want to go. It was a moan, I moaned about it, I hummed and hawed I just did not want to do anything. I did not want to give him happy memories. He did not deserve happy memories. Why would I want to give him happy memories? My best friend the lying cheating scum bag who still cannot be honest with me. This man knows I have worked my fingers to the bones for this holiday, this man knows I have been up from 4am every morning until 10/11pm at night. All that time working and saving to give him a surprise holiday like this and he lied to my face. I want to take his face and smash it off one of the machines until the jackpot lights come on.

We are in Las Vegas the city that never sleeps, it is always buzzing and happy, we should have been buzzing and happy. This should have been a holiday of a lifetime not the holiday from hell. This is supposed to be my best friend, the guy who knows me inside and out, the guy who knows I would not moan and piss away a holiday like this. This is how clueless he is. He thinks he has been so clever, and I am so stupid. The best part of the holiday was the plane home. Two guys behind us, they had been on the piss all day and drank more on the plane, the guy was so drunk he shit himself. He was directly behind Dexter and it was howling. Dexter has a weak stomach at the best of times, and he was heaving. He was trying to hold the sick in. The male air steward offered him a can of air freshener and said there was nothing he could do. There were no extra seats to swap with. I was beside myself inside. He was raging. It was the perfect end to the perfect holiday he had to sit and smell shit for nine hours.

When we got home, Dexter went back to work. Things went back to normal or as normal as could be. His shifts were all over the place, one day he would be earlies, the next day lates but always a 2-hour break in between so it worked out perfect. It was the best thing ever because he was away from the house about 14 hours of the day and it meant I only had a few hours with him. It did not take long, and he was at it again. My so-called best friend. You just know. The only thing was this fucker still did the whole. Oh, I love you. You are my world. You are my best friend. I cannot live without you. I love my family, you mean everything to me. it just rolled off his tongue like I am going to the shop for a packet of crisps. His phone was like a limb. That phone went everywhere he did. That phone was in the shower with him and you know it is not to listen to music. That fucker is away into the shower for a skelp. What bird is it this week? Now he knew that he was not being faithful and yet this fucker still wants to move to a new house. He still wants to go and buy a house knowing fine well he is speaking to other women. Me? I am bleeding like the river Nile. My bleeding has taken a turn for the worse as far as he is concerned. All that nice underwear has been packed up and put away. I am on Bridget Joan's knickers. I am no longer lying naked in bed. I am no longer putting on nice underwear for this fucker. In fact, I even offer him an out. I say my body is fucked, if this bleeding carries on, I do not think it is fair to you. I think you would be better off starting a fresh. I want to see if he is even now going to be honest. I want to know is there a shred of decency in him. I revert to the shower incident. Again, this fucker swears on all our lives. I beg with him if anything did happen tell me, at least if you tell me. I want to know if he has the balls to tell me. Still he lies to my face and swears down on all of us he is telling the truth. I would never lie to you, that is not how we are, we are honest with each other. You fucken lying sack of shit. I know and you know that you have dipped your dick elsewhere. You and I know that you have been talking to other people. You and I know, it was not many years down the line of marriage. It was only a few months. You could not keep it in your pants longer than a few months. The minute you must hide anything is the minute you know that it is wrong.

Chapter 35

Now we are getting a new house. I know you are thinking why the fuck are you even going through with this, because I want to know how far this bastard will stoop. He has already turned my secret against me, the most heinous thing ever and he has used it against me, he has sworn on all our lives, he has sworn on his dead brother's life. This fucker will swear on anyone's life if it suits him and works in with his lies. He is a liar. Now me the arsehole is thinking back to when we first met. Was all that lies about Lorraine. Was her family the people he made out. Was that poor girl what he made out? All their friends stuck by Lorraine and he told me they were all money grabbing bastards. They chose money over him. Lorraine's parents had money, he was making out as if she were buying their affection. I was calling them all the bastards of the day and I could not understand why he spoke to them. Justin, his so-called best friend, still spoke to Lorraine. Now I know Justin's mother half brought him and Joanne up, so I could not understand this. I had seen Justin. I really liked Justin. He is my kind of guy, but he still spoke to Lorraine. Why the fuck did I not see this before.

Paula who is Justin's sister was more of a sister to Dexter. He hated his own sister. He thought she was a selfish bitch, yet he loved Paula. So why did Paula take Lorraine's side in all of this? Dexter told me that it was to do with money. Paula and her husband Daniel chose money over him. He had known Paula before Daniel and both chose Lorraine over him because they were money grabbing Bastards. This is what he told me, and I stupidly believed him. I believed his lies; we were supposed to have been honest with each other. From the very beginning I was nothing but honest with this person. This man was my best friend and the person that I confided in. Now I am thinking the whole relationship has been based on lies. It is all been lies and me like an arsehole fell for the lies. This is what hurt the most. The lies. If he had just been honest with me and told the truth. I would have been hurt, of course I would but I would have had so much respect for him telling me the truth, yet this arsehole lied to my face. He knew that I hated lies. I told him from day one lie to me and that is it. I do not care how bad the truth is, but I want the truth. Not lies.

So, am I going to get a house? Too fucken right I am because it has just given me the perfect excuse to work 24/7 and not spend all my time with this lying sack of shit.

Chapter 36

Agnes has taken a turn for the worse. This woman is wheelchair bound now. My mum and my sister have fallen out while on holiday. Was I close to my mum? No, she is my mum, she brought me into this world but no, I am not close with my mum. My mum and my sister are close, this is why they always fall out. I am more like an outsider. I do not fit in anywhere. I am like the missing part of a different puzzle. Wee jean next door has a puzzle of a tiger, Wee Ann has a puzzle of a giraffe. They both go to do their jigsaws, and both are one piece missing. Wee Jean has Ann's bit of the puzzle and Ann has Jeans part of the puzzle. This is how I feel. I am a tiger with a missing bit of Giraffe. It sounds fucked up but then so do I. I just do not fit. I wanted a different puzzle anyway. So, I am going to try and build bridges with my mum. I take her over to see Agnes and Harriet.

Nothing of Agnes is working anymore, she has gone from the sticks and frame to the wheelchair. This woman is in a wheelchair all day, and she does not moan. It is not a case of you go over and all she talks about is her illness. This woman needs a hobby or something, my mum can crochet, and she is going to teach Agnes and Dexter's gran Harriet. They had only met once before and that was at the wedding. The first meeting was ok, it was not brilliant, but it was ok. It was not like the first time I met Frosty, if I were not there, I think they would have all been doomed. My mum takes a while to get to know you and so does Dexter's mum whereas me? I would talk to four walls and get a friend. That is just how I am.

Now I know that her son is a lying sack of shit, but Agnes? She has not done anything to me, in fact when I was in the hospital, I had to tell her why. Not the whole your son was dipping his dick elsewhere. The other part. You know the part where my loving husband turned my worst nightmare against me. I told her about my childhood. I think she knew anyway. Remember when I saw her that night I knew, I just knew she was fucked in the head. So, she must have saw that in me too. I cannot explain why you know. You just know. The more people try and hide things the bigger their secret is. It was Agnes who did not have a good feeling about me. Not anyone else and sure as fuck not my husband, so am I going to give up on this woman? No, I am not. I really care for this woman and I need to think of a way of taking down her rat bag of a son with as minimal damage as possible to Agnes. The day went ok, and we would do the same next week. Bearing in mind, this is not my mother, this is Dexter and Joanne's mother. Dexter and Joanne know that this woman is taking a turn for the worst. Is Dexter there on his days off work? No, Dexter is too busy trying to get his leg over his next victim. Joanne she is in a whole different league. This bitch, can see how bad her mother is and instead of doing something to help her, what does she do? She drops the kids off. To the woman who cannot do most things for herself, she drops the kids off at her house. This is not just when she is at work, oh no she has been working all week. She needs time for her and Nigel. Nigel the moaning face get. Now before the whole hospital thing I would make an effort for Dexter's sake, now? I do not give a flying fuck. If they come in, then I go. I do not need or want to spend any more time with these 2 human beings. He is as bad as her, if not worse. They now have a daughter together called Blossom. These 2 are supposed to share responsibility of the 2 kids. If he is off work, then he will take the kids to Agnes and Bert and sit and play on his computer. Now this woman cannot do things for herself and these two selfish bastards just drop the kids off. It is one of my pet hates. I totally get parents need to work, but if you decide you want children then you should take the responsibility of looking after them. No, not these two Muppets, they hand the kids out like smarties. Have their date nights, sit and play computer games like Jesus Christ man up and take responsibility for your children. Now I already knew that Agnes and Bert brought Jack up, Dexter told me all of this and how selfish his sister was, but like anything else I was going to make up my own mind and he could not have been more right about anything in his life. These two are perfect for each other. Two selfish bastards swimming away in a fish bowl together.

Chapter 37

Things at home are swimming away. This house idea must be the best yet. Arsehole needs to work extra hours. We need wage slips for the mortgage, so he takes on a new Rota of all spread over shifts. Brilliant, he is out of the house for 14 hours a day. By the time I wake him up he needs his wee routine of two energy drinks and half a dozen fags, and he is out the door. Cheerio you are lying sack of shit. Love you. This idiot thinks he is so clever, and I am so stupid. This idiot is supposed to know me inside out, yet this idiot has not picked up on we went to Vegas with not even a fifth of the spending money, he thinks I was so stupid I did not know about the hotel surcharge or deposit. He has not realised I would have known how much it was for water etc., he has not picked up on the heat thing in Vegas, I am bleeding that much even I think I am bleeding. All the underwear is in a bag put away and its granny pants. I am not giving him sex anymore why the fuck would I? Suck your own dick mate. I work from the minute I get up until it is time to go to bed. I am eating that much shite I am piling on the weight too. I have gone from wearing normal clothes to jogging pants and a t shirt. I look a mess. I would not want to shag me. No chance. I was never into designer clothes or makeup, but I loved wearing nice underwear and clothes. He knows, underwear has always been my thing. It makes you feel like woman. Right now, I feel and look like a pensioner and instead of hip hop and happening I am more hip replacement. Now you can defiantly see the age gap. It went from mother and son to gran and grandson. All of this is going on in front of his eyes and this idiot is that stupid he cannot see it. This idiot is to self-obsessed with his phone, snap chat and messenger that ignorance is bliss. Every now and then I would need to throw him a bone the same way you would a dog. My husband is a dog.

I am still dying inside, I am trying to keep dealing with my secret from my childhood and that my husband is a lying sack of shit. I cannot drink, if I drink, I am going under and this was all for nothing. I still need something to help me get through this. I need something, anything. I do not have Steven. I most definitely do not have my lying sack of shit husband to talk to I cannot go down again. The only thing keeping me going is revenge. Plain and simple. So, what do I do? I hit the shops, but this time I need more I am carrying two things about with me. Inside I am not dead I am flatlining every single day, and every single day I am on that same battlefield. The minute my eyes open I am on that battlefield and there are no good days anymore. I am not living. I am simply existing. The only thing keeping me up is revenge and the want to smash that fuckers face in. Every day he lies to me. Every day he sends me messages I love my family I cannot live without you all. You are my best friend. I love you to the moon and back. I could not live without you. Everything that he had said to me before. I believed all his shit right up until I had that feeling. You just know. You cannot say oh it was this or that you just know. Or I knew when he was going for sex because the hairy bush would get a shave and he was out the door, cheerio! Love you.

So many times, I would drop wee hints just to see what he would say. Are you ashamed of me now? Jesus even I would have been ashamed of me. I look a mess, I look hellish. I have gone from a size 8 to border line 14, my hair is like rats' tails. I would have had to put a black bag over my own head to have sex with me I looked that bad. You are not liking my posts of Facebook. Now you know what I think of Facebook. It is true because half his bits on the side came from face book. I hardly post anything on my personal page on Facebook. You are lucky if I post one thing in months, I will purposely post something about us, just to see what he would do. Now this fucker lives on Facebook. This fucker has seen my post and you know it, yet he ignores is. He does not like it, he just blanks it. Why does he do that because he is telling them the same bullshit story, he told me about Lorraine. My marriage is over my wife is a boot bla fucken bla. Well now she is yeah but you do not know that. You are too busy shafting anything with a pulse. I need attention. You would know when he had someone on the go. I used to do this wee stupid game thing. When I knew there was no one on the go I would pick a wee argument just to see what he would do. Would he go to his mum and dads? No, would he fuck because he did not have anything else waiting at the other side. This man needs to be with someone. This man cannot be on his own. This is when I would bring up the Facebook posts, and what did he do? He lied straight to my face again. Every day he lied. As far as I am concerned, he lied to me every single day when he would not tell me the truth about the first time. This fucken idiot thinks he is Al Capone. This idiot grew a bit of weed and thought he was scar face, yet most of the people still owed him money except his uncle. He was the only person that actually paid him. He was the worst drug dealer ever. Yet this fucker is lying to my face every single day. I am so stupid, and he is so clever.

So, this time I am not going to the shops for stock cubes, oh no I am away with half the fucken supermarket. This arsehole thinks it is great. This arsehole has not picked up on the fact I hate the shops but every time he is off work, I make him come with me. I am doing it because I need some sort of release and he is on cloud fucken nine. He just does not have a clue, because he is so clever, and I am so thick.

Chapter 38

It is his brother's anniversary now I always did something anything to help him through it. Even though the sack of shit never done it for me. The dogs are mine. This arsehole does nothing for them. He does not walk them, feed them, play with them anything. Even though Salem was his and he wanted Doris. If we go away for the weekend and come back, the dogs will run past him and straight to me. The dogs are clever. He does not even bother with Pricilla. I shower her every day. Thelma has run away from home now twice. Clever cat. Now he does like Thelma, even though he is a dick, when he comes home at night, he has time with Thelma. I have an idea. Why do we not go and get another sphynx cat for Thelma. It might stop her running away and it would give that arsehole something to love. I have covered the anniversary thing, it will give him something else to focus on instead of me although he is that stupid, he has not got a clue what is going on. Jesus if the shoe were on the other foot I would have twigged straight away. Our routine did not change when he was doing it the first time. I just knew my husband inside out and I knew something was not right. This fucker has fireworks going on in front of his face and he has not got a fucken clue. But I am the stupid one.

We go away down to Kent and get another sphynx, it should have been a brilliant and fun day. We always used to have so much fun in everything we did. I cannot remember the last time I had a laugh with this man, and I am the stupid one. I moaned all the way there and I moaned all the way back. I did not even take a memory back with me. Now no matter where we went, even if it were just out for dinner or something, I would always take a memory back to put in the memory box. I have not put anything in this memory box since that happened and this idiot has not picked up on that either. Yet I am the stupid one. All of this going on in front of his eyes and he has not picked up on any of it. We have gone from the brilliant couple that everyone said they could see why we were together to gran and grandson. Not even mother and son because I am not bothering with myself at all. I do not dress nice, I have not bothered with my hair. It is like rats' tails. It is a mess. I do not shave my legs, I do not shave the vagina, sometimes I do not shave under my arms and this guy still thinks he is so clever, and I am so very stupid. I am not giving this man a good-looking wife or a happy wife. I am going to make this two and a half year as miserable as possible without getting caught and all this is happening right in front of his eyes and he cannot see it. Yet I am the stupid one. That fruit machine has been ringing on jackpot for ages and this idiot still cannot hear or see it. This idiot is so self-obsessed with his phone that he cannot see it.

We get back to the house with Zack, this is what we called him. He is a beautiful bluey/grey colour. He is so loving and caring, you can tell straight away. The total opposite of Thelma. We put him down and immediately she hates him with a passion. She hisses at him and she gives Dexter this look of you are cheating bastard. How dare you do that to me. Dexter was the only person Thelma liked. Their time was special time. Like what our time used to be. Like the time I felt cheated out of my time with Dexter that night David stayed. This is the look she is giving him. She was going to be cheated out of her time with Dexter for this cute bald cat. She was raging. The dogs? Ah they loved him. They licked him they got to play with him, they loved that because Thelma never gave any of the dogs the time of day. They wanted to play with her, and she just always gave them the Fuck you look. Dexter loved him immediately and vice versa. Brilliant, that is his happy wee diversion. Not that he needed it because he is thick as fuck.

Chapter 39

We have been going to see Agnes every week with my mum and Harriet. It is a weekly thing, we do it every week and I call it fat club, because all we do is sit and eat shite and talk shite but its company for Agnes and she loves it. It helped me and my mum too as we are starting to bond. I love fat club. This is the only real thing that is real anymore. Everything else is fake and lies except this. We laugh, we talk and its brilliant. Agnes is getting worse and worse, as the days and weeks go by her health gets worse. Yet this woman does not moan, she simply joins in whatever way she can. Now I know I am lying to her son. I know what her son did was nothing to do with her so why should I ruin my relationship with her because of him and it is not as if him or his sister are bothering their arse to help her. No, do they fuck. He chooses to use his spare time skelping one out or chatting to other women. Me? I do not know if I will ever trust a man again, but I have no need or want for a man. I am trying to keep that carpet away from the ceiling before all this comes flooding out in one go and I am fucked. I am not burying one secret now, I am burying two. I have not fell apart yet for what this man has done to me. I have kept it bottled up since that day. Now my washing machine has dark clothes, miserable memories, lies and deceit that is all it has swimming about in that machine. There is no bright clothes or happiness anymore. The washing machine is miserable as fuck. I do not know who is worse. Me or the machine.

Joanne and Nigel are getting married soon and I am to be bridesmaid. Bloody wonderful. This is going to be the day from hell.

Things are still the same at home. He gets up, he goes to work, when he is off. I am either working or I make him go to the shops or we sit about and watch TV. We never watched TV. We never had time for TV our lives were full of fun and laughter. We had no need for a TV. We lay in bed at night talking while a candle would burn for the noise. I have not had a candle in months. We have never seen so much TV in months and I am the stupid one. We sit about and I stuff my face with sweets and chocolate. I never even ate chocolate before this. I am a crisp person.

More savoury than anything else yet I am sitting about with jogging bottoms watching TV eating shite and I am the stupid one.

We have not been camping, we have not been to Blackpool, we have not been to the caravan. We have not been anywhere, and I am the stupid one. I work from sunrise to sunset making money to buy a house that is going to be based on lies. It is all lies. This person knows that he is skelping them out with other people, this person knows he is going to buy a house, yet he is talking to other people. This man thinks I am daft standing here working all day to put money together for a house and this man does not know If I was not working from sunrise to sunset I would be on a heap on the floor. This man does not know that the only thing keeping me going is revenge. This man does not know there is a shit load of stolen shit in the house and yet I am the stupid one. This man is going to go through with buying a house when he knows exactly what he is doing. Oh well yes, we will buy a house, but we will buy it my way. It is only going to be in your name and your name alone.

Chapter 40

My friend Debbie has just messaged me. I have known her for years. If you saw her you would be shit scared of her. She is covered in tattoos, scars piercings and she is as butch as anything, again she is the same height as me, short hair. If I showed, you a picture you would think she would smash your face in until you meet her. Mind you she still would smash your face in, but she also has a loving side. Her mum Susan has an African grey and she needs to rehome it. Now I have told no one about what has happened and what my intensions are. No one. I know what is going to happen so I should not take on any other pets and then she says it is a wee bastard. It hates everyone and it bites. The bird has issues. Ok, I will take it.

We go to Susan's house to get the bird and she is right, this bird hates everyone. This is the first time I have met Susan, I have known Debbie nearly 30 years and it is the first time I have met her mum. Surprise surprise she is the same height as me and she has issues. Susan has a voice box. She had cancer. Now I have never met this woman before and yet I am drawn to her. The woman with the voice box. She has dark short hair and glasses, like Debbie she is covered in tattoos maybe in her 60's. The birds name is Jimmy, they thought it was a male and called it Jimmy, but it turns out to be a female. This is great it might give Pricilla a friend. Pricilla is not snapping her feathers anymore buy she screams. Now I know parrots are noisy, but I think she is screaming for her sister. She missed her sister. She was snapping her feathers and now all she does is scream. She is a pain in the arse, but she is our pain in the arse.

Jimmy was the best thing ever for Pricilla, Jimmy was a good talker, Pricilla did talk but it was more the screaming. She would talk then scream. Talk then scream, but now she had a wee friend and her talking improved and she did not scream as much. Do not get me wrong she did still scream at times but just not as much. Jimmy taught her to swear. They were like a wee pair of fish wives. You would get up in the morning and then they would start having a wee conversation. It was so funny. If nothing else, it gave Pricilla some happiness. I think she just missed her sister so bad. Jimmy was a brilliant distraction for her, and the screaming got less and less, and they say animals are stupid?

So, this is it. This is our family. It is a fucked-up family, but it was our family. Again, arsehole was still sending all these messages and cards and lovely texts about his family and how much he loved his family and then the next text would be to whatever bird it was this week. You always knew when he was talking to someone and when he was not. I never picked an argument or said anything about Facebook or that when he was talking to someone because I knew he would walk out the door and his time was not up. He took two and half years of my life, so I was going to take two and a half of his, but I sure as hell was not going to make them easy ones. I still have not given this man sex. I do not know where his dick has been. He could be dipping it in the Clyde for all I care but he sure as hell is not dipping it into me. Not a fucken chance. It was probably the same old shit anyway. He only knows lick me suck me turn around. So, I have not given this man any sex, I say I am constantly bleeding the big fat warning bells should have been where the fuck are the sanitary towels, and yet I am the stupid one. I was bleeding irregular but not to the extent he thought. Jesus even I started believing I was bleeding all the time. I could count with my hands the amount of times we had sex afterwards. It was like throwing him a bone, I knew I would need to do it every now and then, yet we were like rabbits, and I mean rabbits. I do not want just one shot on the swings, oh no it is on the swings have a wee rest then down the Shute. I want to go all round the swing park. We were always like this. Ok you have had a wee rest lets go again and yet I want his dick nowhere near me anymore. I do not know who or what he is shagging these days. I do not know what he has got but for me there must be something for the sex. I felt nothing for this man. There was no passion no love no lust nothing. He would have been as well getting a set of jump leads to get me going. I did not need him for sex. I was going through vibrators like they had gone out of fashion. I knew exactly where they had been. Yet I am so stupid, and he is so clever.

I did need another operation to fix it. I knew I did. I was bleeding on and off but as far as he was concerned, I was practically bleeding all the time so where were all the sanitary towels? I was a heavy bleeder, my periods were awful I should have had a shelf full of them. I went from lying in bed naked to granny pants and pyjamas. The more covered up I was the better. I used to sleep naked or with something sexy on. All of this is happening in front of this man's eyes and I am the stupid one. I knew this man inside out. He must have known me outside in because he still has no fucken clue. Our whole life has changed. Everything has changed and yet he has not seen it. He is too busy on his phone to notice that heaven has become hell.

They had tried quick fix ops, but they just did not work. My stomach is like the road map of Glasgow. The surgeons had no place left to go. They did not want to do a full hysterectomy because it was too dangerous, and I was high risk. That operation was going to be worse case scenario, but now we are at worst case scenario.

Chapter 41

He has got a mortgage; he only went and got a mortgage approved. Ye fucken ha. I have a reason to work nonstop but also a back handed deal. This mortgage is going in your name and your name alone. I know this fucker has been talking to multiple women on snap chat and messenger. This man is going to go through with a commitment of buying a house, knowing it is all based on lies. Ok, you get a mortgage, but my name is going nowhere near it. My excuse, I am self-employed. I trust you that much I will let you put your name on the mortgage this is how much I trust you, you are my husband and I love you. I love you enough that I know you will not shaft me over and kick me out in the streets. That is not the kind of man you are. You love me. Of course, I do you are my world Murrin. Why would I ever do anything like that to you. I love you to the moon and back. Every day lies lies lies, just constant lies and I love you rolls off the tongue. Did he ever really love me? I no longer know. I just know that everything was so happy. My world was bright and now not only are the sunglasses back on, but the wall is back up and there is bullet proof glass round it too. I feel nothing inside, I am empty. There is nothing there but revenge. This is what is keeping me going, this is the only thing that is keeping me going. This bastard in my head is having a field day. He is rotten to the core, but he is in his element just now because all he knows is badness. I have not even dipped since all that happened. Not even a dip because I am so focused on revenge, I do not have time to dip. If I dip, then all of this goes to fuck. I think it was more the fact I did not want this piece of shit in front of me to get one over on me. I was never going to let that happen so I kept everything bottled up, but I knew it would all come to a point, I just hoped to God I lasted the rest of the time. I needed to last to the end of the time, and would you believe it is going to happen at Christmas time. Maybe this will be the game changer for me and Christmas who knows. All I know is I want this lying sack of shit out of my life the minute the time is up. He is going nowhere before it even if I need to throw the fucker a bone.

Agnes is getting worse and worse. I did not think this poor woman could get any worse. She is losing the muscles in her hands and feet now. This woman cannot take herself to the toilet. Bert must do it. Joanne's wedding is coming up and the hen night and this woman cannot go to the toilet without someone helping her. Joanne is her daughter, Joanne the selfish bitch that knows her mother cannot do anything for herself and yet she still takes the kids to her to watch. Not only when she is at work but when her and Nigel want date night or to do housework. This woman cannot do housework with her kids in the house but her mother who can do nothing for herself can look after them. Now this is when I expect her lovely daughter to step in and say I will help you mum. You do all these things for me, you need help and what does she do? Fuck all. None of them. Joanne is too busy with her date nights and housework. Dexter is too busy skelping one out to whoever it is this week and I say I will do it. This woman, their mother needs help and these two selfish bastards could not give a flying fuck. She is mortified that her daughter in law will do it for her. Like everything else I turn it into a joke, and we laugh about it. After the first time it was easy after that. It did not bother me and after the first time, it did not bother her.

The hen night comes, before all this happened, I would go to family functions and join in. I would even try with Joanne for Dexter's sake, now I do not give a flying fuck. I do not want to be with these people any longer than I must be, but Agnes will have no one to take her to the toilet. So, I need to go. I thought well Agnes will need me and Nigel's mum Jacqui would be there. Nigel is an arsehole, but his mum is not. When I first met Nigel and he went on about how cruel and horrible his mum was, again I will listen but judge for myself. I was half expecting her to be like the witch out of emu's world, but when I met her, I loved her. She is like me, mad as a brush, same height and blonde hair. She is not an arsehole she just knows how to enjoy herself. Joanne cannot stand her and yet I thought she was fab. I loved her, however, she did not go. I was gutted. I spent the whole night in the toilet with Agnes.

The toilets were a nightmare It was too awkward to try and get her on the toilet. It ended up a great night. Us and the toilet walls. When Agnes said she was not going to go back to the toilet again, suddenly, I felt ill and phoned arsehole to come and get me. It was the lesser of the 2 evils because at least I would be home and in my own bed with a great excuse I was ill. I just did not want to participate any longer than I needed to.

I was the flippen bridesmaid. I was so ill lately I think even I started believing I was ill. I would be able to work in my room from sunrise to sunset, although when it was Dexter's day off. I was ill, it was always one thing or another, but I was always ill. The dramatic change in our lives from being oh so happy and wanting to spend every second of the day with each other has gone to do not even touch me. The lying-in bed at night talking to each other has become just tickle me so I can go to sleep, or I was in bed before he came back from work. The happy memories are no more. I did not put one more thing in that memory box. I have not given him sex, I do not even kiss him properly any more it gives me the boak and I am the stupid one, and he is so clever.

That bloody jackpot machine is on fire it is been lighting up and rattling that much and still this fucker still has not noticed. He has gone from seeing bright to blind as a fucken bat. If I was not ill, then we would lie about and watch tv and fill my face with shite. I looked a mess. I would have passed me in the street as a tinker. My hair is a mess, I do not even put mascara on anymore or the Rox for my eyes. I do nothing. I am still wearing granny pants. There still is not a shelf full of sanitary towels, and I am the stupid one.

I have lost count now the amount of people that have flitted in and out of his phone. I could not care less, see all that hatred it turned to nothing, just nothing, the only thing that kept me going was revenge. That was it plain and simple.

Chapter 42

We have our new house. Not only did I get him to put the mortgage in his name only. I got him to take the maximum mortgage he could take. He was allowed £100,000 maximum and the house we wanted was £110,000 so we had a few months to pull £10,000 out of our arses. Now, he knows fine well he has been unfaithful on numerous occasions, he knows exactly what he has been doing yet he still wants to go ahead and buy a house. He thinks I trust him that much that I say its ok just to put the house in his name, he knows fine well what he has been doing and still he goes ahead with it. Borrowing money off his parents and my mum.

Now this lying sack of shit knows that his parents do not work. His dad gave up his job to look after Agnes, they are not throwing £20 notes out the window, yet this sack of shit accepts money off his parents and money off my mum. The rest of the money and lawyers bill we worked for; well I did but it was better for me it was a distraction. That was my excuse of not spending any time with him. The least amount of time possible I had to spend with this fucker the better. So, I worked and slept, worked and slept.

My operation was due to come back up. It had been cancelled too many times and I was starting to think I would not get it done in time before the two and a half years were up. In fact, it was rearranged for the time of the wedding and there I was wishing my life away again wishing that it would be then so I would not have to go to the bloody wedding, but it got cancelled again, so I had to go to the bloody wedding.

All we have heard about is this bloody wedding. If nothing else I just wanted it out the way because I felt as if years had gone by listening about shit from this wedding. The wedding that started small like ours to never ending story. Fuck you, fuck the wedding just get the day over and done with but I cannot get drunk. I am so near the end that I am not spoiling it now. Not a fucken chance. By this time, I am fat, well the fattest I have ever been. I look at myself in the mirror in disgust. I have gone from a size 8 to a touching size 14 sometimes. I have all these clothes I cannot wear because I am a fat bastard and all my clothes are my old normal size. I am like a walking advert for KFC. Don't cha wish your girlfriend was fat like me? Don't cha wish your girlfriend loved KFC don't cha.

I walk about in a t shirt and jogging bottoms and that is it. I do not pluck my eyebrows, I do not shave my legs, the vagina needs a lawn mower and my husband thinks life is wonderful and happy, and yet I am the stupid one.

We all had to be at the house first thing in the morning, two bloody hours we were booked into the hairdressers for hair and makeup. I do not wear makeup. I did not even wear make up to my own wedding. I do not want to look like Coco the clown for a day and my eyebrows are a walking advert for Nike. No thanks. I told the makeup artist this and I will give the lassie her due, it took ages I thought I was going to look like a clown, but she did do it subtle. All that time for that? Jesus woman I take my hat off to you all. I am a 5-minute wonder. Hair straightened and out the door. I am not a beauty queen, but I am not a total minger either. I am just natural.

God some people you need a hammer and chisel to take the makeup off. When I shared a flat with Steven this girl would go to bed with makeup on and then get up before him in the morning to redo her make up before he saw her. Like when does your face get time to breathe. Yeah, make up is not for me.

The wedding was what it was ok, boring as fuck. It is all that waiting about I cannot stand. After they are married you wait about to go to the reception. You get there and then you wait about again before dinner, then wait about for the disco. It is all the waiting about and the I do not even want to be here anyway, but Agnes needed me. I have talked her into getting a catheter, so it gives her a break and she will not spend all the night in the toilet and miss her daughter's wedding. I thought if I could do the toilet for you I would and spend the night in the toilet. It would be better than at the actual wedding. Whereas before I would have made the effort, I would have joined in, but I just did not care anymore. I did it for Dexter at first but now Dexter is a complete dick, a lying sack of shit who has had god knows how many on the go. Still lying to my face every bloody day. Sending me messages and love and bullshit.

Agnes has a problem with the catheter that day and night so again happy days I spent most of the time in the toilet. When she said she would not go back where did I go? Into the car to go to sleep. I did not want to join in and be around his family creating happy memories for him, did I fuck. The dramatic change in the Murrin he met when he walked through the door to the Murrin in front of him with the bleeding, the messy hair, gained 3 dress sizes, unhappy, miserable, not giving him good memories, no sex nothing. He did not see, I would have been as well with that sandwich board again saying you fucken idiot look at your wife, look at what she has become, look into her eyes and see if there is any shred of happiness there. That fun-loving happy person has gone, all that is left is a shell and you are too busy with your phone skelping one out to notice, yet I am the stupid one.

Chapter 43

It is my quiet season at work and the time is getting nearer, Now I learn by my mistakes. I have been in a situation like this where I got locked out. I was not going to put myself in that position again. Oh no, I was going to learn to be a locksmith. I would have been as well saying I am going to become a lap dancer. It is never going to happen he said. Clearly, he does not know his wife. That became apparent ages ago. That happy bubbly person with love and happiness is gone, totally gone. The Murrin he knew and loved had disappeared right in front of him and he did not know. Yet, there was no change in our routine before all this happened. I just knew my husband and knew something was not right and yet I have gone from one extent to the other in front of his eyes and this fucker does not know.

The more you tell me I cannot do something the more I want to do it. I am not one of these people who say something and do not do it. Oh no, If I say it, I am doing it. By the end of the day I had found a locksmith willing to take me on. He was going on holiday though and I can start with him when he gets back. Fuck you Dexter.

We are at fat club, Agnes is not having a good day. I am bonding with my mum which is something we have never really done before. When we left the house, my mum said something about Agnes's hair and right there and then I felt like an idiot. Why the hell did I not think of that. This woman cannot use the muscles in her hands. Before arsehole done the dirty, I wanted and needed nice underwear. It makes you feel nice and sexy. Have your hair done, mascara, clothes on matching underwear. It makes you feel different. Right now, I do not give two fucks I am doing this for a reason. This woman is not. I do not do hair and makeup shit. I would not know how. She would look like a dog's dinner. Her daughter on the other hand does not walk out the door without make up on. Why the hell has she not thought about this. It is her mother, she is into hair and makeup and yet she has done fuck all. Still drops the kids off willy Nilly of course she does because that benefits her. If it is for someone else, she does not give a fuck. I cannot do make up I know that for a fact, but she always liked having her nails done I am sure I can do that. That day there and then I go and order everything for gel nails. How hard can it be to learn how to put gel polish on. I can learn to do gel polish and locksmithing at the same time. Happy days.

Chapter 44

I started working with Charles. Well I say working. I was more talking the ass off him. God I can talk for Scotland, but I will not speak to you on the telephone. I hate it, I do not know why but I hate it. I have always been like that. I will speak to you face to face just not on the telephone, but I will text you. It gets to the point and that is it. This man fascinated me, guess what? He is not that much taller than me. He was in the army. I love the stories he tells me in the van. We go from one job to another and so we have time in the van for talking. It is great. I am paying attention to everything he does, and he lets me do bits and bobs, but all the time I am paying attention. If something interests me then I absorb it like a sponge. If it is of no interest to me then there is just no point. It is like Nicam.

I love this, it is like a jigsaw. You just need to solve the jigsaw. The only thing I do not like is the die grinder, Jesus Christ it is like the drill at the dentist. Oh my god, and I need to get sedated for the dentist. I cannot get sedated to go to work. Most of the jobs you can do without it but when its metal on metal oh my god. It is like the crying baby thing. I cannot stand crying babies and I cannot stand the noise of this machine. I know I got over my fear of birds, but this is different. I did not need to get sedated to go and see the birds. Oh my god. Luckily, it was only one time that day he had to use it so that was good. We went from job to job and all I did was talk.

Now this arsehole has messaged me asking me how my day is going? Are you joking? Mr. oh you will never be a locksmith. Now he is interested, or at least acting like he is interested. It was not five minutes ago you were saying I would never be able to do it. Take your text and shove it right up your arse, but instead I said I love it and that I was too busy to message him. I was not letting that arsehole ruin my day. This was my day. I have been looking forward to this. I have been on you tube finding out how to pick locks. I have spent the best part of the week practicing picking locks.

In between Charles going away and starting work we went to the caravan. It was miserable, I love the beach and the water and how peaceful it is and this time it was shit. Everything was shit. I hated it. I hated the beach even though the dogs had a great time, I just did not want to be there, or I just did not want to be there with him. The difference between the first time going and this time could not have been more different. This and camping were my go-to place. These were my two favourite holidays. I do not care about fancy things and money. It has just never meant anything to me. I was happy, we were happy, we were in love and now all I feel is empty again and just wanting away from this man who shattered the only organ I had left that I never damaged. He cut me open, took it out, stood on it then reversed over it and did not bother to put it back in. This man has gone from being my best friend and husband, my everything to one stage below my abuser. This man took the trust that I had given him, told him my true feelings and fears then used the worst part of my life and turned it around to suit himself and his lies. This man who swore on all our lives and his dead brother's life lied to my face to suit himself. I gave him more than one chance to tell me the truth. Not once did he have the decency to tell me the truth. He allowed me to think that something so heinous that happened to me as a child had ruined our marriage. The only thing in my life that I cannot get past this man used against me repeatedly. I tell you what you can do with that text you lying piece of shit.

Chapter 45

All the nail stuff came, and we took it up to Agnes for fat club. We were like a pack of cackling witches. I mucked it up though. I never did it the right way. I thought it was the LED lamp thing that was broke and so ordered another one. Maybe I should have you tubed how to do nails too. Eventually we got there in the end. I would take the nail stuff to fat club every week and do the ladies nails. At least it was something. There would be hell way and no way I could do make up. It was pointless but I know someone else who could have done it, but they did not. Neither of them has done anything to make this woman's life a little better. The woman who brought them into this world they could not give a shit. The woman who is already dying inside at what has happened and these two just could not give a fuck.

I am loving the locksmithing. Charles is starting to show me stuff and he has told me of his plans. He wants to teach locksmithing, so him training me up would work to his advantage because he could teach, and I could go do the labour work. Jesus Fuck, I am on cloud nine. Someone believes in me. This guy believes in me not like my arsehole husband. Someone believes in me. He has no longer said it and I am ordering tools. I have been paying attention to what he says. I have been paying attention to what he is doing. I am actually getting the hang of this. Even the die grinder. I found a way round it. Ear plugs. There is always a positive out of a negative you just got to find it. Things are starting to come together. I have a job I am going to like, my operation will be coming soon, and my two and a half years prison sentence is coming up. Things may be starting to look up. Let us face it. They cannot get any worse, and then I get the letter.

My operation is going ahead. It means I will have had my operation and after it my prison sentence is finished. Dexter puts in for a few days holiday to go to Blackpool before it, which means I will have to be alone with him for a few days but it does not matter because after it I am done, finished and he can go and skelp out as many wanks as he wants. I do not care. He took two and a half years of my life but used my abuse as the excuse and it was the biggest god dam mistake of his life. I may not have been able to stick up for myself when I was younger but I sure as fuck can now. The only thing is I need to do it with minimal damage to Agnes.

Chapter 46

Blackpool was hellish but I knew that was going to happen. We were not there and happy and in love. There was hell way and no way I was going near any strip club. I just wanted to make it through the last final trip away together. It is only a few days. A few days and that will be it done. The difference between the first time and this time was dramatic. Why can this man not see that. There was no laughing, there was no dressing up. There was no sex on a dirty bed in a dirty hotel. There was no love in my eyes. That look was well gone, the look that made me go all gooey did not even want me to smash his face in anymore. I just wanted rid of him. I went from happy, to sad, to venom and now I feel nothing. I look at this man in front of me and I know that once upon a time ago I would have done anything for this man. The love I had for him knew no bounds. I would have stood in front of a loaded gun for this man as he gave me life, He showed me what it was to have love and happiness. True happiness and be able to trust someone so much that I shared my true feelings with him, but then he ripped it away from me, he shattered my heart into a million tiny pieces, if he had just shattered my heart it may not have been so bad but this man in front of me knew my feelings. He was the only person I told my true feelings to and he took that information and he turned it around against me to protect a lie. If he just did not want me anymore, he should have just told me and none of this would have happened. Yet he took the worst part of my life, and he used that against me, allowing me to think that my abuser had wrecked my marriage and how dare I even think to ask him such a thing.

We went to Blackpool and Charles went away on holiday. He did not contact me when he got back. The story of my life. After buying all those tools, he obviously thought the same as my husband. How wrong they both will be.

Chapter 47

Its operation time, here we go number 107. This better be the last. It is a full hysterectomy, but they need to open me up and down the way again. The problem is I have so many scars and underneath the scars is more scaring. I am a surgeon's worst nightmare. I am the kind of person you do not want on your table. Fuck that send her back. Now I have just been told I have a stomach hernia that I did not know I had, and they will do everything all at once hallelujah.

I have a steel rod and pins in my leg and scaring. I get 300mg of dihydrocodeine daily. All of this is given to them with my medical records. Just get me to the operating theatre so I can get this done, get back on my feet and rid of the lying sack of shit. It is all going to fit in perfectly. We have 3 dogs, because of him. I know he is not going to want they dogs.

I am sure he has been speaking to someone else, but I am not 1 million percent sure as in right this minute speaking to someone, so if I time this right, he will go, and here comes the cherry on the cake. He has just taken out a credit card with the same bank he has the mortgage with. He takes this out because I am the one who makes all the money at Christmas time with my work. I will not be able to do much seasonal work for Christmas. We cannot live on his wages. Not a chance. He has a motor bike to pay for his phone bill is through the roof because he has the watch and the latest phone. He smokes fags and drinks energy drinks like they are going out of fashion. He can hardly live on his own wages before any bills are paid. So, he takes out a four-grand credit card.

I go under the knife. Oh, my god I have had operations let me tell you, but I swear to god someone has just opened me with a Stanley knife and there is a group of men sitting having a bonfire. If I were not in so much pain, I would have gone to the shops to get them marshmallows. Oh my god it hurts. This is pain. Jesus Christ this is like the same feeling I had when I walked in the bathroom when he was having a wank but this time there is people inside sitting round a campfire and it is all going on inside me. Jesus Fucken Christ because I get so much dihydrocodeine at home the morphine is worthless. It is doing nothing, absolutely nothing. Will you just get these fuckers to fuck away from me and build a fire somewhere else? Eventually they checked my medical records and saw my meds and changed them. Hallelujah Someone put the fire out. By the time I got back to the ward and the meds wore off I went through the whole situation again, but this time what did they hand me after being cut from ear hole to arsehole. Paracetamol. Two fucken paracetamol I could not believe it. I was going to take the tablets and literally shove them up her arse, but I was in agony. It had to be the last operation that was the one from hell of course it did.

 It was a pain in the tits. I had the worst two days of my life. I got my operation on the Friday night and walked out of the hospital on the Monday morning with a catheter in. Fuck you and your meds. I am going home. I can endure more pain than the average human being. What I feel inside is absolutely nothing to what is going on outside. I just wanted home to recover and get rid, simple as that. This is how badly I wanted him gone.

Now I have just been opened from earhole to arsehole. I cannot walk three bulldogs. Even I am not that good. I need to recover and get rid. This is all I have in my head now. Recover, get rid. My mum is up staying just now because I cannot do everything myself while Dexter is at work. I am in pain, but I do not care. I am going to recover as quick as possible. Time is running out and I did not want to spend any more time with this man than I had to. The venom was starting to come back. I think I had buried it for so long that I felt nothing, but now all I feel is venom. I have never allowed myself to feel any emotions of what happened because I knew I would lose it. I cannot do it just now I can see the finish line. Please do not fuck this up. If you blow it now you have all these pets to care for and no one to do it. My mum is a pensioner she cannot look after and walk three bulldogs. It is just not going to happen. I know that. I feel as if I am starting to get better then boom. Something is not right,

I feel it I am getting worse instead of better. I think do not you dare die, not yet. Please just hold on, the finish line is there, can you see the wee man standing there waving the flag? Do not die now. I command you not to die now. Now I knew something was not right, you know your own body and I thought to myself. You bastard, you fucken bastard. Of all the times I have wished and dreamed of dying and you are going to cheat me out of this revenge. You fucken bastard. How dare you do this to me. I know something is not right, my body is not right.

I need to be losing a limb or something for me to want to go to hospital. I had not even had 48 hours out of surgery and I would rather go home and be in pain so you know it is bad if I need to go to hospital.

It was bad, I had sepsis. Just my Donald duck. I had to go back to the same hospital that I wanted away from. The same god dam nurses. The same god dam meds. Another three days in hospital to get rid of the infection through my body but then my scar took an infection and it all burst the day I was going home. Of course, it did. Why wouldn't it, I have no luck except for bad luck. I could see the finish line, I was nearly there. My 2-and-a-half-year prison sentence was up. The man who done so wrong to me would soon be out of my life.

I was only going to do to him what he did to me with minimal damage to Agnes. It was not her fault her son was a lying sack of shite sowing his oats all over the place. She did not know what he had done. Well I hoped she did not know, not after everything we went through together. I would be livid. That would be the straw that broke the camel's back.

I pray no one ever needs go through this. Oh Jesus. I took an infection in my scar. Oh god, the surgeon says we can do it here and now and you can go home. Ok do it, just do it. Anything to get home. He comes over with a big tube and sticks it in my wound oh my god I think my tits fell to my arse. Jesus Christ. Is that it. No, I need to keep doing this oh my fucken god. I wish I had just gone downstairs and got it done now but hurry up and finish. I literally think my tits and arse have swapped places. I do not know which way is up or down. I was supposed to get that same thing done for two whole weeks. Up and down to the hospital every day for two whole weeks. I am not ashamed to say I was shitting myself. Thankfully, it only happened another three times.

I am back home again; I just need to get rid of this infection then I am home and dry. I went up and down to the hospital to get my wound done. It is getting closer and closer and I can start to feel the emotions coming back again. The venom that I had for what this man did to me was starting to come back again. I knew it was nearer the time and I just needed the infection to clear. That was all I needed. If that cleared up, I would be home and dry. I knew I would not be able to walk the three dogs just now. I am going to have to wait till after Christmas.

Chapter 48

Its Christmas Eve, I am practically home and dry. The infection has gone. I wish it had gone sooner but that was that. Now, I have not had my proper Christmas season because I was in hospital. Whatever money I had Dexter thinks it was all spent on Christmas presents. Now he knows that I will not have one penny to Valentine's day. I can feel the emotions starting to boil again. Everything that I have buried for so long. Everything that I hid away, all those feelings and emotions. The love that I once had for this man was the greatest love of all. I opened my heart and my feelings to this man. This man knew I had never done anything like this before with anyone and for me to do that was like putting myself in a bedroom with lions. He knew this, this man knew everything about me. He knew that this is a part of my life I cannot get over no matter what. No therapy is helping there is no tequila guy at the bottom of a bottle, there is not enough stock cubes in the world to cure what I have or need, and this man knew all of this. And yet he used it against me in the most heinous way ever. What he did was as bad as the actual act itself, because he took something that was so personal and so powerful and he rolled it into a ball and hit me with it, just to save his own arse and his own lies. I knew, I already knew. I just wanted him to tell me the truth. If he loved and respected me like I did to him he would have been honest with me from the beginning.

All his lies have come to this. To where we are today. The woman in front of him, his wife the person he was supposed to love more than anything in this world was standing a broken woman and he could not see it. Or he simply chose not to see it. The more I thought about it the more I thought I did not want to be with this man on Christmas Day. I knew for a fact if I got my mum so drunk, she would not have been able to make Christmas Day. I knew it. I also knew if I took a drink on Christmas Eve there was a big chance of this coming out and I did it. I only had a few days left to go and yet as the minutes went by the emotions were starting to come out.

Christmas morning, I knew my mother would not let me down. She was not seeing Christmas Day. I did not want to spend Christmas with any of them. I knew it was coming to an end. I knew it. I had prepared for this for two and a half years. Like Jesus, it was going to be the last supper. Now not only were things coming to an end, but I got the best Christmas Present ever. Dexter was talking to someone else. He met her at a funeral. This idiot thought she was stealing him. I always said, never underestimate when a woman wants something. She will stop at nothing to get it. She had just handed me the bullet and I was going to deliver it on New Year's Eve.

Chapter 49

Now I know he is away to see her the day before New Year's Eve. Of course, I knew this. I knew everything. He was away to see her and when he got home, I questioned him, and he did was he always did. Went on the defensive. This man is so predictable. Again, he takes it and turns it round on me. This time I am about to spit feathers. This time I do want to kill him but not yet. Just like before he has been caught out and he is fuming. Every time he gets caught out, he is fuming. The times on snap chat, on messenger in the shower. This guy is raging, because his so stupid wife is not so stupid after all. I am playing the long game. I want to know how far this sack of shit will stoop. How far down will he go. What will he do or use this time to get him out of shit? Although for me there never was a going back. I may not have died that night, but we did. Oh, hell yes, we did. I told him from day one. You lie to me and you are out. There is no second chance, I am all out of 2nd and 3rd chances with anyone. Most of all do not lie to me, and what did he do? He lied to my face, and right now he is lying to my face and you can see he is rattling about looking for an excuse or something to hit me with. You are insecure about your past. Ok, it is not as bad as what you said the last time, but you are still trying to blame me. Now all the other times I have let it go because I do not care, I had no intention of staying with this sack of shit from the first time, but he ruined two and a half years of my life.

Now this rat bag got up for work at 4/5am that morning and was on the phone texting her at that time, saying she is going off on one. Thinking it is all to do with this time. I know she is there so I know he will walk out the door. I just need to give him that little push.

I write him a massive message by email. So, he wasted two and a half years of my life, but he also tried fucking with my head. Making me think that I was going crazy because of the abuse. You have not seen nothing yet mate. Your head is going to be spinning in all directions. Just you wait and see.

God I even bored myself to death with the email. Jesus Fuck, this is what has happened from the start. Listing all the things we have done together and where it went wrong. Not the truth. He does not know the truth yet. I was going on about the underwear and not feeling like a woman should feel bla bla bla. God, I think I went on about everything and anything. By the time he came home I knew if something would piss him off it would be me having a drink, so what did I do? Of course, I poured a drink, so when he came home, he thinks I have been on the sauce all day. I am past boiling point, but I cannot blow it yet.

I say I will leave because I know she is waiting in the wind. She is going away to a Gaelic night or something with her parents, but she will be back the following day. I know she is there waiting, and he will happily go. This is his ammo. He needs to have something waiting for him. This fucker cannot be on his own. He is a needy person. He needs someone to want him. This is how he is. She is there waiting, I give the push and cheerio, he is gone.

Now I want to see how far down this fucker will go. I still have a head fuck to give him. I have repaid the two and a half years now it is the head fuck time. He comes home the following day. Now the first time he used my abuse and turned it on me. What the fuck is it going to be this time. He only turns around and blames his dead brother. There is no end to the depths this bastard will go. Now I know she is there waiting. I know they are now going to be happily ever after, and this sack of shit is blaming his dead brother. Oh, my fucken god. You dare to stoop to your own secret and blame your brother. What a lying sack of shit. The only decent thing was he did not blame me this time. Now I ask him about the last time, and it takes him two and a half years to admit it. Two and a half fucken years of lies, not including the ones in between because I did not care. I just was not making it easy for him or giving him any good memories. He is a worthless piece of shit with no moral's no nothing. He takes the worst piece of information from both our lives and uses it to suit him and his lies. This is what this piece of shit does. I think you 2 deserve each other, now this is when it gets even better. I know who she is and what she is. This girl cannot make up her mind. One minute she is a lesbian and the next straight. I do not judge anyone's sexuality. Everyone is free to do what they like, but this lassie has been banged more times than a ketchup bottle. Everyone knows this. She is the local bike. She is already pregnant not by him though, by some other fucker she probably does not even know who. Nothing could bring me more joy than that. All my Christmases have come at once, but I cannot say this yet. I need to keep my mouth shut.

I accept that this is what is wrong with him that his dead brother is playing with his emotions. Now I want to know, how fucken far down are you going to go? What about the house? I already know he cannot afford the mortgage on his own £230/£250 a week is not going to cut it. He walks out the door with a £4000 credit card with nothing on it. He thinks I have no money whatsoever to February.

I have his whole family to feed. 3 dogs, 2 cats and 2 parrots. I have no money for gas or electricity. Let me wait and see how he plays this one out. Now, I will give Agnes her due. She messaged me that day to see if I was ok. I said I am fine; I am hurt but I am fine. Now I am trying to take this bastard down with minimal damage to Agnes. I will wait and see what he does.

We messaged backwards and forwards for a wee while. Now as far as this fucker is concerned, I have just undergone major surgery, I have no money, I cannot work just now but even if I could I do not have any money until February. This is January. There is no wee magic man in the meter saying hold on and I will give you money for gas and electric. No, this fucker decides he wants to take him and her away to a hotel for a few days. Now I know where they are. I am sitting at home with no money or food he thinks with all his fucken family and he is living it up in a hotel with a four-grand credit card.

We go backwards and forwards for a few days. This is 5 years we are talking about not 5 minutes. I was his wife. I am at home with his family and no money. Did the offer of money come? Hell no. In fact, knowing I had no money he cancels the car insurance so I cannot drive the car. My mobile contract was under his name. He wants the phone back. I go to his parent's house to put the phone through the door and his dad is in his car. He thought I did not see him, but I did. Now this other piece of shit knows fine well everything I have done, and he hides from me like I am nothing. His parents now know that he has taken my phone off of me so I cannot phone anyone for help and it is my business number, they also know that he has cancelled the car insurance, he has given me no money for food, electricity or gas. I ask him where my watch is so I can sell it to get food and he has taken it. I already knew he would do this, so I have already taken the box. I do not care about the watch. I just wanted to see how far this piece of shit would go, and he sunk low. Really low. So, I have repaid 2 and a half years but now I owe you a head fuck and strip you of everything like you have just done to me. No problem. A portion of head fuck and everything stripped coming right up as well as the destruction because after all you did that to me.

Now what is the most destructive thing he hates. Humiliated on Facebook and everyone knows what he did, and now I do not need to hold back and worry about Agnes because she did not give a fuck about me.

Chapter 50

I was going to shield Agnes and the family from what happened after all I still went to see her every week, do her nails, go to fat club. I spoke to this woman every day. There was no one else there helping her. Where was her so called family. Where were her sisters and her own daughter? Nowhere, they did not give a fuck. Especially Joanne. All she cared about was passing the kids out like smarties. As far as I am concerned now not only my loving husband threw me under the bus but so did Agnes and Bert. The people that I was there helping. Me, not other members of their family and now these fuckers think it is acceptable that he has walked out the door. Left me with no money to feed all of us and he was the one who chose half of them. No, this fucker has walked out with a clean £4,000 credit card, still getting paid weekly, sold the Tag Heuer watch so him and the bike could have a nice few days away while we are here with no money. Not only thinking we had no money, he cancelled the car insurance and took my mobile phone. That is, it arsehole keep it coming because the more you do to me the worse it is going to be for you.

Here comes the humiliation but I am not posting it on my own Facebook. I never post anything on my own Facebook page, but this Muppet did all my deliveries, so everyone knows him and who he is. I do not give a fuck what other people think of me, but this arsehole and his family do. You have all just thrown me under the bus as far as I am concerned so fuck you, Agnes and Bert. I have near 5000 people on my business page. People that know him and his family. I simply posted the truth. Not the whole truth but what these idiots' thought was the truth. Dexter walked out and left us all on New Year's Eve for another woman. He has walked out and took his £4000 credit card, left us no money, knowing I have just undergone major surgery. Even if I wanted to work, I cannot work until February. My first seasonal work will be Valentine's day. Not only that he has stolen my watch and pawned it to go and have a nice few days away with the bike. He has cancelled the car insurance so I cannot drive and taken my mobile phone.

Oh, he is being called all the bastards under the sun by the people that he delivered my hampers to. OMG they are ripping into him. I knew this would happen that is exactly why I did it. I knew him and his family would be mortified. Me? I do not give two flying fucks what anyone thinks about me. I never have. If you can go through what I have, then worrying about what other people think of you is a grain of sand. The only people I care about are my friends that is it. Everyone ripped into him except one friend. A friend he had before we met. Another friend who he said chose money over him, yet this one man is backing him up on Facebook. One person, the one person he did not deserve because he already threw him under the bus by saying he is a dick, he chose Lorraine and her money over him. Yet this man is standing up for him. I should hate his guts, but I did not. I admired him. I really did. He was the only person to stick up for him. To me that is a true friend. You do not see each other for years and yet you have their back if something happens, and he did. He proudly had his back and he did not deserve this man's friendship. His family backed him publically on Facebook, knowing what he had done. As far as I am concerned now you will all reap what you sow. The whole fucken lot of you. The family that I was going to shield when bringing him down were now on the same ship as him. They are all on the titanic and they are about to get hit with the biggest iceberg in their life.

Chapter 51

Now I have repaid the 2 and a half years and part of the humiliation. Remember I am 2 and a half years in front of this idiot. The idiot who thought he was so clever, and I was so stupid. I have played this scenario in my head in so many ways. The way of taking him and only him down, but now I am taking the whole family down. They did not give a fuck about me. They made that clear as day. Bert hid from me as if I was nothing, they now know he has left me with no money, sold the watch, cancelled the car insurance and took my phone, met someone else, took her to a hotel with the money he got from pawning the watch and thought that is acceptable. Fuck all of you. Now I do not need to hold back. Now it is all out destruction.

I am one person. I have not told anyone any of my intensions. All my family and friends think my life is wonderful. This is a journey I had to go on myself for myself. I had to prove to myself that I am a strong enough person and although I have great friends, I always do everything on my own. It is something I have always done. Do not ask me why, it is as if I need to prove a point to myself. I have lay beside this sack of shit for two and a half years in bed. Just the sight of him makes me want to throw up. I have had to look at his face every day. I want to smash the living daylights out of his face, yet I simply say love you get to work. Could I have done this if he did not have those long shifts. I very much doubt it. It was the only sanity I had. He would phone on his lunch break and I would say what do you want? I am busy at work. All of those 1000's of texts have gone to I do not even reply to one, then he phones because he thinks something is wrong. Oh, mate something is very wrong, but you have no fucken idea because you are still on that fucken phone. It is like a limb. You know he is taking his phone to the shower with him and he is there for an hour. You know exactly what he is doing, and he will walk out and say Hi Sweetheart. We have gone from not being able to be without each other to stay the fuck away from me and stop phoning me because I am busy, but I am the stupid one. The nearer and nearer the time came the more I started to show and become the old Murrin. I changed there and then in that hospital, but he did not know that. That is how stupid this fuck is. There was no change to our routine and yet I knew instantly something was not right. This idiot? I would have been as well walking about with that sandwich board saying you are a lying sack of shit and I am only here to repay to you what you have done to me and he still would have been none the wiser. I am not even attempting to answer his messages anymore, I simply say stop texting me I do not have time to text you back because I am at work. He would phone and I would just moan. This arsehole is still sending long ass messages about how he cannot wait to get home to his family the love of his life. Mind you he was probably just talking to his phone but had to send it as a message.

You took everything from me and now you will get the exact same. See all those people that you chose to look down on at the car boot sale? My friends the people I like, I took all your tools and designer clothes and shoes and sold them to all those people for like a £1. I did not care about the money. I never have given a shit about money but all the stuff you left at the house thinking you and the bike were going to have the house in 30 days because I was to leave. You forgot we were married, you stupid fuck. That is exactly why I made you put the house in your name and your name alone. I was your wife. I had rights to be in the house. I knew that, I had always known that. You were just so predictable the whole way through you made it so easy for me. Even squatters have rights. I had no intensions of leaving the house and what did I care? It was in your name and your name alone. You were responsible for paying the mortgage not me. Your perfect credit rating has just gone down the swanny. I have your new name. New credit. I am fine, you on the other hand are fucked. You thought that you would ride it out at your mum and dads house for a wee while. She stays with her mum and dad. You thought I would pack my shit and go in the 30 days knowing fine well where the deposit for the house came from. This is another reason why your family are now on the same fucken ship as you because they know all this. They thought that was acceptable. Not a fucken chance. Watch this space.

Chapter 52

Reality is starting to kick in a little bit that I have no intension in going anywhere. I have repaid the 2 and a half years and part of the destruction, I have sold all the stuff you left at the house but I still owe you a head fuck, the rest of the destruction and payback to the loving family. I send him a letter to his parents' house telling him half of the truth and a load of shit. I told him that I did not die that night, but we did. I told him that his phone was bugged. I had videos of him in the shower. Photos from snap chat. I told him I had recorded the phone call from the day before he left. The clever criminal found a credit card at work, wearing his bus uniform went into the vape shop with the credit card and purchased 2 vape fags. Now he is on the phone to me while he was doing it. Thinking he was a master criminal. A master criminal does not wear a fucken works uniform to commit fraud, any person with half a brain would know this, but he also thinks I have recorded this. This guy would not last 5 minutes in jail. This guy looked down on people at the car boot sale. Can you imagine what he would think of people in jail. He would be fucked. Well and truly fucked. Criminals are clever, they would see right through him in an instant. This fuckers head is swimming away like soup. He does not know if he is in New Year or New York, so he sends the cops to me. He does not know what part real and what part is not, but now reality is kicking in a little bit. Jesus maybe his wife was not so stupid after all.

The mail is still coming to the house. Now this fucker has blown the whole £4000 on new clothes, shoes. Aftershave. It is all gone. Poof, up in a cloud of smoke. Now all he has is his £250-week wage. This arsehole smokes, he needs 5/6 energy drinks a day and that is before he has even bought any lunch for work, but his work pays for this. They just do not know it. He does not put all the bus fares through. This fucker needs fed and watered. He has a motorbike on HP. His phone bill with watch is near enough a £100 a month. This idiot cannot afford to smoke, drink energy drinks, pay his bike, his phone and insurance off £250. I know this for a fact so where the fuck is, he going to pull the money out his arse for the mortgage. It is never going to happen, and I already knew this, yet I was the stupid one.

So, I leave it for a little while. I already know the bike is pregnant. She is about 4 months on, but they do not know that I know this. I put the cat amongst the pigeons yet again on Facebook. I want to see what this arsehole is going to do or say, and what his family are going to say. I know how this idiot works. I post on Facebook that OMG the time away at the hotel has come back to bite him on the arse and she has fell pregnant as in just fell pregnant. Not that she is about 4 months pregnant. This fucker hates babies. He is that annoying person like me you do not want next to you on the airplane. This idiot cannot afford to keep himself let alone anyone else, yet off he goes. Puts a post on Facebook saying I am going to be a dad and my family are happy and supporting me. Happy fucken days you stupid fuck. I know he is not the dad. He knows he is not the dad. She knows he is not the dad but his one and only friend from work has a daughter who he met at a funeral. This funeral took place just before Christmas. Now it does not take a rocket scientist to work out they have been together for 5 minutes and she is well over 4 months pregnant. How is that possible. I know this man. He might not have known me, but I knew him. I knew after that night we were over finished, no return. I knew when he was speaking to other people. He would do it at work or when I went to sleep. He never sat on his phone in front of me, he probably knows I would have wrapped it round his throat. I was not going to make it easy for him. I wanted to make these two and a half years as miserable as fuck without getting caught. I went to bed early every night to get the fuck away from him. He walks in from work and I need to look at this mother fuckers face every day. I love you rolls off his tongue like hello. He does not know the meaning of the word love. I know 1 million percent if this idiot got someone pregnant while we were still together his arse would have fallen out his trousers. This is how much I know him and how predictable he is, yet he is publically posting on Facebook he is going to be a dad and his family are so happy for him and behind him 100%. This is exactly what I wanted to know and hear. Everything I have done, there has been a reason behind it. So, he is taking responsibility for the bike's child, because he is friends with her dad. He who cannot support himself let alone anyone else and his family are so over the moon he is now living in her parents' house. They are 5 minutes together, they have not had the honeymoon period yet that he craves so much. She was the one to throw him under the bus in the first place and I could not be happier and still they do not have a clue that I know any of this.

Chapter 53

I am still living in the house that is clocking all his debt through the roof. He is now living in someone else's house. No privacy nothing. Taking on another man's child, with no money, a shit load of debt and I could not have wished for a better ending. I do not even need to finish destroying him because he has done a grand enough job all by himself, with his families blessing. I posted that on Facebook because I wanted to see the reaction it would cause and I got exactly what I wanted, now I will finish destroying you along with your so-called family who have just thrown me under the bus.

Now I need a bit of time for myself to take in all this new information and process it and then decide what way I am going to deliver it. The worse the better as far as I am concerned. Do not even expect me to bat an eyelid with whatever route I go down. There is no shred of the nice Murrin left. Well not as far as any of you roasters are concerned. She is away to the land of Oz and they are all out of red shoes to get her back. Your left with Snow Shite. This is what Dexter called me in the beginning. I was a tough nut to crack. I will admit he put a hell of a lot of graft in and I think maybe that is why I liked him. He would say we were like snow white and Dopey although I was the like Dominatrix Snow-white. So, he called me Snow Shite. The other one drifted, but now Snow Shite is back, but with superpowers to totally kick ass.

I have left things for a while, see this is the way I like to work. I do something, it causes chaos then I leave it for a while. You are just starting to feel safe and settled again and boom. I am on you. Now I had his brothers' knife, He gave it to me for my toolbox, you know for the locksmith toolbox that he said I would never be able to do. The one person who should have had my back giving me confidence like I did to him with everything. He wanted to try plastering. I egged him on. I even went and made the £850 for him to do it. He always wanted a motorbike. I went out and bought him all the lessons and test. This is how I roll. If you want to do something then always do it, try it. If it does not work who gives a fuck at least you tried. I supported him through everything, yet I said I wanted to locksmith and he laughed. Said I would not be able to do it, yet now he is giving me his brothers knife for my toolbox. It is not that I wanted him to have it back, it was more of a I know where you are even though you think I do not.

 I got to the post office and I thought fuck that. I am not giving him the knife back. He blamed his dead brother for the 2nd time. This fucker has no loyalty to anyone I thought if I send it, it is kind of like a nice thing. So, I took the knife out and just posted the envelope. Just for a ha-ha fuck you. I know where you are, two streets away you fucken idiot. I have always known.

Although it just so happened at the same time, he had sent the cops to me yet again. This time for his passport. Stuff from eBay had gone to his new address and now he thinks I am running credit up in his name. Eh? Have you seen your credit history lately? You will be lucky to get a penny sweetie on tick. So, the cops asked do you have his passport and I said no, I was not lying when I said no. I did not have it but maybe if they asked the fire pit in the garden, it may have had it at one point when I was trying to get us a fire going. I put your birth certificate and our wedding certificate in too for good measure, and certificates for work or some shit. It all went up in smoke, and we got a wee heat.

The cops left and I messaged him saying stop sending the cops here for your passport as I do not have it. I have sent you Kevin's knife to Maclehouse Road. So now he knows that I know where he is living. This then turned into a slanging match which I knew it would and I only wanted one thing to come out of it, so I pushed his buttons. I knew the thing that would annoy him the most is me knowing the truth about Siobhan, but I knew what his next move would be and this is exactly what I needed so of course I play ball until I get what I want. I always do everything for a reason. So, I hit back with the only thing I know will rattle his cage. I think it is nice your bringing up someone else's baby. Not a slanging match about how dare you leave me and get someone pregnant. I could not care less, he still does not know that though, it was her who replied to my text not him. I know this man like the back of my hand I knew when it was her texting and when it was him.

I already have him admitting to theft, but he always claimed on paper or text there was no other woman. I wanted the truth on my divorce, this arsehole has danced around it saying I made it up or I imagined it because of the abuse I knew for a fact the minute I said about bringing up another man's baby. So now he really knows that I know he is raging. So, raging he comes back and says. Meeting Siobhan last August was the best thing I did and became a father. Happy Fucken days that is all I wanted. I could not care less what you say now I am not interested. I got what I wanted. Our marriage ended New Year's Eve. Now unless I am a complete fucken moron August comes before 31st December. Here it is from the horse's mouth and phone.

Now they are on a rant. I do not really care about anything else, so I just let them rant away. Dexter thinks (this is how stupid he is) I must still love him or why would I go to such an extent to find all this out. This roaster thinks I have gone about to look for evidence of these two idiots because I am jealous. The pair of idiots sent me a picture thing through Facebook dressed as like devils or something saying we are so happy. Fucken brilliant. If you are so happy why the fuck are you messaging me to tell me. I have not bothered my arse contacting any of you. I am too busy working out my next move to worry about you two Muppets. I already know everything, and it is the person sitting beside you that has already told me. She obviously has not told him yet that it was her who contacted me on Facebook when they met.

Yes, I have heard all about you Siobhan. You like men, you like women, but the only men you like are married men. You wait until they split up with their families and then you no longer want them and see if Lynn will take you back. This is your ammo. Lynn did not want your baby. You wanted Lynn to want your baby and she never. So, you found the next available mug. Brilliant. You think you have done me wrong and you could not have made this ending any better for me if you tried.

It is going to be a question of who will crack first you or him. You get the man then it is no fun after that, but this time your fucked because he had nowhere to go and so he is stuck with you. He hates babies, see when that baby comes, and it is here, and it starts crying and he has nowhere to go because he is stuck at yours to live. The pair of you are going to be miserable as fuck. He will not be so appealing anymore he is up to his arse in debt and he is not Lynn and your heart lies with Lynn. The novelty will wear off because that is all it is. You wanted him, and you can keep him. I was finished and you just helped me put the final nail in his coffin. Do I hate you? Do I fuck. You are a silly wee mixed up lassie who just wants to be loved. You are so like Dexter you crave love, but you have both gone about it the wrong way. You know exactly where your heart lies. You have always wanted a baby. Did not need a man just a baby, you wanted, and it just so happened a married man came along at the same time.

You timed it perfectly and if anything, I thank you because if I did not know 100% you were there waiting, I may have had to see the New Year in with the fucker and pick my timing later. You did me a favour. Either way I wish you luck. What makes it all better for me is my husband and his family thought that they threw me under the bus for a 5-minute relationship and not even their own grandchild. They chose to sail me down the Clyde for a 5-minute wonder while knowing he had left me with no money, no food, cancelled the car insurance and my phone.

Oh god I have really hit a nerve because now these 2 will not shut the fuck up. I am done, I have got exactly what I wanted. I do not want to waste anymore of my time on you two humans and the texts keep coming and BANG I thought he did it out of spite, so I just said yeah, yeah. My own fucken mother, who thought I was for the first time in my god dam life happy. Turns around to Dexter on Christmas Eve when I went to bed and said it never happened. It never fucken happened. Are you fucken joking? I thought he was saying it to get a reaction and I did not give him it but then the following text came. Ha-ha we are all laughing at you. You have been playing the victim and we are all laughing at you. Jesus Christ Kill me now. If both were standing in front of me, I swear on anyone's god dam life I would have killed them both at the same time with my bare hands. This bastard knows if anything laughing is something, I would kill someone for and happily go to jail, but I thought he said it because he did not get the reaction he wanted over my mother. Now it is all out war. In fact, I messaged his mother and told her about what he had just said to me now she knew my feelings on this, and it was the straw that broke the camel's back. I did say there are not enough police in Scotland Yard to protect you from that. So, she knew I knew what he said.

Chapter 54

Now I go to phone my mother. Now if this had been say 3 years ago, I would not have bothered my arse. I was 25 when I told my mum and what did she say? She did not believe me. Why didn't I tell her then? Have you not just answered your own god dam fucken question? Of all the people in the world your mother is supposed to be the one standing there by your side. Not mine, fuck she would happily sail me down the fucken river and put bricks in for good measure. I have been trying to build bridges with my mum. Her and my sister fell out. These two are close, too close that they argue sometimes, but this has gone on too long this time. Fiona would phone my mum every day. You would be lucky if I phoned once a year. I just never bother with them. My mum did not believe me my sister thinks oh just get over it that it happened years ago. I could not give a shit about my family. I appear for Christmas or whatever and go. I am not close to these people. I chose my own family. This one is shit and they would stick bricks in the boat before they shoved me down the Clyde. They do not understand the damage that has been done. They do not care. It took many years later when my cousin Susan told my mum and then she believed me. Not when I told her, no. When someone else did. Do you know why? because they handed us out like smarties. My mother cried for five years to have me. Five fucken years she waited now if you want a child that much you want to spend time with the child. You wanted me. I did not shout from my dad's dick and say come here to I shoot you with something to make me, I want to live in your stomach for 9 months then come down the Shute out of the vagina. No did I fuck. She wanted me, she should have looked after me. She should have known something was wrong. The only thing she remembers is one day on a bus full of people I turned around to her out of the blue and said I hate you. No wonder I hated her. She left us with anyone that would look after us so her and my dad could go out drinking. Her social life was more important than my childhood. My childhood was ruined because they handed us out like smarties. My adulthood is fucked too. My whole life is fucked, well at least my head is.

As I got older, I rebelled big time. I did not want to be with these people, Jesus I would sleep out in the streets at night just to get away from them. I would do all nighters with my pals up freezing stairs like arseholes, I was every other mother's worst nightmare friend for their child. Your parents did not want me as your friend because I was a bad influence but then you did not want to be my worst nightmare either because I had all this built up anger inside and I would happily take it out on anyone. Jesus I would get involved in other people's fights claiming to be their long lost relative.

I left home at 16 and never went back, I went down to Butlins to work to stay there to get to fuck away from my house. It was the best god dam year of my life and it just so happens two girls that I lived with there I have just found again. Part of the reason I went there was to stay the fuck away from my own family. See them on social events. That was it, but now Fiona and my mum have not been talking. That means she is on her own. If there is one thing, I hate is people being left on their own so even though I do not have proper family feelings for this woman she still brought me into this world so I will take her under my wing.

Now this is 3 fucken years we are talking about not 3 fucken minutes. I say to her from day 1 the same as I did to Dexter. This is how we roll, be honest and upfront do not do all that shit you usually do with my sister. Oh, I do not really want to come up but really, she does she just wants you to waste half an hour of your fucken time talking her into it. Not me, If I ask you and you say no that is it. I am not asking again. If something is wrong with you tell me do not let it fester like you do with Fiona. If I am a dick tell me. This is the way I work I hate people that pussy foot about stuff. What is the fucken point? Just get to the point. It does not take her long as she is working with us. She enjoys being with us. I take her to Agnes's every week, and she loves it. You can tell that she has real emotion and feelings for this woman but its Harriett. These two are like a wee tag team. Remember I am near enough the same age as Agnes, so my mum and Bert's mum are the ages of each other oh and the 2 of them are like a wee pair of fish wives together. You even get the odd swear word from Harriet and she does not swear. Fat club was the only real genuine part of my life for the two and a half years, I was bonding with my mum, Agnes was happy and laughing all day so was my mum and Harriet. Jesus if Bert was in, he would even throw his 2 pence in or you would just hear him laughing at us. We laughed from we got in until we left or until Nigel came in and we all fucked off.

The point is I have built bridges with this woman and started to let her in. I am even phoning her during that day. Going out for lunch bonding like mother and daughter should. This was good for me. I could spend time with my mum instead of my lying cheating husband. She would come over to the house and help me with work. It gave her something to do and she loved being in amongst the banter. Now if you are in our house you have absolutely no idea what is going on. I still act as if my lying cheating husband is still my best friend. We still do not argue. I do not see the point in arguing plus me arguing could lead to one of 2 things killing him or blurting out the truth, so I simply join in., Dexter loves her, he wants to keep her.

My mum is fun, of course she is Jesus she wanted fun rather than looking after her children. Her and Dexter get on great and its making things a lot easier for me so hell yeah, I will embrace it. The point is it has been three years not three minutes. I have chosen to allow this woman into my life even after knowing she did not believe me. It is something no one in the family ever talk about. No one wants to fucken know. They do not care. It never happened to them. They do not deal with my head every bastard day. Yet I slowly allow this woman into my life to the point I even say I love you mum.

So, I am thinking there is hell way and no way my mother said that. Jesus, she did not know what was happening. She thought for the first time ever I was happy. No way would she do that. Either she thought I was so happy she wanted to ruin it and tell my husband that I have lied to him for 5 fucken years or she honestly does not think it did. She has gone back on her word. Either way it is a bastard and he will know this because he knows exactly what I think, and I have only just allowed this woman into my life. I pick the phone up and call her. Now I know Christmas Eve was my fault I purposely got my mum so drunk so it would fuck Christmas, but she did not know that. As soon as I asked her mum did you say. I had not even finished the fucken sentence and she says oh well I cannot believe it happened. I did not even say anything I just hung up.

Jesus fucken Christ how many bastard buses are coming. Dexter threw me under the bus, Agnes and Bert threw me under the bus now my own fucken mother has just thrown me under the bus after allowing her into my life. After knowing all those years ago when I first told her she did not believe me until Susan said something and now, she does not believe me again. I will tell you exactly what has happened. This woman knows fine well she handed us out like smarties to anyone that would watch us. Not just grandparents, their friends, fuck the dog next door would have been good enough if it barked. She chose her social life over her own children. Why did she not believe me? because she did not want to believe me to save her own guilt that is why. See when I told them my dad rolled over went back to fucken sleep and my mum said she did not believe me. This is what I am dealing with. My head hurts every fucken single day. My head and I are on that battlefield as soon as my eyes open and before I have peed. My head is full of demons. I am a fucken mess inside, and these two fucks do not care because as far as I am concerned it was their fault. OMG there I have said it for the first time ever. It was your faults. You asked for me. Jesus fuck I sure as hell did not ask for you two. I would have picked better parents. God alone knows why I am not in the gutter with needles in my arms. I am still trying to figure that out myself. I would give everything and anything just to have a normal head. Just not to feel so much pain and anger inside. It feels as if the hurt, pain and anger take up my whole body so there is no room for anything else inside, but if I have learned anything from this it is that it can.

Happiness can live in beside the rest of the shit and make my life a bit easier. Everything happens for a reason. Although I thought I met the love of my life, the person I could trust more than anyone in this world. All that fell apart, but it is ok to be happy. There is more than enough room inside for happiness as well as all the other shit.

Chapter 55

Jesus Fuck now my head is away up in that tornado on the way to the wizard that never was. It is all over the place, not only has my own mother thrown me under the bus but my darling husband has just hit my worst fear and he knows it. He knew exactly what he was saying when he said they were all laughing at me. Jesus fucken Christ. This is big. This is a double whammy. My head is about to explode with all of this. What the fuck am I going to do. It must top his, Jesus Christ, that was a good one he got me. I will admit that, but again this idiot does not know his wife.

Now he still does not know the truth, in fact no one knows the whole truth. Everyone is going to find out the whole truth the same way, I had already started this book. I was nowhere near the end, but it painted a good enough picture of how fucken thick he has been, plus since I started writing this I have known, when all of this is over and done with, I am moving beside the water. Now Demi has found me the perfect house on the beach. I have an idea that will kill 5 birds with one stone. If you have been paying attention, then you will know I do not give a flying fuck what anyone thinks of me except the friends and family I have chosen. This book was not finished. I gave it a Mickey Mouse ending and sent it to Dexter and his dad. Jesus, I had not even checked it for spelling or anything I just sent it.

So, they two have a copy of the unfinished book and now suddenly goby is not so goby anymore, but I am not finished there oh no. See the same Facebook page that I have posted everything else over. I am now putting up a new post. Now, remember these are the same people who were calling him all the bastards under the sun. These are the same people who have also been the Bain of my fucken life for the past 2 and a half years. They were the lesser of two evils. I bent over backwards for these people; the amount of times people were not in for deliveries even after I have just spoken to them in the morning. Or they did not pay delivery charges. Oh, they did not know. My fucken arse you did not know. You people do not give a fuck about me. You were only out for what you could get. You made my life hell. Every season was a total nightmare. Have you any idea how many times I wanted to go on that page and tell you all to FUCK OFF. Out of 5000 people I have chosen a handful of friends. The same as the car boot, thousands of people at the car boot in the last 15 years and I have chosen a handful of friends. Oh, I am going to kill so many birds here with one stone. I do not give a flying fuck what people think but, Dexter does, Agnes does, Bert does, Joanne does and so does my mother. She is on my business Facebook page. She was mortified when I put the post up after New Year, just wait to she sees this.

I had to hunt through Nigel's Facebook page to get photos because I burned every single picture of him and his scum bag family but now, I needed a bloody picture. You can always rely on Nigel; he was probably too tired to change the settings on his Facebook page, so I got a picture of Bert and Agnes together and one of Dexter and Joanne together. Now anyone with half a brain will know there is NO such thing as bad publicity. I take the picture of all 4 of them post them on my business page and simply say …. these people think it is funny for children to get abused. Post.

Then I get the unfinished book uploaded onto amazon, call it I only did to you what you did to me. As if that is even something I would say or call it. It is not even finished but I know for a fact what I have just posted is going to cause mayhem and why would not it. People wanted proof, I sent the text message about them laughing what I failed to do was post the one before it about my own mother saying it was not true and that is why they were laughing. Why did I do that? She deserved it. OMG did she deserve it, but I knew that we were in lock down, she still does not speak to Fiona. She has not been coping too well with lockdown and it most likely would have knocked her right over the edge. Did she deserve it. Fuck yeah, but she did not have a backup. If she was speaking to Fiona, then I may have done it but I never. She would have been mortified enough that it was on Facebook. I was no way letting anyone else throw me under the bus, so I threw myself under and publically posted it on Facebook.

Why did I do that? Many reasons. I wanted to see is Siobhan and her father were going to back Dexter like he backed them. It never happened, in fact no one backed Dexter. Not even the one friend he had sticking up for him at New Year (you totally missed the boat on that because that is probably the best friend you ever had and you shit all over him - he proudly had your back at New Year - he was the only one who defended you and you shit all over him). I also wanted to see if the so-called family that were now standing by him, Agnes and Bert to see if any of them dared to say anything. No one did, the aunts and uncles said nothing, in fact not even one person stuck up for them not one. It was Joanne's friends. She has amazing friends; I admired her friends. The first 2 people to have her back though she does not deserve. Her and Nigel hate them, yet they were the first 2 people to have her back. Other friends of hers had her back and I should want to hate them, but I do not. I still do not. They are only doing the exact same thing I would do, and I admire them. She needs to open her eyes though and realise what she has. They are what you call true friends.

Now the punchline, here is a link to my book and what really happened. It is not a finished book. It was a half ass finished book, but I was not ready to tell him the whole truth yet, so I simply posted a link to the book I uploaded onto amazon. Now remember, I have already chosen my friends out of these 50000 people so whatever these other people say or think means absolutely nothing to me. I could not care less. These are the same people who slated him for what he did, but I did not post the whole truth on Facebook. I shielded my mother. Fuck knows why. Well it caused mayhem, absolute mayhem, which I knew it would. That is exactly why I did it. There is no such thing as bad publicity, these fucks have made my life as miserable as he did. I was using them as much as they were using me. They were my get out of jail free card to work.

Have you any idea how many times I wanted to go on that page and say FUCK ALL OF YOU. You gave me a shit two and a half year, the same as him, so daft arse now has half the truth, his parents, him and his sister's pictures are all over social media saying they think child abuse is funny which was true. I just missed the part out about my mum and OMG all hell broke loose. I was getting called all the bastards under the sun, but the people who were calling me bastards and god knows what else paid to read half a book, they slated me so much everyone now wants to know what is in that book. Jesus fucken Christ. I wanted to know what was in the book and I fucken wrote it.

The only people who contacted me at first were people who have been through the same thing and they knew what was going to come out my mouth when I had the conversation with Steven, because they go through the exact same thing. If all my shite helps one person then I do not give a rat's ass about the rest of you. You walk in my shoes for a day or take my head and see how you cope.

The others were other people that I know. People who I have met or been in their life for any length of time. My old boss Hazel, the only one I liked, and OMG did she make us work. This woman made us clean kitchen tiles with fucken corn on the cob sticks. I shit you not. It was a shop like KFC. The same kind of idea and this woman had us pull out all the machinery and clean it with fucken sticks every bloody week and the floor tiles. You literally could have eaten your dinner off the floor in work. She worked us like dogs and yet I respected her. Everyone looks for a scam in work. You are a liar if you say you have never done it. There was my side kick in work Julie. OMG we were a pair, always winding other people up. The shop was across the road from the Evening Times building and it was full of guys. Us two were in our element. We were a pair of wee fuckers. If it was just us 2 on at night we did not pull the machines out on a Monday night (sorry Hazel) but we never did anything to scam because we knew it would come back to bite Hazel and as much as she worked us like dogs we all respected her. She was 2 different Hazel's. The boss Hazel and then after work or if we went a works night out, she was Hazel our friend not our boss. That bastard that owned the place did her wrong and she left, the minute she was out the door Julie and I would go and get our own chickens and bring them into the shop. Cut them up with the bandsaw and sell our chickens as food not theirs. We made a packet, we never did it when Hazel was there but we sure as fuck did when she left and told her.

It was all people who knew me as a person, my girls from college, people that I have previously done work for, people who knew me for me. They knew I would not do something like that for shit and giggles. No there was a dam good reason why I did it. All my other "so called friends" that I have done work for and favours for where nowhere to be seen. These are people who say one thing to you and mean another. They never gave a fuck about me. Do you think for one minute I gave a fuck what any of you thought? No did I hell. It was all my friends and people that know me. There are 2 types of friends. People that you meet through work, school, college. People you have spent time with, and you always say oh we will get a night out together and it does not happen. You have your own life to life and so do they. It is not as if you say it but do not mean it. It just does not happen, but these are still friends.

That half ass book made me over £3000 in a few days. We are in lockdown. I am self-employed. We are all fucked. I wanted this house on the beach and you stupid fucks have just paid my rent and deposit on a half-finished book. Who is the stupid one? It certainly is not me. I could not have given a fuck about any of you or what you thought about me. Did I like some of you? yes of course I did but would I lose any sleep over you not wanting to speak to me again? Hell no, but I have just repaid quite a lot of favours in one fail swoop and made £3000 out of a book that was not even finished. I am sitting here happy as a pig in shit. Through all of this, if there was ever a time for the friends that I personally have chosen to bolt, now would be that time because none of them know this. Everyone is going to find out the last of the truth together. I have amazing friends and I have an amazing chosen family.

Since I started writing this, I have not only learned so much about myself I have become a better friend. All these amazing people have been here and had my back from day dot, and yet it took a stranger to walk into my life and let me see the world through a new set of eyes. Would I do it all over again? Hell yes. I am so walking away from this as a person that I love, OMG I love me, I love how I did all of this on my own from that night in the hospital right up until now. I have gone on this journey myself. I have not asked anyone else to help me or tell anyone else what I was doing. Me, just little old me. Do not get me wrong, I have been to hell and back. I had to hold all those feelings in until the day he walked out the door. I held all of that in for 2 and a half years, but I can do that. Jesus, I hold in the most heinous thing ever and get on with my day. This was a piece of cake compared to that, but I did love Dexter, I genuinely loved Dexter and his family. I trusted them, I trusted him, and they all threw me under the bus one after the other. I am still a human being. This man opened my heart and I let him in, something I had never done before and he took that and ripped my chest open with a Stanley knife and cut it out. That is what it felt like. To love someone and then loose them is like grieving for them. I was devastated but I had to hold all of that in for 2 and a half years.

Chapter 56

When he walked out that door that was when I literally collapsed and everything I bottled up for so long came out, Jesus I went to hell and back again. I am not ashamed of that. If you genuinely love someone like I loved him it hurts like hell. It was the fact I allowed it. I opened my heart to that man, and I let him in. I shared real genuine feelings with him. He was the only person that knew my true feelings about what happened, and he knew that when my mum did not believe me it killed me. The person who is supposed to be there for you no matter what failed me. He knew this and he knew that people laughing at me was the final straw. God I am not joking you have no idea what that feels like, you cannot begin to imagine how that feels to have the actual act itself done but for people to laugh, yes, I could kill someone with my bare hands and I am not ashamed to say it. If you dared to stand in front of my face and laugh at me about it then prepare to die because the only way that is going to end is one of us dead and I would bet my life I killed, you. All that anger and hurt that I have carried about for all those years would come out in one go and there is no way you are coming back from that. No chance.

I have spent the last 6 months looking at myself, the way this whole thing panned out. I have needed this time to myself, I had to re find myself, and I like what I see. Ok I love what I see, Will I always be damaged hell yeah, there is just no getting away from that but look at the person I am. With all the shit I have been through in my life I am still standing. God I am worse than the clap there is just no getting rid of me I keep getting back up, but each time I get back up I get back up stronger. I do not care what you or anyone else thinks of me. I could not give 2 fucks, but I do care about my friends, and things are changing, since writing this my friends have saw a huge difference in me. God I even tell Demi I love her, and I do. I have missed so much of her and the kids' lives because I get too close and I back off again. Demi will be with me until the day I die, that fucker will be in the coffin with me, even if it is just to get the last word, but one thing I do know, no matter what I do, she will always back me 100%.

I have changed again. I am still the Murrin who could not give 2 flying fucks, but I have allowed happiness into my washing machine. Its ok to let happiness in. I have amazing friends who have stuck by me through all of this without knowing the truth and now it is time for change. If ever there was a test of friendship it has been through this journey and I am going to be a better friend. I am going to let my friends into my life. I know I can trust them 1 million percent and now this is my time to shine. I may have been to hell and back again, but everything happens for a reason. It is just a pity it took a stranger to show me that it is ok to be happy.

There are still so many things I want to do. I want to go to Thailand, see after I get my new house on the beach, my next thing is Thailand but now it is time for the rest of the truth so I can begin my new journey.

Chapter 57

It has maybe been a week or so since I posted on Facebook. Now daft arse will think that is it finished thanking fuck. No, I simply needed time to get my head around my whole mother thing. So, after the last charade of texts I honestly cannot be arsed with them and I need to sort my head, so I block his number, his mums, his dads, everyone. I just do not want to have to speak to any of these human beings any more than I need to but, Murrin may be great with lots of things, but technology is not one of them. I can break into a house, but I cannot work a fucken phone. I have blocked him and deleted him but now I am ready for the end and I do not know how to unblock him. This is how stupid I am with technology, but I have another phone, my works phone. Now the last time he was mouth almighty before he got half the truth now, I am going to send the final blow. I text him, wait to you see what I have planned for the finale, you will love it. I cannot remember the exact words, but it went something like now you know why I never kissed you, you gave me the boak, I had to sit and look at your fucken lying ass face every day bla bla bla. As soon as I sent it, I blocked the number because I do not care about anything he has to say. I have not cared for a long ass time but now I know he is shitting himself. No fucker backed him up on Facebook, not even the friend who is the dad of the Siobhan. He is willing to accept responsibility for a child that even she does not know who the dad is and none of them, not one have backed him up on Facebook.

This man knew my feelings about people laughing at me, he knew he said this but now he has half the truth and knows his wife is not so stupid. I know what his next move is going to be before he even does it. He has no one backing him up. He knows his wife would kill you quicker than look at you and now the arse has fallen out his trousers and he calls the cops again. He phones the cops to protect him, he probably thinks I will kill him and her, but you could not be any further from it. I love locksmithing, in fact I have been teaching myself auto locksmithing during lockdown. I need to be CRB checked to locksmith. You mate have done far more damage to yourself than I could have done. A tanking would be over and done with but now you are stuck living in the house of the person who threw you under the bus's parents. You are living in someone else's house, bringing up someone else's baby and up to your arse in so much debt. I could not give a flying fuck about either of you, but you do not know what the finale is, so you go running to the cops. I already knew you would. You have been so predictable the whole way through.

Chapter 58

I bloody missed them. I had waited all day expecting them to come
because I knew he would call them. I knew it. It has been so nice outside
we are all in the garden all day. Jimmy is out as soon as she is awake,
Salem and Doris love being out so I am out. We are our own wee family
now, wherever one goes, we all go. So, we have been in the garden all
week. I got up in the morning and there was a card through the door
from the police but no number. I thought its ok they will come back
later tonight. Oh no, I am out in the back garden with the bikini on
during the day. The tits are out, the scars are out (another thing I do not
care about, my stomach looks like the road map of Glasgow I have so
many scars and I wear them with pride. I do not give a fuck) the garden
is all fenced in and then I hear someone shout for me. I stand up and
low and behold the police have come during the fucken day. They put 2
and 2 together and instead of coming up with 5 they came up with 4
and came around the back fence. Clever cops saw how nice it is and
thinks, garden. There I am standing tits on show and yeah hello.

They came around to the front of the house, that let me run upstairs
and put a jumper on. There are two of them, they are both about the
same height, one is bald and one has short dark hair, they are both
laughing no flippen wonder, great start to an arrest, but they just have
this aura about them, as in a welcoming one even though I know I am in
the shit. In they come, now they know I have done it. I know I have done
it, am I going to waste their time saying it was not me? No, if I do
something, I will take the blame of it. No point arsing them about. Yes, I
did it. While laughing (because of the whole bikini thing) they tell me I
do not have to say anything. Now these two men in front of me have
just seen me half naked great start, I am not wasting their time and
saying prove it. Yes, I did it, they are not jobs worth cops where power
goes to their heads, no they are genuine nice guys. Although they knew
I was in the wrong they did not treat me like a piece of shit. No, very far
from it. We had a chat in the car, they explained everything that would
happen at the station and basically treated me like a human being even

though they knew I was wrong. They did not need to do that. They said that they would make it as quick and painless as possible. These people know I do not have a criminal record, this is not something I do on a weekly basis.

We get to the station and it is a separate part. It is like waiting in the queue at the chippy, it was only us there. One of the officers went through the doors to say why I was there, the other officer explained everything to me in detail about what would happen and so forth. You can see through the glass, and there is an older man at the desk, and he looks cute and sweet and I think can I get him. He just had one of those loving faces. Oh, please be him, I asked the officer is that the man I am going to get, he said yeah, either him or the sergeant oh fuck do not be the sergeant knowing my luck I will get the sergeant.

In we go and it is the nice man, he kind of looks like father Christmas without the beard, he is wearing a blue polo shirt kind of thing and he explains that he has to ask me all these questions and off he goes, now I need a pee. I do not know if it is a nervous pee, but I need to pee. This other lady comes with a black t-shirt on attractive looking woman, taller than me, dark hair tied back, no makeup on just naturally pretty and she takes me to go to the toilet. Again, this woman knows I have done wrong and she is nice. I cannot remember if it was her who said something about being searched or the two officers that brought me in. I am thinking oh fuck it is going to be like telly strip and cough. There will not be much stripping going on because I have no fucken knickers on. I was in the back garden getting my tan on working from the garden. She takes me to this cell, it has what can only be described as a silver bowl and you pee, but there is no fucken toilet paper, where is the toilet paper? The nice lady is outside the door waving a few sheets at me.

We get into the interview room, now they have already asked me if I want a lawyer, I said I did not want one. There is no tape. In the telly there is a tape recorder thing, no he pulls out an iPad thing. Why am I not surprised? They ask me did you send Dexter a message saying X, Y and Z. Yes, I did, do you want to think about it, no I was in the wrong, they have not judged me, they have not been awful to me they are doing their job. I am not arsing these 2 men about. I did it end of. Can I go home now?

They put me in a cell until the paperwork was done. Now while Santa was asking me questions another younger man came, tall short dark hair, good looking guy, same blue polo shirt. I was in that cell all like 20 minutes maybe and that guy came down and asked if I was ok? All these people knew I was in the wrong and not one of them treated me like a piece of shit or made me feel degraded or disrespectful in any way. Not one of them.

Now as a society we are bastards, we do things to suit us, it was one of the questions I asked the officer with the dark hair. How the hell do you manage to take all the shit people give to you and say to you without wanting to smash their faces in. I watch TV I love police interceptors. I do not know how these people have the patience to deal with half of these morons. They shout and scream at them hurling abuse, but see if Jimmy next door has been on a bender for the weekend and has drank his way through half the off sales and partaken in some drugs and he is now standing in front of you with a loaded gun? You are not going to phone wee Jean down the road to help you. No, you are going to dial 999. You are going to phone the people that half of you call pigs because it suits you. If your child goes missing? Who do you phone? These people are out all hours searching through woodlands and bins, drains gutter everywhere and anywhere and yet you do not give them the respect they deserve.

Like war veterans, these people gave up their families and loved ones to fight for our country. Most of them lost their lives. We owe them our lives. Jesus fuck I swear to god if they could see what we have become now they would not have bothered their arse and what do we do for those people who went years without seeing their families, lived off of practically nothing fought in all kinds of weather and we give them one fucken minute silence a year. One minute out of our lives a year for everything they went through, with a red fucken poppy. We should be ashamed of ourselves.

I was looking around the cell and I had to laugh, on the wall it says something like if you destroy the cell you will get into shit basically. There is nothing to destroy, it is 4 walls, a silver bowl and they give you one of the gym mats you used to get in PE that is it, there is nothing to destroy. I did have a wee chuckle at that. I was only there maybe 20 minutes and as true as their word they came and got me to take me home. It only turns out to be the nice lady who took me to the toilet was the sergeant. She went over my paperwork, explained everything to me and all this madness started going on. People were appearing from everywhere. Then another man appeared behind the desk, again same blue polo shirt, he was laughing at me. Not in a bad way, I had said something that embarrassed him, the gentleman that had been out in the sun all day, I did not even get to find out his name, but If you are available as in totally available it just so happens I am too. I think it is my time to shine now. I will be changing all my numbers and my address, but I will need to update them at Coatbridge Police Station. Just so you know, I may have a communications act charge against me, but it was worth it. It will not affect my locksmithing. I bet it is the first time anyone has asked you on a date through a book. The 2 officers took me back home, again the journey home was the same as the way there we chatted about normal stuff, and I remember the name of that other thing to watch if you ever read this. It is called Banshee.

Maybe a wee idea, see if you took kids from school and put them through the whole process of being taken away to the station, processed at the front desk, interviewed and in a cell for a wee while, there might be less crime. I know if I ever thought about doing it, that has put me off and you were all lovely. I do not get why people who have been through that choose to keep committing crime and going back. You are all off your nut. It was an experience but not one I would like to do again.

Chapter 59

Everything that I have done the whole way through this has been for a reason. I found out a lot about myself as a person. I found out exactly what my husband and his family were, I have the most amazing friends ever and I am going to start a new Chapter of my life. I know the minute I leave this house I will change all my numbers; I have found a house on the beech that you morons who slated me has paid for. I am going to start letting people in. If anything, this journey has pushed my friendships to the limits, and they are still standing by my side. All my friends are finding out the whole truth the same way, this is something I have seen through the whole way myself. Dexter has no friends; he fucked the only decent friend he had. He is now living in someone else's house, stuck with the person who threw him under the bus, the person that he has publically said he is the father to her baby, supporting her and her dad (his new friend) where were they? They were not there backing you up. I specifically did everything the way I did for a reason. The rest of your family were not there backing your mum and dad, Joanne has amazing friends and I really hope that one day she realises that before it is too late.

She needs a reality check, if she would take herself off that high horse then she may even be a nice person. If you choose to have children, then you should be prepared to look after them. You chose them, they did not choose you. Children are not smarties; they are the most precious thing ever. You have amazing friends, you have parents who support you, and Nigel's parents. Get off your high horse and let Nigel's mum in. You are no better than she is. She is an amazing woman. Who cares if she smokes, so do you? Get over yourself.

Agnes and Bert, I hope your children step up to the mark now and help. They are both selfish bastards I kind of understand why you stuck up for him, but you most definitely went the wrong way about it and that was your downfall. I was going to take him and him alone down and shield you from it but the minute you threw me under the bus I did not give a fuck. Think back to the very beginning when all this started. I kept all of you out of it. I had no intention in getting any of you involved until you threw me under the bus and then reversed over me.

To my darling husband, ah there are no words to describe you. One person will never be enough for you, the grass is not always greener on the other side, your wife was not as stupid as you thought and that you learned the hard way

Mother, you and I are done. You may have brought me into this world but you sure as fuck are not taking me out.

Lorraine, well to you it seems I do owe an apology. I spoke to your mum after the post was put on Facebook at New Year, I stupidly believed what he said but after speaking to you and your mum it seemed as if you did not care up until that last post there when I put up the half ass book. You did still care; you were still in love with him. For that I apologise because I saw you in the shop so I should have confronted you and asked you about it but I never and that is on me. I genuinely believed him and with all that texting I could not understand why you would allow that. I did not know you were still in love with him and whether you accept it or not I apologise. There is one thing that you can take away from this, well two. Money cannot buy you love. There are two things in life that money cannot buy you. One is love and the other is health. I only met you a few times and you seemed a nice enough person. Why would you not stick up for yourself? I hope if you have found someone new that you are genuinely happy, and you NEVER allow another man to treat you like a door mat. Now I understand why all your friends stuck with you and not him. More fool me for believing him. He called them all the bastards under the sun because he said they chose money over him. Take comfort in knowing that one person will never be enough for him and he is now up to his arse in debt, about to bring up someone else's baby and stuck living with her parents at his age.

Chapter 60

This chapter is for you my darling husband. I have planned this the whole way through, I knew exactly what date I was bringing out the truth on the 7th of June, your birthday. It is my last birthday present to you. Love the Birthday Fairy. Enjoy!!!!!

Your wife was not as stupid as you thought. You fucked up. From the very beginning when we started talking, I said to you ONE lie and that was it. No matter how bad the truth was I would have rather had the truth. I knew straight away something was not right and our routine had not changed. That is how well I knew you. I just knew something was not right. I begged and pleaded with you to tell me the truth. You did not love and respect me enough to be honest with me. Had you been honest with me, it would have broken my heart yes, but I would have respected you for telling me the truth. That was your first mistake.

You lied to my face. In fact, you lied to my face for the next 2 and a half years because as far as I was concerned you and I finished that night. Even if you were trying to get your leg over someone else you could have supported me through the you are fucked. You were the only support I had. You knew I did not have Stephen. You were the one I spoke to about my true feelings and you knew exactly I was heading for a you are fucked and yet not only did you lie to my face you let me spiral out of control with nothing, no help. You knew what the stages were. A dip, a pothole and you are fucked. The signs could not have been any clearer. The garage was full of knocked off gear. I was drinking, I was drowning, I was going out of control because you were telling me that my past was making me think you were talking to someone else.

We were only just married, it was not as if it was millions of years down the road and I am taking my false teeth out to give you a gummy. No, we had not long said our wedding vows.

You took the only part of my life that I cannot get over and you turned it against me. You were standing there lying to my face saying it was all in my head because of the abuse. You my dear husband were the person I opened to. You knew my exact feelings. I had said to you before I was scared in case my past would fuck us at some point. I openly said that to you because I trusted you. That was my worst fear. The most heinous part of my life would fuck up the happiness I now had but it was not my past. It was you, you took the worst information ever and used it against me to protect your lie. You would rather let me think my worst fear was happening rather than you just be honest. You got me into that state. You knew exactly what that would do to me and yet you chose to use the thing I feared the most against me rather than just tell the truth.

So now not only have you cheated on me. You have now destroyed me by using the thing you knew would hurt me the most. You knew exactly what a you are fucked is. You know that there is not much chance of coming back from a you are fucked and yet you chose to put me through a you are fucked and walked out the door. That my dear was the biggest god dam mistake of your life.

If there is ever a time, I am grateful for coming back from a you are fucked it is so this time. I lay there in that hospital bed and the new improved Murrin was completely gone. What you had done to me was worse than the act itself because you knew my true feelings and fears. You, my best friend and husband. The person I trusted more than anything and any one I opened and let you in. You had no idea of the damage you had done but let me tell you this my nearest and dearest you would soon enough find out. Jesus fuck would you find out. I was a child when my abuse happened. A child, I could not stick up for myself but I sure as fuck can now and you my dear are fucked.

You thought I would let you enjoy Vegas after that? Are you fucken joking? I will tell you a little thing about Vegas, shall I? It was nearly just me coming home myself. I was minutes away from slashing your throat in Vegas. What stopped me? Not your mum, I was still livid at this point. If I killed, you it would have been over and done with far too quickly. I wanted you to suffer. I wanted you to suffer like I did. You ruined 2 and a half years of my life as far as I was concerned, and I was going to do the exact same back to you as well as destroy you.

Did you enjoy Vegas? Did you fuck, I moaned the whole week. You forgot I stayed in South Africa you arsehole. I can take heat. I had £5000 spending money for Vegas, I had been to Vegas before. I know how much things cost. They do not change that dramatic, and I took £1000 anyone that has been to Vegas knows you are having the worst time possible for £1000. Let us watch TV lol. Even £5000 would not have been an amazing trip but it would have been a whole lot better than £1000 and we even came home with money. It was the worst holiday ever but there was hell way and no way I was letting you have any fun. Not a fucken chance.

I moaned about the heat. I moaned about the prices. Hell, I moaned about moaning. I was even annoying myself. Now if you had half a brain you would have known that even if we did only have £1000 we would have made a laugh and joke about it just like we did about that stinking hotel in Blackpool and found some sort of scam to have a laugh and enjoy Vegas. This is just the beginning of your 2 and a half years of hell and you did not even twig in Vegas, Jesus you were going to be easy to fool you stupid fuck.

Do you think I did not know when you were talking to someone? I would even drop hints now and then about Facebook and snap chat. This is how stupid you were, and you thought I was the stupid one. You did not even twig when all the underwear went into a bag and put away in a cupboard cheerio, away to the land that never was. I had no intensions of making the next 2 and a half years easy ones.

Where were all the sanitary towels for my bleeding? Do not get me wrong I had some problems with irregular bleeding, but Jesus fuck you thought I was losing pints a day and where were all the sanitary towels. I was a heavy bleeder when I took my periods. Jesus I would have 3 or 4 of the large kotex towels on and still soak into the bed sometimes. How the fuck did you not think if she is losing all the blood for 2 and a half years is, she not dead. This is how stupid you were. I should have had at least 100 packs of sanitary towels to last a week and where the fuck where they all, and you thought I was stupid.

Before that night when did I ever eat chocolate except when my periods were due? It was the only time you would ever see me eat a bit of chocolate. I was always a crisp person. Now I am eating chocolate by the bucket loads. I am a fat bastard. I cannot even look at myself in the mirror for the wanting to throw up. Why did I get rid of all the mirrors in the house? When did we ever sit and watch TV all the time before that night? We always had fun or made a laugh out of things. We were sitting about watching TV all the time if I was not working because I did not want to give you anymore happy memories.

Jesus fuck, I could stand in my room for 18 hours a day to work, yet when it was your day off at work, I was ill. Jesus I was ill that much I was even starting to believe that I was ill. I had undergone 106 operations. I had major surgery, still had my staples in and I was away doing a Minnie Mouse job. I can take pain. You know I can take more pain than the average human being, yet I had all these stupid illnesses that stopped me from doing things. I cannot go camping because of my bleeding. We cannot book anything because you never know if I am going to be ill or not. You know what I went through with my accident and yet you are accepting I cannot do x, y and z because of ulcers or bleeding. They said I would never walk again with my leg and I proved them wrong, but you accept stupid illnesses as excuses as to why I cannot do things. No far from it. I was just not giving you happy memories or a happy wife.

Now I have never been one to wear makeup, maybe mascara and lipstick if I am going out but I always loved underwear and wearing nice clothes. Now I have Bridget jones pants, I have not even bothered to get my hair cut in 2 years. It looks like rats' tails. I am walking about in jogging pants and crocs, I have gained about 3 dress sizes. I do not pluck my eyebrows, I do not shave my legs, sometimes I do not even shave under my arms, I need a fucken lawn mower for downstairs and I am a walking mess. Jesus I would not even want to kiss me let alone shag me.

Your wife turned from wearing nice clothes and underwear to a fat ugly bastard right in front of your face and you did not see it. I could not have made it any more noticeable and yet you still do not see it.

I cannot kiss you anymore, as in properly kiss you. It gives me the heave. I did not kiss you except a peck and you still have not twigged. You are lucky if we had sex maybe 5 times in 2 and a half years. I was throwing you a bone like a dog. I always flinched when you touched me, and you did not even notice. I did not even come once. I just said and did the right things. Have you not noticed there is now 3 purple surprises in the drawer that is what all the fucken batteries were for?

We have not had any happy memories the memory box that we had to upgrade twice because there was so much stuff in it for the first 2 and a half years has now not got any more stuff put in it and you have not twigged. Jesus even if we went out for something to eat, I would pinch something from the place, or we would keep a napkin. That box has had fuck all in it and you have not twigged.

Before I went into hospital for my operation I specifically turned around and said to you I think there is a reason Jane and Donna (I worked in Butlins with many years ago) have come back into my life. Dropping a fat hint and nothing. It just happened in November last year before I went in for my hysterectomy.

Just before I went into hospital for my operation, I purposely made a board thing and put all the pictures for the first 2 and a half years in it for a reason. I wanted to remind you that we were happy at one point until you fucked it up. There was not one picture of the following 2 and a half years. Only the first part. In every single picture we were laughing and happy, there were also pictures of our fucked-up family, but they were our family. The family you chose to forget about and disregard like rubbish.

You walked out of that door thinking we had no money. Not one penny, I had just had major surgery 2 surgeries in one go. Even if I wanted to, I could not work. The last operation just had to be the one from hell. Yet you walked out that door with a £4000 credit card and still getting paid weekly and gave us nothing. I am still at home with our family. It is the middle of winter. It is a 5-bedroom house that needs heat and light. You thought I used all the money I had left to buy your family Christmas presents. So now I am myself with 3 dogs who are £8 a day on dog food. 2 cats that are £5 a day on gel cat litter before I have even got them food. The birds are ok they do not cost much but I have all these animals to feed and heat and you thought I had no money. To throw caution to the wind you cancelled the fucken car insurance and took my mobile phone. So, I am now no money, no food, no gas or electric, no phone or car. This is how you treated your wife. You did not know I had money. You thought our marriage was hunkey fucken dorey and you sack of shit thought you left us up shit creek without a paddle.

I knew you had already taken the watch. I know you like the back of my hand. You had the phone watch on when you left but you came back and took the Tag Heuer watch, your Stone Island shit (you forgot the jumper by the way but I sold it for 50p) I already knew you would take this but I had the box with the receipt. I know you are not getting full whack for it without the box and receipt. I am 2 and a half years in front of you arsehole. All you wanted was your designer stuff to show off. Like you always have. Me and my £1000 jacket. You made sure you took everything that was of value and off you popped thinking we were fucked.

I purposely asked you for the watch to see what you would say. I told you we had no money, no food, that I had gave the dogs all the human food because I had no money for dog food. I wanted to know how far down you were going to go. None of these animals that we bought chose us, we chose them. They are our responsibility to feed and heat and you did not give a fuck. All those messages about how you love your family. The fucked-up family that you loved so much you walked out and left them nothing. You disregarded them like a piece of rubbish.

I purposely sent all those messages about not feeling like a woman and this is how our relationship has gone from that night to now. You thought you took my confidence away; this is what you thought, and you could not have given a fuck. Everything I have done I did for a reason. I wanted to know if there was any decency in you, also the worse you treated me the worse you were going to get back. All of this is clocking up the miles. Right now, we are sitting at you cheated, umpteen times now. No, I was not always sleeping when you were on your phone. You think I did not know you were on your phone at night when I was asleep. I could not have given a fuck but I sure as hell was not making it easy for you. If you had even attempted to sit on your phone in front of me, I would have rammed it right down your throat and you know it.

You have walked out for another woman leaving us all up-shit creek. No money and no means of making money because I cannot drive the car without insurance or work because I have no phone. God you are clocking up the miles.

There was always a reason behind everything I did. I was basically setting traps and you walked right into every single one. You and Siobhan sending me messages with pictures saying you are so happy as if it was making me jealous. I did not care, if you are so fucken happy then why do you need to send me messages telling me? This is how stupid you are. How stupid do you feel now?

The age thing never bothered us, I would forget what age you were most times because it seemed you were more mature for your age. You were an extremely intelligent man, who had a fountain of knowledge about loads of things, but you had no common sense obviously. I loved listening to your stories and the things you had learned off the internet. Your face would light up like a Christmas tree when you told me things and you knew I was listening. You fucked up Dexter, you totally fucked up. If you read the beginning of the book and how happy it sounds. Everything sounds bright and happy, until you get halfway through and it is like a car crash waiting to happen. You did that, you and only you.

You put me through hell and back, but I would not change a thing because I will walk away from this a stronger person with my head held high. You and your family should dip your heads in shame. You are scum, plain and simple scum. You treated your wife like a piece of shit on your shoe and your family not only stood by you but threw me under the bus.

I did always say I would one day write a book and you always asked you if you would be in it. You are the star of the show. I have even dedicated it to you. How is that? I am not one of these people who just say things for the hell of it. I do it. Do I care if anyone else reads it? No, do I fuck this is how I wanted you to find out that your wife was not as stupid as you thought. You just learned that the hard way.

I truly did love you, I trusted you so much I shared my true feelings with you, and you used it against me. This is the end. This is everything written down from the beginning to the end. It was only me. Just little old me against all of you and I am still standing. Your wife was not a mug, and no one will ever treat me like a mug and get away with it. Enjoy your new life Dexter. Goodbye.

To wrap shit up

What have I learned from this? I am a much stronger person than I give myself credit for. It is ok to let people in and to be happy. It is ok to add happiness into the washing machine. Just choose wisely who you let in. Maybe what I have needed has been right here in front of me all this time and I did not realise.

Pricilla went back to the person she loved and missed the most. Her sister. She is as happy as a pig in shit. She is away back to Aberdeen, back to her sister and loving life. Teaching her sister to high 5.

Levi got the peace from her daughter that she wanted so much. She has gone to a lady called Jacqui who has been through the same thing as me, although she has nobody. I met her when I was out with the dogs having a chat and I just knew. Levi looked at me and I knew. Selfish bitch that I have kept her for another few days. It was my way of saying goodbye. I knew the minute Doris came I lost my baby. I just knew it.

When Jacqui came to the house, she went straight to her and I knew I made the right decision. She came up to me to say goodbye and I knew she wanted to go. She never wanted a child. Just like I didn't yet I never asked her. I chose to make a memory with my husband over my own child. I fucked up. She was my baby and my responsibility, and I will regret that for the rest of my life. Giving her up broke my heart but I knew it was the right thing to do, and OMG it is she is happy as a pig in shit. She is the only dog; she gets constant attention and most of all she is allowed inside the bed with her and on the couch. Jacqui sends me photos. Levi takes up most of the bed and Jacqui is left with fuck all. This was the only thing that Levi loved. Getting on the bed. I love my pets they are my children, but my bed is mine, so is the couch. I have been down that road many times before with bullmastiffs and bulldogs and it does not end well. You end up with no Flamen bed. I will allow them anywhere just not in my bed. So, she is in Levi heaven.

Thelma and Zack did not do good at all. They poor cats sat behind that door when that arsehole was up collecting some stuff and they cried for him and he did not even see if they were ok. He did not even just open the door to see if they were ok. He knew fine well they cats loved the bones of him. He would carry Zack about like a baby. Thelma? Fuck Dexter was the only person she liked. From day dot every time he finished work out of all the pets him and Thelma would have "their time" at night. They were not coping without him. They started peeing all over the place. Zack cried every night waiting for him to come back. Thelma sat at the top of the stairs every night waiting for him for "their time" and he never came. He did not even open that door to see if they were ok. They were crying at the door for him and he ignored them as if they were nothing. They would not have coped without him. Zack stopped eating. All he did was cry for him. Thelma just waited on the stairs and they say animals are stupid. They two cats cried for him and he did not even bother to see if they were ok. That is how little they meant to him. My friend Sandra found a great home for them. They are with a couple from the BBC. They took a few days to settle in, but they are much better now.

Half of our fucked-up family that we chose is now separated. If there was anything of emotion left inside of me, it left when half of my family did. I know I done the best thing for them, just not for me.

Me, Salem, Doris and Jimmy, I know what we are going to do. We are heading straight for the beech.

I went back to my size 8 clothes, and I stopped stealing. Will I do either of these again? I can never say never but I am a survivor and I will not let my past dictate my future.

I am going to start afresh, who knows what I will do. I can make money out of anything. God I could not walk after my accident, my rent was £950 a month, how did I pay the rent? I sold pishy knickers. No word of a lie. It was me and Stephen that were living together at the time. I was selling off stuff on eBay. I had an underwear set, a new one. A guy messaged and said If you wear it first then I will pay extra. My immediate thought was you dirty bastard and then I thought wait a minute. I Googled it, and it is a thing, omg people pay money for worn pants. I bought pants from Primark for 50p and sold them for £20. I made a website for a tenner, took a picture of a hot looking woman off google, god I fancied myself. I called myself Ursula I was a hot blonde with huge tits from Sweden. I joined a dating app thing and sent people the link to my page. I could not keep up with the orders and wearing the pants, so I pissed in a bottle, sprayed the pants with the piss and posted them. I can make money out of anything.

It is a new beginning for me. I have many skills but there is so much more out there so who knows. What I do know is happy clothes will be in my washing machine and only those people nearest and dearest to me will know where I am.

Was I ever going to send this to a publisher? Hell no, I wanted this to come out exactly the way I would say it. No publisher in their right mind would print this the way I wanted it, plus it had to be the 7th June. No fancy grammar or fancy words, just the Murrin way as if I were telling you my story. If you have been paying attention you will know that money means absolutely nothing to me. If it is handed to you on a silver platter then you do not appreciate it. Well I do not, I would rather work for it.

I have really enjoyed doing this, I did send it to friends before I sent it to Dexter and Bert, just to see if it were something they would read. It was the same, a half-finished book but I wanted the people I cared about to find out about my childhood from me. My life has had more up's and down's than a hooker's knickers and I probably have another 5 books in me. Even if it is just for myself, I am going to write them. This has been the best therapy ever. Maybe I should have listened to my physiatrist ages ago and wrote shit down.

I do not care if people buy this or not, these are my words, and this is exactly how I wanted my loving husband to find out the truth. My way, with my words.

I do not hold grudges against anyone who backed up their friends on Facebook, I admire you for what you done. I would have done the exact same myself.

Enjoy your new life Dexter because I know I am going to enjoy mine xxx

I am just an ordinary girl telling stories – I write my stories the same way as if I was talking to you – there are no fancy words in my books – there is no perfect grammar – I call a spade a spade in real life and this is how I write – If you like the way I write then you will like my other books and short stories I have

Payback is a Bitch – Growing up in Sighthill – Butlins WonderWest in Ayr – What an expensive night that was - Fuck you Landlord – Book night – A night on Ecstasy and many more

Thank you for taking the time to read my book – I hope you like it

Printed in Dunstable, United Kingdom